A SMALL SILENCE

By Jumoke Verissimo

CASSAVA REPUBLIC

Abuja – London

First published in 2019 by Cassava Republic Press

Abuja – London

Copyright ©Jumoke Verissimo 2019

A CIP catalogue record for this book is available from the National Library of Nigeria and British Library.

The poem 'Not My Business' has been reproduced with permission from the poet Niyi Osundare.

UK ISBN: 978-1-911115-79-3

Nigerian ISBN: 978-978-975-034-4

eISBN: 978-1-911115-80-9

Cover & Art Direction by Michael Salu

Book design by Tobi Ajiboye

Printed and bound in Great Britain by Bell & Bain Ltd., Glasgow

Distributed in Nigeria by Yellow Danfo

Distributed in the UK by Central Books Ltd.

Distributed in the US by Consortium Books

For
S/he OLUDUMARE

And
Four oracles, who in their prime, revealed the riddles of the dark: Femi Awote, Felix Okadigbo, Oluwatosyn Bucknor, Pius Adesanmi.

'Darkness is your candle.
Your boundaries are your quest.'

"Wetness and Water" in *The Big Red Book*
Jalāl ad-Din Rūmī

1

Prof turned off all the lights in the house when he returned from prison. He bathed, cleaned, ate, and slept in the darkness which devoured the whole flat. When he did not have any cleaning or cooking to do, he would sit in his chair reciting passages from books he had memorised. He cooked his meals on an old kerosene stove whose red and yellow flames leapt out of the whorled burner and lapped the sides of the steel pot. The light from the fire made him wince and mutter, 'Ish, ish, ish.'

His house was not always dark as soot because the wan light of an electric bulb drifted in at night through the only window in the sitting room and sat on the arm of the chair opposite his. It irritated him. In the daytime, the heavy curtains his mother had hung covered the room in a thick shade but could not prevent the sun's intrusion. The slight parting in the curtains allowed a thin stroke of light to fall on the floor of the sitting room. Prof tried though, to keep in the darkness. He adjusted the curtains, but they always fell apart, inviting shadows to lay claim to new spaces in the room.

It was dark, but never dark enough.

Prof soon grew tired of aligning the curtains. He turned his attention to staring at the shadows which formed beside the furniture, moving around the house like a blind man born to his handicap, sensing when something was not in its rightful place. He regained confidence in knowing that the flat was as familiar with him as he was with it. He crept in and out of rooms, floating like a paper lifted by the wind. Sometimes, he strayed into a room where he grazed an object, took note of the positioning and counted his steps backward and forward to avoid hitting the same object twice. As he moved from one room to another, filling spaces, he dreamt of dreadful ways in which his enemies — those who made him go to prison — would die.

On the nights that his irritation filled the room, he defied his fear of the electric bulbs on the streets and took a long stroll around Jakande Estate. It was at these times that he bought kerosene or some foodstuff that he needed. Carrying an empty four-litre jerrycan, he would brace himself with his praise names before leaving the house with a walking stick made from a rusty iron rod which had once served as a curtain bar. He walked out onto the street, covered from head to toe like a woman in a burqa, his ears catching distinct conversations in the mix of clamouring voices, car honks and sometimes bleating goats finding their way home, alongside the music that blared from roadside CD/DVD kiosks.

Prof stopped by one of the kiosks defaced with campaign posters for the just-concluded election, which had seen President Obasanjo elected for a second term. The poster that caught his attention was torn and what was left of it was the lean face of Muhammadu Buhari, the name of Chuba Okadigbo, his ANPP running mate, and the words: "WE'LL NOT DO... IT'S A PROMISE."

Prof wondered what the lost words could be. After ten years of absence, this was what he had returned to; two former military heads of state contesting for president. He tried to dismiss the thought of Nigeria's politics from his mind, but he could not.

'Obasanjo of the 70s contesting against Buhari of the 80s, and this is 2005!' he blurted out. 'How can this country move forward when it seeks the dead to bring revival?'

People stared at him but turned away before their eyes met. It was often this way; people hurried ahead or crossed to the other side of the road once he turned to look at them. He was more interested in those who walked ahead of him in a pair or in threesomes, sharing neighbourhood gossip or intimate stories. It was through them that he discovered his neighbourhood was the black cauldron that cooked rumours for several other blocks of flats, lit with bright fluorescent lamps, to savour.

Prof overheard one such rumour of himself and his flat on one of his infrequent night strolls. As he walked away from his home that day, he listened to two straw-thin teenage girls selling plantain chips tell the story of his life as they must have heard it.

'That is the home of the man I was telling you about, the bastard one that came back mad.'

'Is it that professor that Uncle was talking about yesterday?'

'Yes! His father was a landlord here, before he died.'

'Does the man even come out?'

'Out? That is trouble for us in this neighbourhood. If you go to his doorstep you are as good as dead!'

'Uncle said that if he kills, nothing will happen as he is a mad man — he'll be free of guilt.'

'How does he live inside that place without coming out for lights?'

'Uncle said he has iron bars on his doors and windows.'

'How does Uncle know *sef*? What does he eat? I think he will eat only cockroach and rats.'

The girls took furtive glances at Prof's building and when one tried to point towards it, the other one hit her on the shoulder to drop her hand.

'Stop it! Don't point.'

'What will happen if I do?'

'Nothing, just don't point to that mad man's house.'

'He could even be dead.'

'Until his dead body begins to smell, and council comes here, we can't even go near that place.'

Prof walked behind them. He listened with a little smile sneaking onto the corners of his mouth, till it gave way to a small chuckle as the girls hurried away. It was at that moment that Desanya came to stand beside him. She often joined him on his excursions, and they would stand in front of the building to compare his flat to the others. His flat was noticeable, the way one notices a missing incisor tooth on a young woman.

Prof observed the way the darkness of the flat established itself before the world around it. At these times, he would tell Desanya of how bothered he was that the little brightness encroached on the darkness of the area. Sometimes, he told her of how, while standing outside, he considered what would become of him if light flooded the rooms. But once he stepped into the flat, the darkness in the room enveloped him and he settled into it to brood over his past. Desanya left him at these times, evanescing from his thoughts the same way she came.

2

Desire sprawled on the bed with her arms and legs asunder. The only piece of cloth on her was her panties but she could still feel the heat. Her phone beeped, and she read the text message Remilekun forwarded to her from the landlord with a smile. He was asking for the month's rent, again. She and Remilekun always replied to his messages with, 'How much is it again?' They both knew he couldn't reply because Mama T, Remilekun's mother, paid the rent automatically from her bank account. Yet, the landlord would always send a text on the 28th of every month, requesting the month's rent.

As Desire turned on the bed, her thoughts moved to the irony of the insomnia and discomfort she felt on a mattress with coiled springs, compared to the way she had slept like a log on a cardboard or mat on the beach where she spent her childhood. *What does it mean to be comfortable?* Desire thought. There had been a time when she yearned for a bed and now that she had one, she wanted the breeze-cooled beach of her childhood days.

Desire didn't like living in Abesan. She hadn't wanted to live in Abesan Estate but because Remilekun was infatuated with a young man at the time, whose face was shaped like a camel's, she succumbed to her friend's choice. The next step had been to convince Remilekun's mother of their preferred residence. She could still hear Remilekun pleading, as she made a sorry face.

'Tell my mum that living in Abesan is better. You know, because of cultists.'

Desire had looked into Remilekun's eyes and sniggered. 'Stop it! I'm serious. Tell her cultist activities on campus is too much around Iba, or even Ojoo, and those places are the closest areas to the university, but—'

'But you want to go and collect strokes from Mr. Longface.'

'What strokes? Is he a teacher?'

'Hahahaha, I hear you. Whatever you people call it. You want to be close to Mr. Longface's thing.'

'Please! And please stop calling him Mr. Longface. He has like... like... I don't even know. Seriously, have you seen his eyes? They just enter your body. Like, they practically leave his eye sockets and move into your body.'

'Remilekun! All of this for a man who does not even notice you! You want us to go and live in that place that is almost one hour from campus even without traffic?'

'We will have time for ourselves.' Then realising that something sounded odd about what she had said, she rephrased it. 'We will have time to do whatever we want. You can even bring your boyfriend, I would never talk. I'll even leave the room for both of you.'

'*Abeg*, this is you asking me to do that for you when it happens.'

So, when the time and choice of accommodation came, Desire did not find it difficult convincing Mama T with stories of student cultists in uniform chasing professors from classrooms, tales of rape and limbs staring at you first thing in the morning by the gate. She embellished her stories as much as she could from newspaper reports that carried vivid photographs: mangled bodies found in front of campuses; students running from their classes as cult factions fought openly on campuses with guns and knives.

It was easy narrating the horror stories to Mama T. The university was close to a transit centre managed by *agberos*, who called themselves area boys, because it showed that beyond being ruffians, they had a claim to the money they extorted from the buses passing through the area. Inevitably, fights broke out because of power struggles between different factions. Because the university campus was close to the *agberos*' territory, there was usually no distinction between the ruffians' fights and students' protests. After a while, the regular occurrence of this led to some of the students coming up with even more horror stories, to emphasise that their university was more gangster- like. It was a badge of honour to be in a university where you could always act like the hero in an action film.

Mama T was so concerned by the violence that she asked Remilekun to forget university and join her in her wholesale business.

'Or you people can go to the university fwom my house, *abi?*' Mama T suggested. Mama T's Yoruba, and even pidgin or English when she spoke, carried a zest because of her inability to pronounce the letter "r". Yoruba words like "rara", "ranti" or "eran" carried an urban corruption of Yoruba which added a "w" where the "r" should be.

'How would we cope with reading with all these visitors who come to see you at home?'

'The distance, *nko?* Have you regarded the distance from the house to the campus?' retorted Remilekun.

'It is a diwect bus. Just one bus.'

'Ojo is not far-o. Iba too.'

'Mama T, the cults are always fighting in those places.'

With the mention of cults, Mama T sighed. 'God will *kuku* pwotect you fwom all these childwen bwinging their afflicted head from home to the campus.'

'*Amin-o*. And we don't even have lectures every day, so we can stay home and read. It is convenient for us,' Desire lied.

'But there's never light there, *abi?* Don't you know that Ipaja area never has power? At least you need to be comfortable where you are rweading.'

'Is there light in Surulere here? Is there light anywhere in this country? Are we not all living in darkness?' Remilekun said, with a laughter that caught on.

Mama T shook her head, 'Me, I'm going to the market. Just try to find a good place in Abesan, okay?'

Once Mama T agreed, they went searching. Their story of

living in Abesan, however, began with the landlord telling them that the previous tenant had left without paying his electricity bill of three years and so there was no power in their room.

'I will just tap light from the pastor's room next door.'

'How now? You're connecting us illegally after we paid for electricity!' Remilekun snapped at him.

'How now *bawo?* Don't you want light? Or what kind of question is this?'

The landlord had already climbed a chair and was twisting wires in the ceiling before they could protest. Remilekun had almost fallen over laughing at the sight.

'You people don't know that we just have to make things work, somehow, *somehow*, in this country. We don't have a government. We find ways to do things. Somehow, *somehow*.' It did not matter whether they wanted electricity or not because three weeks went by and the entire area was in total darkness. The estate's transformer was carted away for repairs and no one knew when it would be returned by the power authority. The landlord never came to see them either after they moved into the house, he only sent reminder messages:

'It is month end. God provide. Pay up. Stay bless.'

Desire dismissed the landlord's text from her mind and, turning on the bed, closed her eyes; when she next opened them, night had fallen. She looked at the clock and saw it was just a few minutes from three in the morning. The sound of footsteps drew close to the door, signalling Remilekun's return.

Remilekun staggered into the room, although no smell of alcohol drifted in with her. Desire remained still on the bed, heaving slowly like she was fast asleep, while listening to her friend's movements as she took off her clothes—which would most likely join the heap on the floor. As expected, she felt hot air against the side of her face, indicating that Remilekun was hovering over her. Remilekun, as usual, was not deterred by the fact that Desire seemed to be asleep; she jumped onto

Desire's bed, screaming and laughing while tickling her to ensure that Desire stayed awake to listen to her.

'*Oya*, wake up, wake up. Let us talk.'

'Stop tickling me,' Desire feigned a sleep-induced voice to calm the laughter thundering out of Remilekun's mouth as if it needed to settle into Desire and fill her up with gaiety.

'Remilekun! It is past three in the morning!'

'So? I can't miss my friend again? I mean you've not seen me for three good days!'

'*Abeg*, let me sleep,' Desire turned to the wall.

'You better turn and face me, or I won't give you the real gist.'

Desire remained quiet, facing the wall.

'*Hehn*, I have to tell you something.'

Desire ignored her, even when she tapped her shoulder.

'See, I'm serious-o. It is about that man you're always talking about. The professor guy.'

Desire turned to face her, sitting up on the bed. She held herself still, nerves pulled tight like dried cowhide.

'Prof? What about him?'

'Yes, the Prof guy. He's out of prison,' Remilekun said, flinging a newspaper at Desire's chest.

Desire focused on the pages of the newspaper, flipping slowly, despite her racing heart, until she got to the page with Prof's story. She raised her head and was going to ask if she could keep the newspaper but Remilekun was off again.

'Do you remember Toks, that guy with the cute rabbit teeth? I saw him yesterday at the party.'

'Mmm?' Desire nodded so Remilkun would just get to the point. She however noted that her infatuation and the major reason she made them move to Abesan Estate was no longer Mr. Longface, but now the one with the "teeth like rabbit" and Remilekun seemed eager to talk about it.

'We talked a lot! I didn't even know he was so much fun to talk to.'

On another occasion, Desire might have poked fun at the

rabbit teeth and what was cute about them, but this time she was eager to hear about Prof.

'Mmm,' she grunted.

'He has his own clothing line and he said he's travelling to London this summer to see about a new business he is thinking about.'

'Mmm.'

Remilekun realised she was losing her audience, so she returned to Prof's story.

'Toks gave me the newspaper. The party was at his father's house in VI. From what Toks told me, people are saying the professor is not normal again-o. They say he lives on cockroaches and insects. He only goes out at night and things like that. A lot of this and that, like, they've heard screams inside the house. Maybe, he eats people that go to his doorstep or something. I don't believe that one, *sha.*'

'You really shouldn't believe anyone would be capable of eating someone in a community like this. Not in this twenty-first century. How did your friend know?'

'He is a big boy now. Everybody knows he is a rich boy who is living in this area, for whatever reason. People would want him "to drop something". So, to get money from him, they'll feed him stories about the area, even when he doesn't want to hear them.'

'I hear you.'

'My sister, leave that matter, *abeg*. What is there not to believe? Was Clifford Orji not a man? He was killing and roasting people in broad daylight, at a place where people commuted, and he wasn't found out or arrested for several years. Where is he today? Prison or madhouse? Didn't they tell us Clifford was a mad man ignorant of his actions? Madness! It's the reason the world has gone under. And let me just tell you something, there is no one who would go to a Nigerian prison for more than six months and come back sane. That man, according to the newspaper, was there for ten years! Have you been to the police stations? Now, imagine what the maximum prisons are like, *abeg*, hell is closer than we think!'

They both laughed and Remilekun added, 'Even the average policeman behind the counter looks like a prisoner dressed up for interrogation. *Abeg!*'

Desire laughed out loud. It was again one of those few times that Remilekun talked politics. Remilekun's jokes didn't anger her, instead they helped lighten the anxiety that followed her realisation that Prof was close by. Now, with the knowledge that he was living in the same vicinity, she decided that she must have talked about him so much that the universe connived to bring a twist into her life.

'The interesting part is that I know where he lives. It is close to us.'

Remilekun waited for Desire's eyes to enlarge, but instead Desire, trying to control the feeling inside her which she could not recognise, said, 'Well, good to know he is close by.'

'Is that all you will say? I mean you are always talking about this man.'

Desire smiled.

'In fact, if you weren't always talking about him, I wouldn't have known of him,' Remilekun said.

'You? You that was enjoying in your mother's bosom and always got what you wanted, how would you know anyone? For me, Prof is my hero. He saved me. This university education I have today is because of him.'

'I won't accept that one. Your present education is because of *my* mother. Isn't she paying your fees and even giving you pocket money?' Remilekun laughed and hit her playfully on her arm.

'Stop! You know what I mean. It is the motivation,' she raised her voice.

'Okay, seriously. I don't understand you. Here is a man you saw as a child. How is he a motivation?'

'He gave his life for this country!'

'What life? Did he give Nigeria her independence?'

Desire realised the argument was going nowhere, and instead, was making them both angry. She lay back on the bed and closed her eyes, signalling the end of the conversation.

'Now that your Prof is close by, perhaps you'll sleep better,' Remilekun moved over to her side of the room and flopped onto her bed.

Over the following weeks, Desire pretended she did not care about the news but memories of Prof's visit to Maroko bothered her; she wanted to know if he had changed from what she remembered. She began to wake up each morning from dreams of Prof asking her to come for a visit, telling her how she had abandoned him.

One day, she returned from the campus and grabbed Remilekun's arm as she entered the room.

'Do you really know where Prof lives?'

'Who is Prof?'

Desire rolled her eyes; she was not in the mood for Remilekun's games.

'Why do you need to know?' Remilekun stopped to face her. She dropped her bag from her shoulder and dissolved into laughter. 'Don't tell me you want to go and see him. No... no... no!'

'At least, someone should know if he is as crazy as they say,' she said, humouring Remilekun's derangement story. 'And what if he isn't mad?'

'If people say he went mad in prison, it could be the manageable type. The neighbours say he goes out only to the local market at night and wears a cloth that covers him from head to toe. Is that not madness? What is he hiding?'

'What could he be hiding? He was in prison, he probably just wants to be on his own. Think, rethink, you know.'

'Rethink? What is he rethinking? I mean, he was in prison for ten years! Many of his colleagues who were jailed, died there. He returns, and he is rethinking—rethinking what?'

'I just said that—'

'See, I don't even know why you are so interested in him. It doesn't make any sense.'

'All I want is to get an interview. For the campus paper.'

'Hmmm! You make me laugh! When did you start writing for the Campus News?'

Desire ignored the question, letting the discussion die, but that night she made Remilekun take her to his block.

When they reached Prof's address, they stood in front of the building, Remilekun daring her to go up and knock on his door. Desire acted defiant and walked up the stairs and spent the next few minutes staring at Prof's doorstep until Remilekun, exasperated, marched away. Desire turned away from his door with a frown. She ran to catch up with Remilekun who seemed irritated by her lack of boldness to knock on the door.

The next day, Desire returned to the house. She stood in front of his door and raised her right hand to knock but it slipped down to her side without hitting the door. After several tries, her knuckles landed on the wooden door, and she rapped it like it was a drum, and then, as if something hit her, she stopped, turned around and rushed down the stairs and ran into the road.

3

Prof was asleep in his cell the day his mother and friend came for him. A warder had told him some days earlier that the president had freed some prisoners, but he hadn't thought he was one of them. He no longer expected freedom.

He stirred as one of the new warders tapped him on his leg. 'Prof, or what do they call you? Get ready, there are people here for you.'

He raised his head up from where he lay in his cell and uncurled himself into a stretch.

'*Oya*, come, let's go,' the warder said, and turned around immediately to call out to someone, 'Give that one any cloth you see. Who dey keep cloth for here?'

Prof followed the warder with his head bent low, his steps slow. He veiled his face with his threadbare khaki shirt, stopping when the warder dawdled to greet or reprimand a prisoner in a cell, until they reached a front desk with other warders and a few unfamiliar faces smiling at him.

'Home beckons,' someone said to him. He noticed the man clasped a small gadget, later identified as the new GSM phone, in his right hand. 'Mr. President has freed you.'

Prof placed his hands behind his back and observed the ghosts before him; his visitors—Maami and Olukayode, his childhood friend, whom everyone now called Kayo because Prof had, a result of not being able to pronounce his friend's full name as a toddler. Maami and Kayo watched him, and exchanged quick glances, between turning to listen and respond to the warders. He could tell from their looks that they were examining the way his shoulder blade was chiselled into his flesh, burrowing a visible hollow in his neck.

'Take,' Kayo said. Prof did not look at his friend's face, even as he accepted the handkerchief that he passed to him. He put it in his pocket, eyes fixed on the Nokia mobile phone which Kayo clutched. He tucked his grey vest into his trousers and swapped the prison uniform he used as a veil over his head with the flower-patterned cotton shirt they gave him to change into. The sunlight was bright, and it penetrated the shirt as soon as he stepped outside. He winced every time he needed to raise his face to the light.

As he walked out of the prison, he noticed a calendar with the picture of a young girl, smiling with her eyes shut. She reminded him of Desanya—who had often visited him in prison. He was going to turn away when he noticed it was a calendar from 1995 and it displayed the month of October—a month and year he could never forget. His eyes landed on the date he had come to prison: 3 October 1995. It was two days after Nigeria's independence celebration and four days before his 45th birthday.

He thought back to that day. He was trying to avoid the cars swerving towards pedestrians who filed down the broken sidewalk of Bode Thomas Street when a man in an army green T-shirt and khaki shorts gave him a scissor kick that saw him kissing the ground. Before he could gather himself to stand, he counted seven men, all wearing the same clothes, bent over him. They punched and kicked his ribs until he spiralled onto the ground like a millipede.

In that moment, he understood what it was like to be a ball being rammed about by tennis players, as one of the men asked him, 'Who hit you? Guess!' The sun's rays boiled the blood and sweat dripping from his flesh, split open by the strike of cowhide whips. He raised his swollen, bloodied eyes, and caught a name graffitied on a wall in white: MKO. Moshood Kashimawo Olawale Abiola, the billionaire businessman who was in prison for treason, because he had declared himself president four months after his victory was annulled by the government. He considered that they might soon share a prison cell. The white letters of the politician's initials faded slowly to a light grey, blue-grey, then charcoal; until everything became so black he felt outside of himself. He stopped struggling against the men and watched his motionless body as he could no longer resist the darkness that possessed him; until he woke up handcuffed with a hood over his head, in a vehicle that smelt of dried faeces and what he would later identify as dried blood. This was how Prof Eniolorunda was to become disconnected from the world he fought for, for ten years.

Prof placed his hand on Kayo's shoulder, 'Take me home. I want to go to my father's house.'

* * *

Prof dug into his pockets for a handkerchief as his mother excavated a phone from her bag. She punched the keyboard for light and explored the walls for the switch. Prof placed the handkerchief loosely over his eyes, as a blindfold, to avoid the light of the 30-watt amber bulb which came on as he stepped into the house. The cloth covered his left eye but the right eye, which was left partially bare, made him squint. He turned towards the curtain and felt the coarse settling of dust on the thin lines of the fabric's weave. The dust rose into his nostrils and he sneezed. His mother moved closer and slowly stroked his back. Prof did not turn to face her. He listened to her low voice as she spoke. Kayo walked in after him and sank into a chair. Prof walked towards the farthest corner of the room, observing his mother and Kayo.

'I'm still wondering why you'd choose to come to your father's house, and not mine,' Maami sighed, before adding, 'I would have washed the window blinds or changed them for one with a brighter colour, *so gbo*.' She rubbed her temples and looked out of the window, before moving restlessly around the room.

Prof moved to take her place at the window. His eyes

roamed over the row of houses with peeling paint, stopping
at the faded signpost with "LSDPC Low Cost Housing Estate,
Abesan" painted on it.

However, everyone called the estate Jakande Estate, after
Lateef Jakande, a former governor of Lagos state who built it
and many others around the city to tackle the city's housing
problems. Years after, not much changed. The blocks of flats
remained as ugly as he remembered, only now there were
more discordant noises leaping from generators and pepper-
grinding machines competing for attention. He rearranged
the curtains, turned away from the view, and found himself
facing his mother.

'The curtains are really dirty. Are you sure you don't want
to stay with me—in my house?' His mother waited for him
to reply and when he didn't, she added, 'At least for some
months, you can live with me. I'll cook good food. I can also
bring people to clean this house and air it as well if you want
to return.' He stayed quiet, her words disappearing into the
air as if she never spoke. 'Kayo knows the right people if you
need a job,' she added. 'You know how it is, big-big women
and big-big men are everywhere in this country.'

Prof held Kayo in his stare for a long time; no smile, no
attempt to show appreciation for the kindness spoken about.
Kayo, on his part, grunted.

'You needed to remind them of me?' Prof asked.

'*Haba!* You're a man of the people now-o. Don't you know?
We can also turn on the radio, I'm sure it's in the news,' Kayo
turned around to switch on the radio on the stool beside the
chair. 'Mr. President released ten prisoners, but you're the
most significant one. You're probably the headline.'

'Don't put it on. It isn't necessary!' Prof growled, staring
down at his feet as the crackle of the radio filled the room,
'Please turn it off.'

Kayo waffled but turned off the radio. Prof turned to look
at his mother, studying the lines which had formed on her
forehead, the corners of her eyes and the sides of her mouth.

He imagined tracing them with his hand. Oblivious to the turn of his thoughts, Maami attempted to court him with stories that started off with 'Do you remember when...' He wondered if what he saw in her eyes was fear, although he couldn't say what for. He began to hum a birthday song he had heard on the car radio. She stopped talking.

Kayo chuckled, 'Do you miss celebrating your birthdays?' He moved closer, their shoulders brushing, and whispered, 'Remember how I used to get you drunk the night before your birthday?' He hawed.

'*Abeg*, let's see your face. Remove the shirt over your head, now. *Abi*, you are now Captain Hook?' Kayo slapped his back and neighed. 'Do you want me to get you a generator? The power situation is still terrible-o.'

'How regular are the outages?'

'Ha, I can't say it is regular, as we don't even have a pattern. There's been no light here for four months. Even though there was a name change, the problem persists.'

'What name change?'

'Oh, they changed the name from NEPA to PHCN— Power Holding Company of Nigeria—when the government privatised electricity distribution.'

'Hmmm?'

'We have seen no benefit so far. In fact, it is worse. We have gone from "Never Expect Power Always" to "Problem Has Changed Name."' He sighed, and with an added intensity to this voice, said, 'We have not had light for two years now in my area. They carried our transformer away and three months ago, some people stole the cables. We use the generator, morning and night.'

'Hmmm.'

'Well, it is the way it is. This is our life. We have accepted it,' Kayo laughed. 'But there's regular electricity here. At least, you can do some things with power. You get four hours out of twenty-four hours. It is not that bad.'

'Really? How could anyone tolerate light which brought

even more darkness?' Prof asked. He adjusted the cloth from his face to shade the light a little, before walking towards the bedroom.

As he moved away, he overheard his mother saying, 'It will take a while, but we will try to bring him back to proper life.'

Prof moved down the passage into the bedroom, more certain than ever that he would keep the light out of his new home.

'You can't exist here—You should ask them to take you back to prison. I mean, that's home now—for you, for us—Think, man, think!'

'How can prison be home? He should stay here. This is where he belongs.'

'What is this one saying? Home is where your body settles even in the dark. The prison is home.'

'Is this one okay? Was his body ever settled in prison, lest being settled in darkness? Please, Prof, don't mind him. Take your time and relax. You can make up your mind later. Seriously, when did prison become homely?'

Prof felt the voices in his head increasing as each one tried to be heard. They wanted to drown out Desanya's voice, which was usually the loudest, and the one he ended up listening to. He focused on her voice; *'Nothing has changed since you went to prison. Okay, there are now GSM phones,'* Desanya said with a giggle.

The moment her voice came in clearly, he knew the other voices would go away and leave Desanya to speak to him. This was their routine.

'Hey! How are you coping with the new attention?'

He smiled and didn't respond. It was always how they started their conversations. She did most of the talking and he listened.

'I see you're considering turning off the lights.' He remained silent.

'Here's something for you as you ponder; "Someone I loved

once gave me a box full of darkness. It took me years to understand that this too, was a gift.'"

'That's profound,' he murmured, turning around to see if his mother or Kayo were behind him.

'Yes, that's Mary Oliver. Remember her?'

'Not sure I do.'

'We—you read her to me when some Canadian NGO visited the prison with books.'

'Oh, I did?' He pondered over the words. Desanya had come to him as a gift. When he had been thrown into solitary confinement, the many voices in his head wouldn't stop talking. He would press his hands to his ears and scream, but that did not stop them.

Until Desanya came to him. She whispered, 'Breathe, breathe, breathe.' He listened to her and the other voices left. She stayed.

Desanya was different. She didn't have a name when she came to him. He just thought of her as The Voice. He wanted to give Desanya a personality so he started with a name. A name from a memory that would not go away. He gave The Voice the name of a little girl in Maroko—an area for low and middle-income earners who bragged to be homeowners, even though they waded through potholes to arrive to a house sinking in the mire. The location appealed to the country's big men and the people of Maroko were given an eviction notice over the radio and asked to vacate the area by the following day. Prof was in a caucus meeting of activists when he heard the story, and he hurried over to the area.

As he spoke to the thousands of eyes staring at him, hopeful that something could change, his gaze landed on this little girl with eyes like water in a glass. He picked her up from the ground and carried her in his arms. The feeling he felt holding her was close to nothing he could compare, except to once in life when he felt he was going to eventually be a father. It was just a moment, one he tried not to think of. Yet, as he looked into the little girl's eyes, he felt as if cold water was running down his entire body and he shivered. A strange feeling overcame him. He felt a sudden yearning which was not for want of a daughter, rather, she made him want to become a little girl. He wanted to feel vulnerable and be so innocent he could share his emotion without fear of judgement.

He asked for her name—she whispered into his ear like someone blowing off a candle in three breaths and he heard, 'De-san-ya.' He left Maroko with her presence still filling the corner of his arm where she had rested when he carried her, filling a place that had become empty at a point in his life. Many weeks later, with his heart buried in a vacuum, he returned to look for her, and someone told him that a pillar had fallen on her and killed her. He left the place emptier than when he came. *You have lost another one*, he told himself.

The name "Desanya" suited The Voice. It filled up the emptiness that came with the loss, with warmth. While he could not see this new Desanya, he could always spread his arms along the prison wall, begging Desanya to come for a chat. There were times she did not come. Those times, he cried as he pined for her. Those times, he felt lucky to sight an ant in the cell that he could talk to and express how much he missed Desanya. He would jump with an hysterical happiness and then smile at his luck when an ant waited for a few minutes to listen to him whine. At other times, when he was overcome with weakness, he would strain his ears to listen to the echoes of laughter, groans, or deep sighs from the other cells.

Desanya interrupted him and he stirred from his thoughts. *'You should go to your mother and Kayo. You're spending too much time alone.'*

4

Maami and Kayo startled as Prof hurried out of the bedroom. They stopped talking. Prof, ignoring them, began pacing the length and breadth of the sitting room, counting his steps and measuring the distance between the kitchen, the bedroom and the bathroom, and the spaces between the furniture and the walls, loudly. He closed his eyes as he did this until he felt he was familiar with the spaces around the house and then he returned to the side of the sitting room where Maami and Kayo were now talking in low tones. When he turned to face them, he observed how Kayo and Maami, now quiet, conversed with their eyes, their throats bopping up and down as they swallowed spittle.

Kayo's heavy breathing and Maami's quiet humming sounded like background music to an anticipated act. Prof watched his friend's travelling eyes, which moved about as if trying to leap out of the sockets and ascertained that his friend kept something from him—many things from him.

Theirs was a friendship that was almost natal and bore many good stories of the past. In their childhood, they were like conjoined twins; seeing one meant the other was close. Prof was the one "who had sense" while Kayo was the one "whose head was not correct". The community threw this readily at Kayo, for it was common knowledge that his coarse voice was because of the *gbana* he smoked openly from the age of nine. Kayo never hid behind uncompleted fences or deserted schools like the other children who smoked marijuana. He went about, smoking it openly like a cigarette—which itself was seen as bad enough for teenagers. Kayo would take a puff and roll the whiff of cannabis in his mouth until it gathered into fumes that formed mushroom clouds which he blew into the faces of the children that gathered around him, while their mothers cursed from a distance, taking care not to come near him. They feared Kayo for his unpredictability. Yet, Prof knew he was timid, that his actions were a cover-up for his many fears. He could not confront anyone who stood up to him, those who were not hassled by his upfront hard ways which were actually a way to distract others from his diffidence.

Prof saw himself and Kayo running to the stream to watch naked girls take their bath, plucking fruits from neighbours' trees, and running errands for older people for a fee. There were also the distinct stories of selflessness and sacrifice. One time, Prof stole books from the office of the headmaster of the only secondary school in Ilese, and Kayo, who accompanied him was the one who was caught. Rather than relaying the story of how his friend lacked books but loved to read so much and that he had accompanied him to steal the books, he let out the first words which must have made sense to him in the convenience of defending a crime he knew he could not disentangle himself from. He looked up at the guard who caught him and said, 'I just finished shitting, sir. The paper was for my *yansh*.' He placed his hands over his buttocks to emphasise the purpose and place of the paper. Later, on the assembly ground, in front of the other students, he screamed, 'The paper was for my *yansh, sah!*' into the air, but not once did he mention his friend's name.

Many years later, unsure of what to do with their lives in the village after they completed university, they both moved to Lagos, and their struggles were soon forgotten, with regular visits to Abe Igi, the open food and beer joint where journalists, artists, activists, writers, and poets gathered under the leafy cover of almond trees at the National Theatre. They spent hour after hour there with other comrades and artists; talking arts, politics and imagining sex, until alcohol turned people into grouches cursing even their beer bottles, or simply laughing into the air with their fantasies.

As he stood facing Kayo in a room years after they felt they could have died for each other, he wondered if their younger selves might have screamed in disbelief at the way their eyes now tore into each other as they considered the possible consequences that could result from the other's defiance.

He walked past Kayo and his mother and walked towards the switch for the light, then flicked it. Prof ignored Kayo's curses at the power outage, straining to study the outline of his mother and friend in the shadows.

He let the fatigued silhouettes swallow as much silence as they could before saying in a quiet voice, 'I turned off the lights.' Adjusting the cloth over his eyes, he moved towards the curtains and adjusted them to give the room an even darker shade. He waited, expecting Maami or Kayo to make a comment. When none was offered, he added, 'I have been thinking about lights for a while now, and—' He closed his eyes, and then opened them again slowly into the dimness, 'I don't think the light is important.'

'Which one is this again? What has light got to do with your return?' Kayo asked. He took a few steps forward, but stopped as Prof began to talk.

'I'm fine. I'm just saying, I'll be staying in the dark now,' Prof replied with his eyes closed. There was a sound and Prof could not make out if it was a chuckle or a throat being cleared. He also could not tell from whom it came.

'You want to live in the dark,' Kayo said. It was a statement, meant as a question, and he did not respond to it.

'So, how long are you going to live in the dark? Mr. Man, you're funny sha. Electricity is never regular anyway, so, what's with the drama?' Kayo stomped towards the switch, laughing. His voice juddered with the laughter, until it reached a truck-horn pitch.

'Don't. Don't do it,' Prof said, making sure his tone conveyed both his annoyance and desire. He waited, half hoping Kayo would be defiant and challenge him. Kayo walked three steps towards him then stopped.

'This is not funny! And what would you do if I switched on the lights?'

'I can't tell,' he replied in a whisper.

'Why are you doing this? May we not live in dark times, man.' Kayo said, turning the situation into a prayer, as was typical of the Yoruba. His voice was as low as Prof's, who was listening for footsteps, so he could tell when his friend moved towards the switch. He sensed that there was something different about this Kayo, different from the one he grew up with, but he could not make out what it was. There was a streak of confidence in this one. He seemed sure of the things he could make possible.

Prof stepped in front of Kayo, placing his hands on the switch, and with clenched teeth, he muttered in one long breath, 'I could kill if the lights come on.' The iciness of his own words baffled even him, and with his back against the wall, he puffed out aloud. Except for the whirr of his breath, the room was quiet. He straightened up and said, 'I think it's time you leave.'

'Leave for where?' Maami jumped in. She did not wait for an answer as she added, '*Oya, joko*. Sit. You need to relax. You're too tense.' Maami then turned to Kayo, 'Be patient with him. You know how prison is. He has—' she paused and then said, 'He needs time, okay? He has gone through a lot.' Prof walked towards the door. He turned the knob and opened it. In his younger years, he would have spent several hours revising how to look straight into his mother's eyes to defy her wish. He sighed. The frail light of evening streamed into the room and he stepped into the shadows. Neither Kayo nor his mother moved.

'Kayo, I really think you should leave now. I want to be by myself. Thanks for your kindness. Thanks for your concern. Please leave. Maami, please, you too.'

Prof wanted to shout the words at them to express his heightening exasperation, but he found himself whispering and gesturing with his hands towards the door—right, then left, then right again—like a dance routine. His mother took a seat and Kayo continued to lean against the wall.

'Am I talking to two deaf people?' he asked.

'Are you okay? Or has prison made you delirious not to know that I'm your mother?!' Maami said, glowering at him. Prof listened to his mother's sniffling. He wondered how she could cry with the smell of undispersed dust in the room.

He snuffled. He looked towards the window and noticed the grey colour that settled over everything.

'You want me to leave your house? You! You! *Se o mo nkan ti o'n so sa?* Do you know what you're saying? Do you? I'm sure it is this accursed house. I should have taken you to my house from the prison. Kayo and I should not have taken charge of this house. We should have allowed the government to take it. This place is evil,' she said, finally letting out a small sob.

Prof moved closer to his mother. He nudged her on the shoulder, clasped his fingers around hers and compelled her to walk with him towards the door, 'You really should go now, go home,' he whispered, unlocking his hands from hers. He tightened his fist as tears stung his eyes and he struggled not to let them fall down his cheeks. 'Maami. Please. Go.'

'Let me help you. I'm your mother. I will help you. I don't know what they did to you there, but you can be sure the reason I didn't die was to take care of you. Don't you understand? I prayed, I fasted, and God made sure I am alive to see you again.' She cupped his face with her hands even as he tried to resist, 'My son, please don't send me away.'

The corner of his lips pulled down, and he bit his tongue until he tasted blood. A sob stuck in his throat when he tried to respond. Unable to take his silence, his mother howled, 'Eni!' her voice beating as her body vibrated with the velocity of the words unfurling from her lips in the company of sobs that rose with each syllable of disbelief. 'Eniolorunda Durotimi Akanni, whatever you are, you are still my son. They may call you Professor. They may call you activity—or is it activist?—

these breasts fed you!' she said, grabbing her breasts with her hands.

Long seconds of silence followed between them, before she repeated, 'You're my son, you will not send me out of your house. Do you know what this means? To send me out of the same house where my things were flung from the window? Do you know? Do you know this is an abomination happening two times?' She spoke with as much energy as her choked voice could allow.

Prof could hear all the things she did not say. He heard the groans from carrying heavy baskets of cocoa from the farm to the market so that she could pay his school fees, while she saved up for her typing and adult education classes. It stirred up the loud wails reaching his prison cells any time she came to agitate for his release. It was also the wail of the late nights of his younger years when he listened as she returned from work as a farmhand because her petty trading was never enough for his school fees. He winced at each thought, yet he resisted putting the lights on or asking her to stay. This house was not the place for her. It was the place for him, and this was not the time for explanations. It was time to make a decision—an immediate one. She had to leave.

Among these preoccupations, he heard Kayo placating him with words. He was not attentive enough to know what his exact words were at first, until he turned to him.

'Please, let us stay. *Ma binu*. If I have offended you in any way, forgive me, please. Forgive me for bribing the warders. I know you don't like things like that.'

'I just want to be on my own for now.'

'You have been through a lot, so you don't know what you're doing. Maami and I can help you. Let us.'

'I don't know what I'm doing, right?' Prof shook his head, suspired and turned to his mother, 'Maami, go home.' He was tired and needed to sit on the floor without being told to do so, to sleep on a bed, to put out the lights and put them on again at his own discretion, if he ever wanted to do so.

He knew there was a weariness in him, but he could not tell
where it came from. He was tired of his mother and Kayo's
presence, and all he could say when he felt he had as much
strength as he needed was, 'Please, please go.' Prof fell to the
ground weeping.

Maami and Kayo rushed towards him. He didn't know
which of them placed a hand on his shoulder, but it made
him snap. And with his body vibrating he screamed, 'Go! Go!
Go! Just go!'

'Stop! Stop! Stop this!' his mother yelled back before she
lowered her voice. 'Eni, my son, no, no, don't—' She stopped
suddenly, and the silence that followed showed that there was
a lot unsaid between them. Prof stepped aside as his mother
and Kayo walked ahead of him, taking slow steps towards the
open door. With them, they carried the words they wished to
say.

When they hesitated by the door, he said, '*E se*, thanks.
Thank you.' And like he needed to assure them that this was
not a total disconnect, he asked, 'Will you bring provisions for
me? Every two weeks? I will appreciate that a lot. You may
leave it by the door when you bring it. Thank you.'

'I have an extra key. I can always drop the food in the house
anytime,' his mother said in a defeated voice that still held
some pride. It was a small way of emphasising that she could
have her way if she wanted.

Prof did not respond. Maami understood the silence. Her
tone changed to one of resolve and she said, 'There's a GSM
phone on the table, in case you need to reach me. If you
need anything, let me know, okay? There's a young girl selling
wosiwosi downstairs. You can send her to me, she knows how
to get me. *So gbo?*'

Kayo lingered for a while at the door and he failed to
surrender his hold on the door midway. The silence between
them matured into grief as the distant noise of traffic filtered
in. The smell of *akara* wafted in, but it did nothing to affect the
tension in the room. Kayo finally let the door go, slamming it

shut, and the lock's tumbler fastened after them. Prof rested against the wood, which vibrated for a long moment as his mother banged on the door, each strike resonating in his body.

'Eni. *Ha! O ma ga o*. If this is fair, it's okay. But you must know that this is too heavy a load for me. I waited for your return and cried to sleep every night. But God knows best. Just seeing you alive from prison is succour,' his mother said in a cracked voice.

Prof placed his head against the door and listened to his mother sing his paternal *oriki,* each line punctuated by a pause. *Apa'n jara omo olokun esin, omo a boba jokuso, abo ba jaro, omo yokoto yokoto nikun ajifa, igba te ji fa, emi le ni ikun la si, ara agba sin, abikuko bi eni rebi, omo poranganda, poranganda ti n koni le yin okan...*

He remembered how these words placated him as a child.

They were the same words he repeated to himself, as an adult, when he felt like he was disappearing from his skin; with a cannibalistic void taking the place where he should be. He would be there, but suddenly feel absent and inexistent. These words reminded him of who he was and where he was from, the things that he thought were expected of him.

His mother stopped singing his praise song. Prof tried to continue the words, but he could not remember them. And then he tried to translate them into English, to see if it would taint how the words grounded him to his childhood and his mother's embraces. '*Apa'n jara*, child of the horseman, who holds the king's rein, the one who is to descend with the king into the dark place, he who delights in the innards of the fortunate. For if you are not fortunate, why do you celebrate a paunch? The child of *Agba-sin*, who saunters into the afterlife. Child of *Poranganda, Poranganda* who breaks the front teeth...' He couldn't remember the rest of the chant; it felt like another loss and a bigger emptiness ate at him. Prof sank to the ground. He listened to his mother and Kayo's footsteps until only silence and echoes of their presence remained with him. The sounds that seemed frozen when they had been there now sneaked about the room.

He heard a scream languishing in the distance, some jolting laughter, a baby's cry and the buzz of traffic and again, the smell of fried *akara*. He shut his eyes as he felt his stomach crunching inside, as the pain in his head cascaded to every part of his body. He tightened his fists and then unclasped his hands for the burst of a wail which seemed to diffuse into every part of his shoulder. His whole body shook. Although he did not feel better, he felt like each time a tear stung his eyes, the small parts, the little parts, the fine cracks of his broken heart, mended. He picked up the **GSM** phone and tried to understand how it worked. After a futile attempt, he realised how much more things had evolved in his absence. He opened his mouth and breathed out, ashamed at himself for his inability to operate the **GSM**. At his inability to sing his *oriki* in full.

5

At the age of nine, Desire Babangida's mother started to speak at length with her shadow, but the other children treated Desire as if nothing had changed. They played pranks on her. They joked about the smell of the food wafting from the different houses and how she salivated. They wondered whose mother's snores kept them awake through the night. They laughed at how their parents, who were also neighbours, fought amongst themselves over the smell of burning firewood which entered their rooms. In the evenings, as the children ran home to their parents, Desire walked towards the side of the road where Iya Mufu sold *tuwo* to the community in the evenings.

'I have come,' she said, genuflecting towards Iya Mufu.

'Welcome. *Oya, oya*, join Abudu. You people should move those hands fast, so I can answer my customers,' Iya Mufu screamed as Desire settled to squat by the open drain, next to Abudu, a mute boy who always smiled at her with his eyes. They washed the plastic plates together in two big bowls, one for washing with a tattered sponge and the other for rinsing. Desire then stacked the plates and hurriedly placed them by Iya Mufu, who was surrounded by a small crowd of impatient customers stretching their naira notes at her. Iya Mufu would grab the closest one to her, pick a plate from the pile by her side, and dish out a portion with the steel spoon paddle from the two black, round cauldrons—one filled with white *tuwo* and the other a crimson stew, which sat by a smaller pot with *gbegiri* soup. She served until the last drop. To signal that the *tuwo* was finished, Iya Mufu banged on the side of the pot and lifted her hands in the air, proclaiming 'The end!' with a huge smile on her face. A slight murmur would rise in the air, a little hesitation, but in a few minutes the crowds of customers dispersed slowly, leaving Desire and Abudu to clean up the place, while Iya Mufu counted the day's earnings.

Abudu smiled at Desire as they washed and packed the utensils into a wooden box, before both departed into the night with a bowl of tuwo and a 20 naira note.

Desire did not ignore the changes that came from her mother. Whenever she was alone in the room, she watched her converse with her shadow. 'You have not treated me well at all—at all. Is this the life I asked for?' Sometimes, Desire's mother screamed at the shadow. She moved from one side to another like one moving to a song, before breaking into a loud wail, panting. At times, she would turn to Desire and with a smile hovering over her lips say, 'You know I love you. You know, you know, you know *abi*?'

Desire stood by the door or a wall and watched as her mother talked and gestured to her shadow. She moved towards her mother and stroked her arms gently, 'There's no one here. Only me.' What she wanted to do was rush towards her and shake her out of the conversation with her shadow until she stopped. Instead, she let tears run down her face, until her body convulsed against her mother's. When Desire calmed down, she stared at her mother, unsure whether to leave her alone. But she did, she always did. She walked to the door and leaned against its frame, her body straddling the wall. She remained this way until she fell asleep standing, only to wake up bent like a broken branch.

As time passed, Desire learnt to move to a corner of the room and focus on the noise outside, instead. Sometimes, she rushed out to play with her friends in the neighbourhood and returned to the room at night after helping Iya Mufu sell her *tuwo*. She tiptoed so as not to wake her mother. This was the rhythm of her life until they heard the seven-day quit notice on the radio for all the people of Maroko.

The eviction changed everything. Soldiers carrying guns covered Maroko, and although it was acknowledged as one of the most populated areas in Lagos, where the music never stopped, it entered an eerie silence in the afternoons. Things were like this until the day the man called Prof came around to speak to the people.

Throwing off the long silence which had taken over the area, the people of Maroko shouted, wept and clapped all at once as Prof stood on a makeshift podium, speaking to them. Caught in the throng, Desire ducked her way around until she was in front of the crowd, and within a few minutes she found herself on Prof's shoulder, hearing the roar from the crowd but not understanding what was said. On his shoulder, she felt a calm descend upon her. The empty spaces inside her appeared to fill up as Prof whispered something in her ears as he tried to put her down on the ground, but she couldn't hear him well because of the noise around them.

Desire could never forget the look in Prof's eyes as he released her from his arms. He turned immediately towards the government officials who were carrying out the demolition and wagged his finger at them. He screamed slogans into the air and Desire believed for many years that he smiled at her, his eyes saying, 'You see, all I am doing is for you.' All around them people were fainting, rolling on the ground as the place they called home became rubble, but she alone saw the way he stood for the people—because of her. It was what she believed. It was what she knew. Prof was there with them, to save her. He ran down from the raised platform he was on and ran towards a tractor. The tractor screeched to a halt, almost running over him as he tried to stop it from grinding a man's personal belongings to the ground. In the hours of arguments which transpired between him and the government officials, the people salvaged what they could from their falling homes. Prof returned to her. He smiled and pushed a book into her hand. She genuflected, accepting the book, keeping her eyes glued to the ground. She did not want to look into his eyes, lest he saw her embarrassment, because she had not yet learnt to read well at that time. In a staccato, she read the title in her head: *How to be a Nigerian.*

She took the book home and read the title to herself when she was alone. Then she left the book by her sleeping area. She did not open it for many days even though she wanted to. It confused her that Prof had given her a book on how to be Nigerian. She wondered if she was from somewhere else and if he knew and needed her to know that. She went about for many days repeating the title of the book to herself. She ignored the discomfort of its edges rubbing against her skin where she tucked it in her skirt at night. The book remained unopened beyond the first page for many weeks. But everything changed the moment she read the first sentence in the preamble of the book: *It is not easy to write a book. First, you have to get a book: then you have to write it.* Desire was intrigued by the idea of consuming another person's difficulty. The more she thought about the process of writing and how much the writer must have struggled with thoughts and ideas, the more she was determined to become a fluent reader. She imagined that Prof wanted her to read, and that must have been what she heard.

Once she started to read, she learnt to build a world with the words she found in books and stopped minding that her mother spoke with shadows. Reading, however, came with its own troubles. She needed books to read and they needed to be bought or stolen.

Desire stole from neighbours, she stole from her friends at school. She stole books and nothing else.

The woman Desire stole from the most was a woman she worked for during her secondary school holidays. Madam, as Desire called her, was a high school teacher who brought home books from school. She would fall asleep sprawled across the sofa, limbs stretched as far as they could reach.

Desire stole one book a week from the house, or sometimes two if she finished one too quickly. She took it into the toilet with her when no one was watching, and it was in the toilet that she wrapped the book in a scarf over her stomach, adjusted her gown and returned to work.

It was going smoothly until the woman asked her one day, 'Desire! Can you please check if some of the books fell behind the shelf? Or maybe the children threw them under the chairs. The shelf is almost empty.'

Desire moved around the house performing the task of cleaning and searching for books she knew were in her house. She lifted the chairs, upturned the tables, and the shelves. She swept the inner corners and arranged her face into a look of despair before walking up to the woman in the sitting room.

'Isn't it possible that Taiwo and Kenny have been taking books with them to the neighbours? I think I saw them going there yesterday.'

'What! Which of the neighbours? Is it that woman?'

Desire did not talk, but merely grunted, to agree with the woman's suspicion without exactly burdening her conscience further with guilt. Especially, as the neighbour the woman suspected was one Desire knew Madam would never ask about the books.

'Ha! And you could not stop them. Didn't I tell them to stop going to that woman's house? These children won't kill me.'

'I can go and call them now.'

'I thought they were in their room?'

'Sorry Madam. I was cleaning and taking care of the house, and—'

'See, Desire, I know you are here to clean, but please, also help mind the children when you can. I don't want my kids to go to other people's houses, okay?'

Desire genuflected again, looking down.

'Oh, I think the kids are in their room. I made a mistake.'

'Okay, go on and continue your work. And please, just make sure you stop them if they ever try to go to that woman's house again. I wish someone would just evict her and let a normal human being come into this compound.'

A week later Desire sent a message that she could no longer work there because it was affecting her health. By the time she left her boss, she had stolen 33 books.

She arranged the books in a high pile in the room, and it took the place of the furniture she and her mother did not have. They joined several other stolen, picked, borrowed-and-never-returned books. By the time she was 16, she had so many books she could have stocked a library with them if she wanted to do so. She only stopped stealing books the day she watched a mob burning a thief for stealing from a stationery shop.

6

As the years passed, Desire decided to find out more about Prof, beginning with his full name: Eniolorunda Durotimi Akanni. At first, it was not a conscious effort to know more about him, but the news of him found her as the years passed. His stories filled her ears wherever she went. His news came to her between caring for a mother who was now not just talking to shadows but was now a shadow herself, a shrunken body on the mat mumbling to herself, waiting to be bathed and fed. It was from the news going around that she learnt that the university had sacked him because he would not *dobale* for the Vice-Chancellor, a man who asked that his lecturers lay prostrate before him at every meeting. Desire learnt how he led so many student marches and followed with labour union action.

She watched Prof on the television sets arranged side by side by the roadside electronic shop, varying only in size as if to make their presence noticeable in their difference. She watched as Prof wept over how much he loved his country. It was so unexpected. One minute he was screaming out slogans, and the next, he let out small sobs, and then he would let out a howl that left the few people standing around him with open mouths, before they drew close to him and touched his shoulder. He sniffed and shook his head, his grey suit slipping down off his shoulders. He wiped his eyes with a handkerchief that someone handed to him, and returned to roaring about his passion to save Nigerians from the clutches of "foxes from hell".

'This is a violence against human rights! And I will not be here and watch you suffer. I am ready to die for the people. My people,' he was heaving and puffing, gesticulating as he spoke. His upper lip twitched as he spoke of how citizens were being cheated out of what should be theirs.

The following day, Desire walked up to a discussion of the "Free Readers' Association", men who gathered at newspaper stands to read for free. Most FRA members were men on their way to work that bored, with no work that bored, or looking for work that bored. They gathered and argued over political analysis, which led to lengthy complaints on the sorry lives of Nigerians.

'Bro, country is very hard-o. I go collect salary like dis, begin cry.'

'*Sebi*, you even dey collect salary. If me I see work like dis, na to begin use my company name as my surname.'

This remark made the others laugh. Desire stood with the men, their hands whipping the air as they described life in Nigeria with the magnitude of their anger distorting their mouths and widening their eyes. They talked about monies that travelled in and out of the accounts of those in government. They bemoaned the absence of Prof in the country. Although it was common knowledge that the police had arrested him, no one knew where he had been taken.

In the weeks that followed, the newspapers stopped carrying stories about him. Before the newspaper stories, the news of his arrest was all over the city. As the weeks multiplied, people stopped talking about him openly except at the newspaper FRA. This was where Desire heard them discussing the killing of another activist, Ken Saro Wiwa, and eight other Ogoni, and she wondered if Prof would end up in the same way. One morning, the men at the FRA were discussing their fears that Prof would die, but were interrupted by a truckload of army men with whips, who dispersed everyone there for "illegal gathering."

Prof's disappearance and the demise of the FRA came about at the time Desire started to work as a porter for Mama T, a big trader at the Balogun Market. Mama T, shortened from

"Mama Terror", always wore her face in a frown. She could throw tantrums that shamed thunder. The few times she smiled were when she counted money placed on her elephant thighs and it was on one such day that Desire's grief for Prof, who she feared she would never meet again, overtook her. She focused on the open book in her hands as she suppressed her tears, only to look up to see the successful trader eating her up with a look that burnt into her skin. Desire clamped the book shut. She knew what those eyes were telling her, '*You are here reading a book while the others are working, abi?*'

'See this *olowikowi*, you sure do not have a head on your neck *ke?*' Mama T tapped her on the shoulder as she carried in the last bundle of lace fabric.

Mama T bent over her, slapping her hands together like clapping cymbals. She turned away from Desire and faced the other labourers who were busy loading off batches of cloth from trucks into the shop.

'*Se*, you're learning how to cawwy material from twuck to shop inside the book? Do you think that is how we make money in Lagos?'

The other porters found this hilarious.

'Mama T that is tisha-o. She like book too much. She even know everything *sef.*'

Desire put the book down and hurried to do her work, muttering an apology even after Mama T's eyes were no longer on her.

'Tisha? Me, I'm not looking for "Madam Tisha" here-o. I want pwoper somebody whose muscles are not made fwom plastic. I need an *akilapa*—sturdy and stwong hands like iron. *So gbo?*'

Desire hurried to meet the others. She dropped her book on one of the bags of sachet milk as she did. Mama T picked it up and studied the cover. 'War and Peace? What kind of book is this? Leo Toy-toy? What kind of name is this?' She held Desire in a long stare before saying, 'Come for your big book with the stwange name when you finish your work-o. *So gbo*? Who goes around reading this kind of big book inside the market?' Mama T shook her head and paddled her heavy buttocks to her seat.

In the evening, as the market became empty, Desire walked up to Mama T. She thought of words to express her apology, but none came to her. When she stood in front of Mama T, the first words she said were, 'I love reading.'

It was not what she had meant to say when she knelt on the ground in front of Mama T. It was what came out. She thought over her words again and said, 'Do not be upset, Ma. It won't happen again, Ma.' She looked at the ground and prayed in silence. Mama T said nothing to her. Desire felt her eyes on her, scanning her body from top to bottom. Mama T shook her head. She stood up and walked away with pouted lips that let out a long '*Issssh,*' and a wave of the hand over her shoulder, 'Go away, unfortunate one. Bookworm!'

Desire hesitated for a while before she ran to pick up the book from the chair. She held it close to her chest. When she left the shop, she knew she would not be doing much sleeping that night. And indeed, she woke several times in the night mumbling prayers that she would not be laid off. The next day, she avoided Mama T, who in turn ignored her until evening time, when she prepared to go home after the day's work.

'Er... you. What's that your name again?'

'Desire.'

'Desire? As in, "the things I want"?'

'Yes, Ma.'

'*O ga o.* Desire, Desire, Desire. What won't one hear? Anyway, ask one of the girls to give you the diwection to my house, *so gbo*? See you on Sunday, by 3pm.'

Desire walked into Mama T's compound scouting for the entrance to the house after missing her way trying to locate the building. There was a chaos of lock-up shops and kiosks in front of the house and the houses on the streets were numbered without any logic. Desire walked past three houses side by side numbered 7, 21, and 49, all the while trying to locate the "house with the sculpture inside it" as one of the girls had described it to her. She found it the fourth time she barged into a house. The sculpture was a mottled mould of an old man facing the house as if he was watching over it. Desire would later learn that Mama T inherited the bungalow from her father, the sculpted old man.

Desire looked at the house. A block of architecture dabbed with brown and cream paint, occupying space and beautifying nothing. It was evident that the designer had attempted to put some finesse into it, but the occupants' mark was more evident than that of the architect. Now the building sat in the middle of the compound, a giant, rectangular antique, surrounded by a cemented floor and whittled flowers leaning against the walls like they were in mourning. She walked past three Land Rovers parked at the back of the house and directly in front of the door. This three-bedroom bungalow, with its entrance behind rather than in front, would become a welcoming home to her.

It was on this first visit to Mama T that she told the rich merchant her life story. Desire told her of her excellent school-leaving results, her dying mother and a childhood spent on the beach. For the first time, she told someone everything— well, almost everything—about herself. Mama T was so quiet as she told her story, that Desire at a point believed she was no longer listening, until she asked, 'Can you help Remilekun do her GCE?'

At first, Desire did not understand what Mama T was asking her to do, until she added, 'I will finance you into university and even give you feeding money, if you do it well-o.'

This was when it occurred to her that she was being asked to impersonate Remilekun and get a "scholarship" for her university education in return. Desire didn't go home to think about it. She agreed on the spot. It did not occur to her that she might be caught or that something could go wrong.

Mama T also made Desire a supervisor in the shop. Desire became responsible for counting the bales of cloth brought in and taken out of the shop. The other labourers, realising the difference in the relationship between her and the Madam, stopped sharing stories like how Mama T winked at some of the salesmen. She lost out on their gossip when she gained Mama T's friendship.

The plan was straightforward. First, Desire obtained an examination form under a fictitious name. Second, Mama T settled an invigilator. It was this invigilator who arranged the seat numbers at the examination centre to benefit Remilekun and Desire. At the centre, Desire looked around to see if there was a way to identify "their man" but all invigilators seemed more concerned with the students' fashion sense than even checking their identity.

'This is a mini gown, right? *Mini*? Do you think you can distract us here?'

Another of the invigilators said smiling, 'This one is dressed like an SU, she is a *konk*, Christian. She is not like all these ones that have come to cheat. Let her go.'

Desire didn't smile back at the man who made the remark. She walked towards her seat, holding an umbrella in one hand and her stationery in the other—her avatar was the stereotypical born-again Nigerian Christian. She wore no jewellery and was dressed in a full flower-patterned shirt-waister that swept the ground as she walked. The scarf tied around her head covered her forehead and looking at her could make one wince at the tightness. That singular experience made her realise how the desperation to achieve one's dream could incur a courage that was never there before. Not once did she look up to see if she was being suspected of anything—until one of the invigilators walked up to her and called her by her real name. She jumped. He smiled. Remilekun cleared her throat.

The process was easy, whenever Desire was done with a paper in the exam hall, "their man" walked up to her, collected the paper and gave her Remilekun's. This was how she wrote two candidates' papers at one sitting—varying her handwriting. When she left the examination hall with Remilekun that day, they nodded and smiled at each other and each departed without speaking.

They both knew they were different in every way and any desire for friendship was smothered by a mutual shame; one for her impoverished finances and the other for a destitute mind. Still, they smiled at each other through the examination, shifting eyes, watching the other's movement and twiddling fingers.

Speaking came seven months later. It was the day they went to the examination centre to check the outcome of the results. 'I had six As and two Cs. It has never happened before. Thanks.' They walked slowly out of the school compound where the result sheets were pasted on a notice board.

'How do you read so well? I really want to read and remember, you know, but—' Remilekun finished her sentence with a laugh. She looked at Desire, expecting her to say something. Desire kept quiet. She walked towards the bus stop, excited more by the promise Mama T made to her, 'Once my daughter passes, you pass. I'll see you through the university, *so gbo*?'

'We have to be friends. I'll have to learn to read very well when I enter the university. You see, I've tried to write this exam four times, but I never remember the things I read.' Remilekun tapped her on the shoulder, 'Are you here?'

'Just thinking. Let's go. In time, we will learn how to remember everything. In time,' she smiled. 'We all forget what we read. That's why some of us keep reading. So we never forget.'

7

'Open! Open! Open this door!' Prof's door shook with each bang. 'Please, please, open this door.'

Prof stood in front of the door listening, trying to decide if he should open it. At first, he was dazed by the audacity, but the continuous banging soon became so constant, he immured his thoughts to it.

'Let us talk. At least you can forgive me.' Pause. 'See, if you don't open this door—I will break it-o!'

In the middle of the screaming and the banging, a loudspeaker sliced the threat with the pump of Angelique Kidjo's *Agolo*, and then swallowed everywhere.

'I just want to talk to you and clear my mind, please,' Kayo shouted over the music.

'Kayo, your redemption is in yourself. Go home,' Prof said as he took a seat.

'I can't sleep. I can't. We should talk. It's one month already and people are asking questions, what do you want me to tell them?'

There was something in his voice that almost pushed Prof to the door, but he held himself and said instead, 'Tell them, whosoever they are, that I have no stories from the prison to tell you or anyone of them, Kayo. Go away.' Prof stood up and walked into the inner room, leaving the knocking to continue.

'Won't you open the door for him? At least listen to what he's got to say, he seems desperate,' Desanya said.

'I won't. And did I invite you here now?'

'Okay, I'll leave,' she said, sulking.

Prof felt a little sorry at first and then he shrugged and went into the bedroom to sleep.

'Mo ti r'anmo n'Ijare o, ko lo ba mi r'obi bo o, ki n mi mu s'ori pele o, k'eleda ma ma gbabode o...'

It was when he woke up that he realised it was the sound of someone singing a Yoruba spiritual that had stirred him from his sleep. There was a song, but it was outside his door and not in his bedroom. His mother was outside singing songs of longing to see him. Her voice lowered, and he knew she was going to stop repeating the songs with that porcelain tender voice that made his shoulders wilt.

For a moment, he wondered if his mother and Kayo came together or whether they planned their visits on the same day.

'You can't make me go through this, Eni,' she said.

Prof listened to her voice. Her pauses. Her sighs. Her shuffling feet made him realise she was tired of standing and waiting for him to open the door, but she was not ready to leave.

'I have the key, but I want you to let me in yourself.'

Prof listened to the heavy thud which meant she had decided to sit by the door. Hearing her sit by the door outside brought back childhood memories of the two of them waiting together at the bus stop after failing to sell any goods at the market. She would sing as they waited, her hands straying into a gentle caress across his body, his head, his back. They sat, stood, squatted and bent at the bus stop, knowing there would be no food to eat that night.

She was outside his house now, waiting.

'I have carried too much, Eni. Do I need to carry new ones in this old age of mine?'

Prof sighed.

'Each time I come here, and you do this, all I can think of is how this house has haunted me. It was here in this house that I was almost thrown down from the window.' She laughed. It was a high-pitched laugh that brought a chill to the bone. 'I can still feel how you snuggled on my back unaware of the things that were happening. Your father throwing down all that I owned in life, on my head, in the rain. His new wife laughing... laughing at me.' Prof heard a sniffle.

'Eni, it was raining. I covered you. *I covered you.* It was raining, and my things were dropping down from the window. I was rushing up and down these stairs with you on my back covered with a nylon while the rain beat me. *I covered you.*'

At first, he was afraid her persistent doorstep drama would stir up some conflict with his neighbours and create a spectacle he did not need. Perhaps someone would request they broke the door. He feared that in a few minutes people would gather in front of his doorstep pleading with her to stop crying, and she would tell them her story, their story, and they, now bold enough to confront him, would call out to him to look with pity on his poor mother and stop acting like a bastard son. He thought of all of this as she banged on the door.

She didn't cry as he expected she would when she got to this point. Her knocks became gentler. Her voice was calm and low as she recounted a story he had heard often growing up.

'I returned home on that day, the rain washed me so thoroughly I felt I would get a new skin. I returned to my village in Ilese with you. Now, I am here standing in front of the same house...' She took a long pause before she added, 'locked out again.'

Then he heard nothing.

'I will keep coming. You will open this door, I know. Here, take this for your upkeep.' She slid some money under the door. 'I will leave provisions by the door, okay?' she paused as if waiting for some sort of response.

Prof walked into the corridor and closed his eyes. He was afraid of the things he was hearing in his head. But he immediately returned to the sitting room and leaned against the door to listen to her recite his praise-poetry while his body swayed as her voice droned on. He waited for half an hour when he suspected she might have left, before he opened the door to pick up his supplies and take them to the kitchen. There was a part of him that wondered why she didn't defy him and unlock the door with her extra key.

He wanted her to come in and confront him. He wanted to

resist being confronted for not opening the door, for choosing to put the lights out. He wanted to stop thinking about her hurt, all the pain she was revealing, one day at a time, at his doorstep. It was not unfamiliar to him. He knew the pain she was talking about and he had tried to shield her from some of it. When his father had requested he should come to see him by his bedside, Prof had gone alone. This was after many years of his father denying paternity and failing to support his mother in his upkeep. There, bloated on his deathbed, the man stopped denying his paternity.

Prof watched the face of the man who for many years made him tell his friends he was fatherless. If he had not seen evidence that his mother legally married him—photographs of an elaborate wedding complete with a smiling couple at the centre—he could have believed he was an accident. This was worrisome for him in his early years in school, and for many years he struggled to come to terms with how the union of two people who fell in love could suddenly dissolve into unresolvable hatred. A hatred which asked that a son should be forgotten or effaced from memory. He stood at the side of the bed and watched as the man struggled with words to fill in for his absence of many years. Prof watched his drooping eyes, thinking of those times when all he had wanted was a recognition as "son", someone to call "Father". He stood over his father's deathbed, lost in the sight of several tubes running across the disappearing body of the man whose attention he had begged for most of his life. Prof listened to the intermittent breathing that came as "Father" struggled to spew out the heavy stories of his absence.

'*Dariji mi. Jo*, you can only forgive an old man who was too young to know the meaning of focus,' and then he slumped. Prof stood by the bed, unsure of how to react to the suddenness of being called "son", while watching the doctors and nurses rushing in; calling, screaming and darting up and down the ward for one instrument or the other to save the man, his father. He stood there unnoticed. His head swirled with confusion as he tried to process his father's last words which remained silenced on slightly parted but still lips. Prof wondered how his father would have recounted the abandonment and neglect as the bidding of death lingered before him, he wondered how he would have been asked to forget that he was a son who grew up feeling he was never wanted by his father.

The lawyer who had brought him to see the dying man, handed him documents of two houses, one in Lagos and another in Kaduna, and said, 'He would have preferred you didn't come for the burial.' Prof stood, looking at the lawyer, who looked at him like one who expected to be challenged with a barrage of questions, his thoughts stuck on those final words.

'You're sure? He asked me to—' he paused and said instead, 'I mean, everyone knows he's my father—he was legally married to my mother for one year... he spoke to me now, he—'

'For your father's sake, just take what he left for you and leave. Forever.' The lawyer made sure they locked eyes before adding, 'Help sustain his memory—his legacy.' Prof looked at the ward and the swarming teams of doctors, the hurrying feet of unfamiliar half-sisters, half-brothers and relatives. He snatched the documents from the man's hand and walked out of the hospital wondering if there was any difference now that he could say, 'My father—is dead,' with a true sense of ownership, without feeling guilt, fear or shame. Although, there was a part of him that knew he could never tell his mother; in death, his father's legacy ensured he felt his place: a bastard.

'He said he loved me. Very much,' Prof told his mother later when he recounted the event.

'He did? Bread-for-brain idiot,' his mother said without any emotion.

Prof moved through the rest of the day after his visitors departed, catching up with the part of his daily routine he had missed while they tried to get his attention. He sat by the

radio at 5.45pm although there was no power to listen to the
network news. He sat down by the radio in silence. He then
went to his bedroom for a short nap. While he waited for sleep
to take hold of him, he listened and identified his neighbours
and what they were doing at that time of the day. He knew his
neighbours' voices. He knew some of their names from the
way they called out to each other.

He woke up screaming.

It was just a few minutes after nine o'clock. He stood up
from the bed and wrapped himself up in his usual burqa
style, with his bed sheet, for a stroll through the streets. Prof
became a ghost as he floated in and out of the night. He loved
that the power was off in the area and he walked through the
streets in slow and unhurried steps. He could tell that people
avoided him from the rustle of their hurried feet disappearing
behind him, to those approaching veering onto another path,
as he walked in their direction. There were, however, a few
times one or two bold ones would walk past with a hard stare.
He didn't mind that people moved away from him. He didn't
look up to confront them. He took his steps, one, and then
two, and then paused. He stared around and started his walk
again, one, and two and three and pause. '*The darkness in the
house sometimes bothers me,*' Desanya said to him.

'Why?'

'*Maybe you should let in some light then. Do you feel it
encroaches on the light outside? I mean—the darkness in your
room?*'

'We do not see in the light; we see in the dark.'

'*Are you listening to yourself? What are you saying?*'

'I never saw in the light. We need to be in the dark to see. I
need to be in the dark to see better.'

Prof turned away from her and eyeballed those passers-by
who shook their heads as they wondered who he was speaking
to. He considered what to do, and asked Desanya if he should
return to his room.

Once he stepped into the house though, he was struck
by thoughts of how living with lights could take him into an
unimaginable gloom.

8

Desire walked towards the university's main gate, burdened by the books in her arm. She ran into a pop-up sale of second-hand books by the Yakoyo canteen.

'I'll come back for this one later,' she said, pointing to Nawal el Saadawi's *Woman at Point Zero*. The bookseller nodded. There was a distant look in his eyes, and she felt he would have already sold it when she returned. It made her sad. On the days she got a good price for books, from authors she loved, she walked with a bounce, but today she could think of nothing but her intention to visit Prof again that night. It was going to be her seventh night knocking at his door since Remilekun had told her about him. Prof never answered.

A coursemate waved and ran towards her, exclaiming, 'You look like a walking library! Are you not coming to the rally?'

Desire nodded, although all she wanted at that moment was to go home. She found herself pulled towards where students gathered under the canopy of neem trees, a popular hangout spot between classes. It was a large crowd for an impromptu meeting. She walked towards the front in unhurried steps, as her coursemate disappeared into the moving crowd. Most times, she tried to avoid the student union gatherings that imitated political rallies. She stopped behind the crowd and watched for several minutes as students backslapped, laughed and talked amongst themselves, as the student leader climbed onto the makeshift podium. She found herself moving further into the crowd for a convenient spot.

The young man on the podium stood silent as Desire tried to settle in the crowd. After a few pushes and uncomfortable jabs from others, she found a spot where she could get a better view. Someone stepped on her foot and she turned, expecting an apology, but the girl simply pointed to her own feet, 'Someone marched on my foot too. This is a rally not a parlour.'

Desire shook her head and faced the podium. This was when she caught him, squatting and talking quietly to some of his colleagues. The white, well-starched shirt and khaki trousers he wore brought an image of him to her mind—a mummy's boy perhaps, chubby-faced and with lips that pouted from regular sulking as a child.

The young man stood up from his tête-à-tête and faced the crowd again.

'He looks—'

'Shhhhh! Ireti is talking,' a student beside her said.

The voice booming from the speaker into her ears sounded familiar.

'Greatest Nigerian students. The one standing before you today is Ghandi Reloaded. Here is the voice of Comrade Iretioluwa Durotimi. You, my friends, call me Ireti, a.k.a Ghandi Reloaded. I'm your man! Your 2011 presidential aspirant for the SUG, the one who will detoxify this campus—' Desire focused on Ireti, the student leader with a full afro on his head. As he turned in her direction and waved to the crowd, she gasped. She turned around to look at the other students, and returned to study his face, carefully. Several beads of sweat formed on her nose—his face, his nose, his hairline. It looked familiar. Desire squeezed herself forward through the crowd until she was right in front of him. Her eyes scanned Ireti's features once again; the eyes, nose and mouth; she was right. Yes, they were like Prof's.

Another time, Desire might have laughed at Ireti. She would have laughed at the way he spouted political rhetoric and sounded like a monologue from a bad play. But now, she watched him as he balanced himself several times on the podium, made from class desks, to avoid falling. The way he moved his hands to stroke his beard and kept a half-moon smile lingering on his face reminded her of Prof. She closed her eyes and opened them again to assure herself she was not dreaming.

'Who is he?' Desire asked the beanie-wearing boy beside her.

He turned to look at her, and with a frown, answered, 'Ireti. The student union presidential candidate.'

'Who is he? What does—?'

This time, the boy looked at her with thinned eyes before responding, 'Who is he? What kind of question is this? Can't you see he's a presidential aspirant for the Student Union Government?' And he moved away from her, turning and shaking his head as he did.

Desire watched Ireti as he slayed the English language with meaningless jargon.

'My fellow comrades, friends, students and highly esteemed associates from other universities, here today. Just as you are here for me, I am here for you. My diaphanous resolution is to protect my fellow students from the incorrigible political campus philistines who want to mortgage and imperil our dream by selling our birthright for a mess of pottage! We, my dear students, will not accept the *floccinaucinihilipilification* process of our future."

The crowd erupted into continuous applause, some shouting "Deep! Deep! Deep!" Ireti waved his hands for them to keep calm, and he continued, talking loudly until the crowd again settled to listen to him.

"Therefore, I am inviting you to join me in this fight, by voting me as your president for the Student Union Government. I believe in our collective power and what can emerge from it. We are, indivisible, irrepressible, ever articulate and ready for anybody.'

Ireti paused and the students screamed. He waited briefly for the crowd to calm down before he continued, 'But before I venture into the calamity we have labelled an education system and its implication on our collective dreams, let me first extend my gratitude for your support and trust. I will not enter into any hokum, but go straight to explain my agenda which is inclusive without being intrusive. I, standing before you, I'm focused on a four-point agenda: the melioration of academics, the security of students, and then, the demobilisation of transport hike and school fees increment.'

Desire wondered how student politicians managed their academic work with school politics. There were stories of a few student union leaders staying for an extra academic year in school, but there were also those who were incredibly brilliant and topped their class.

She looked with increasing familiarity at the banner behind him, with an artist's representation of his headshot and a slogan "Ghandi Reloaded, Your Man" hanging down the tree. How many likenesses of his face had she walked past unknowingly? The many banners and posters were almost a part of the design structure of the campus; they jarred in their announcement of music concerts, religious activities, SUG elections and new eating outlets; wearing the same black ink on fluorescent green or white cotton cloth with two strings attaching them to a tree, and two holding them down with stones.

Where do they even get the money for all of these posters and banners? she thought. Desire had once overheard an argument between her classmates on how some campus politicians got money from the government and used it to relocate their families to the United States and Canada. Maybe there was little difference between the student politicians and the country's politicians.

Desire watched Ireti with renewed focus. She observed the way he thrashed his hands in the air as he spoke, moving his body forward when he needed to modulate his voice. It was clear he knew his crowd. For every word he spoke, even when the students did not seem to understand, the way his body moved seemed to speak more truth than his words. Desire wormed her way out of the crowd. As she walked towards the bus stop to head home, Ireti's voice lingered in her head, along with his face.

9

Outside Prof's dark room were lights from the amber bulbs and fluorescent lamps of his neighbours. Desire stood by his door. She was returning to knock with the hope that he would see her, and as usual she had not told Remilekun where she was going, but she didn't think her destination was a secret.

At first, Desire knocked on the door like a rat nibbling on wood. She considered that he could be asleep, and this meant knocking harder to rouse him, so she knocked on the door like it was about to be pulled down. Yet, the door remained closed. She listened for footfalls. Her ears filled with the congregating sounds of mothers screaming at children, babies hollering for attention, sputtering generators filtering out the monotony of the traffic's hum and laughter sneaking in and out like the disappearing croak of a frog. It was the second week since power had gone off in the neighbourhood.

Her legs hurt but she was not yet ready to head back home. She drummed binaries on the door until her knuckles stung. 'Hello. Hello,' a gruff voice called to her. She ignored it and knocked on the door with even more vehemence. Although the darkness enveloped him, she could make out that there was a man standing at the foot of the stairs. She also noticed his hands were placed on his hips and his legs spread apart.

'See, woman, if you knock until tomorrow, that man won't open the door. I don't know you or where you're coming from or if you knew him before. I can assure you—you will not know him again. He has changed from human being to something else,' the unsolicited advisor offered. 'I see him walk out of his house only at night. So you should appreciate my advice, woman, because that man is not normal again.' He lingered for a while before walking away.

Her imagination took a leap at his words. She pictured Prof opening the door the two of them standing opposite each other without words passing between them. Clods of blood stuck to the hairs of his full beard like the plastered look of unkempt dreadlocks left to define their own destiny. She imagined the way he arched his lips into a crescent, a gesture meant to be a smile but was more of a grimace. She saw the blood between his teeth again and how everything contrasted with his peanut-shaped eyes which were not bloodshot but the white of coconut meat. He would not say a word, he would not laugh. He would bare his teeth at her. She was about to scream when she snapped out of her daydream. She caught her breath and looked in the direction of the passer-by to find him gone.

She took the first step and scanned the environment. She took another step and it felt heavier than the first. She hated herself for coming to see him. She took each step, each one feeling heavier than the previous one until she reached the last step.

Clang!

The sound of the door struck her. She froze. She placed one leg on the last step and the other on the next-to-last. She was afraid that if she turned towards the door, she would realise that she had only imagined the lock unhinging.

The voice came to her, wafting into her ears like the rustling of leaves in the wind.

'Yes? How may I help you?' the voice said to her. It was the same voice she remembered from her childhood. The one that turned to speak warmly to her after spilling several angry words into the crowd. The voice that boomed from a speaker but spoke softly into her left ear, those words she never decoded.

Desire walked to the head of the stairs stiffly. She fidgeted as she tried to meet his eyes. She felt the brightness of his bead-like eyes swallow the darkness in the room. She stopped by the door and looked at the door handle and then down to her legs.

Prof opened the door but remained inside. She studied what was his face hidden in the shadows and tried to smile, but all she could do was pull her mouth into a wide stretch that hurt her cheeks. Her lips trembled in their half-moon position.

'My name is Desire. I know you. I mean, I have—you see, I-I live around here.' She took a deep breath and started all over again, 'Sorry, I was going to say "Good evening, sir."'

The Prof before her did not wear dreadlocks the way she expected. The years in prison had left him with some hair, but it was not locked. Desire waited for him to say something, like, 'I remember you, the young girl from Maroko,' or something that could lead to her falling into his arms and sobbing between masticated words.

Desire shifted her feet on the ground. She turned to look at the stairs and then at the door.

'Are you here to see me?' he uttered. He spoke so softly that she strained to hear him.

She froze as his eyes caught hers. She turned away and stared at the ground again. She considered telling him she came to the wrong flat.

'I – I – I came—need to talk. To you.'

'Me? Need? Why? Uhn?'

She was stiff. Her throat grew narrow. She remembered nothing. She shook as she thought of being accused of trespassing. She turned around to face him, but his intense gaze made her assess herself.

'What do you want?' he probed again.

This time confidence rose from inside of her as she noted the uncertainty in his voice. She sensed an expectation in the way he responded although he tried to conceal it with rashness. 'I came to know you, to see you...' she paused long before she added, 'sir.'

'You came to know me?'—he snorted— 'What are you?' He spoke with such softness she felt the need to be careful.

He paused and made an attempt to talk louder but his voice still sounded like a whisper, 'What exactly do you do?' He cleared his throat and sniffed. Something she would come to know as part of him.

'Sir, I am a student. At the Lagos State University. LASU. My name is Desire Babangida Jones,' she repeated her name with some hope that he would remember. 'Desire,' she curtsied. She still faced the floor as she spoke to him.

'Babangida?'

'Yes, sir. I'm not related to that former head of state Babangida, although my mother said they named my father after a man who got his father—my grandfather—a job at the railway while he was in Minna.'

And just when she did not expect any conviviality, he said, 'Stop sir-ing me-o. Or I will call you big madam! You're not in the army, are you?' he guffawed, 'Er... Madam Desire of LASU, okay. You can call me, er... Prof—my title—or Eni, if you are brave enough to call me by my first name.'

She could tell he was enjoying the conversation more than she was. Her hands tingled. Desire bit her lips. She was now unsure if she would ever get a chance to enter the house.

'Come in,' his voice took the quiet tone that startled her earlier, once again. 'Oh!' Prof unlatched the lock and flung the door open. He disappeared into the room and left Desire to walk into the flat and find a place to sit. The sitting room's darkness stirred up the anxiety in her. She entered the house, acknowledging the fugitive silence that would become a major guest in their many conversations when Desire became a regular visitor. She took a seat, hands clasped between her thighs.

'You kept knocking even when I never opened the door. Why?'

He had recognised her knocks, then. She clutched the arms of the chair, welcoming the darkness and how it kept the secrets of her fidgets.

'I got tired of wondering who it was, so I considered opening

the door today.' His voice was so soft she needed to sit on the
edge of the seat and pay full attention to hear him. He laughed,
'I have some other people—they are my people. They knock
regularly, so I wanted to know who this new person was.'

'Who comes?'

He ignored her question. 'Do you know this story in the
Bible, of the man who kept going to his friend's door to
lend three loaves of bread, in the middle of the night, for his
visitor?' He waited to see if she was going to respond, before
continuing, 'Anyway, the profundity there is in this line; "I tell
you, even though he will not get up and give you the bread
because of friendship, yet because of your shameless audacity,
he will surely get up and give you as much as you need." I
mean who goes to knock on a man's door at midnight for
bread to feed a friend?! The story is about persistence. I think
it is in the Gospel of Luke, you could read it up.'

'I know the passage. I've read everything I could find. The
story is in the Book of Luke and my favourite passage is "For
everyone who asks receives; the one who seeks finds; and to
the one who knocks, the door will be opened."'

'The door will be opened *ehn*? How convenient!' Prof said
and started to laugh. His laughter was soft at first. He then
rushed into a soft monotony of rippling laughter that grew in
tempo until it sounded like a chorus she was required to join.
She laughed, hiccup-like at first, and then she found herself
letting loose.

On that first visit, she was not bothered by the way the
room was lit by reflections of light from the outside. Her eyes
wore the room's shade, familiar with the absence of light she
thought a result of the general power outage. When shouts of
'Up NEPA' rang through the neighbourhood, signifying that
power was back, she wondered why his lights did not come
on. Yet she did not ask him to put his lights on because she
welcomed the darkness, which covered her unease. She said
nothing. As her eyes became familiar with the room, making
the dull, dark shapes into tangible objects, she recognised how

the room was both sparse yet full at the same time, as if it used to have more. She identified that there were three chairs in the room, the one she sat in, which was by the door, and the one Prof sat in and then another which leaned against the wall. There was nothing on the walls. They were bare but for a grandfather clock she did not instantly take notice of until it chimed in a loud tone behind her some minutes after she entered the house. It was 10pm.

Desire looked straight ahead at what appeared to be a curtain in front of her. The rectangular shape and the way its shadow draped made her conclude it was a door that led into other parts of the house. In all her observations, Prof did not make a sound. It was almost as if she was alone in the room, all by herself. She began to fear a conversation might never start between them until he cleared his throat and said, 'You're from LASU, uhn? I think there is more to that university than is known. Anyway, I had to move to the university in Ibadan and er... you know... you know... never mind anyway.'

She wondered if the "never mind" was linked to the story of how he was denied a place in the Arabic Department because he was not practising any religion. She had heard different stories of him from the men at the newspaper stand. It was from one such debate that she had learnt of how he was sacked because he rebuffed his colleagues, telling them they could not see how an academic paper differed from a religious text.

Desire was attentive to everything in the house, so much so that she could even tell when Prof moved to the edge of his seat or relaxed against the backrest. She followed the faint white of his eyes which were comparable to candlelight striving on a windy night. She stayed quiet, sometimes missing his cue for her to contribute to some of the things he said.

'Many of the professors and many professionals left the country to begin a new life abroad in the 1980s. These men carried the remains of what was home with them in their hearts when they left. They were dejected in their chosen exile for many years, not because they left, but because they knew when they returned home to rest from their sojourn, even the faint idea of home they left with, would no longer exist. Many of these professors returned from some of the world's most prestigious scholarships to serve their country, and again left, forever haunted by the inability to serve in their home.'

'They had a choice. You didn't leave.'

'They didn't leave, it was not based on choice, and they were driven by the conditions around them. Don't you understand? And I was not... I mean I didn't have the... I was not a professor then.'

There was silence again.

'Can I ask you something?' Desire asked.

'Go on.'

'Do you ever wonder why the president didn't release you during his first term? I mean, they released many people, so why not you?'

Prof pondered the question for a while. He had realised that something was different when they stopped moving him from one prison to another, as well as no longer asking him to confess to one thing or another. He woke up one morning and learnt that Abacha was dead and there was a new head of state, who released Obasanjo from prison. Later, they told him there was an election and Obasanjo was now the head of state. He woke up each morning filled with the hope that he was going to be released soon. They never did. The warders became nice to him for a while, and then, when they realised that he was not going to be released, they just treated him as their mood dictated.

'I don't know, Desire. I just know I left prison when the president desired a second term. I am one of those who he granted mercy.' He puffed and laughed, then repeated, 'Mercy?'

'Well, isn't that what it is?'

'I was traded for something.'

'What do you mean?'

Prof did not answer her question, instead he asked, 'So, how is it that you make it here in the night? This is Lagos, you know.'

'Well, I live somewhat close. I live in the estate.'

They talked into the night and Desire only realised she had spent almost three hours in the room when the grandfather clock struck 12. She stood up and walked to the door. Prof followed behind her.

As she stepped out of the house, he said, 'Do you write poetry?'

'No,' she said.

'No?' he laughed. A short laugh followed by a sigh, 'You sometimes slip into the quiet of a poet.'

'Really? I feel there are so many things in my head. I'm— I want to listen to them.'

'Hmm. You could try writing poetry. Poetry is the best way to listen to the soul. Well, that's what they say.'

Prof sighed. Once he unlocked the door, he stepped back and whispered, 'See you tomorrow,' as if she had been there yesterday or the day before, and then disappeared into the room once more.

'Goodnight, Prof,' Desire said, wondering if she would return the next day.

10

The first time Prof's mother visited him in prison, they sat in silence for one hour before she released a flood of tears. What followed was the sound of her crying becoming a means of communication between them. Prof listened to the sound of her sniffling and tried to understand her sorrow. As they sat facing each other, his eyes stayed on the ground and she, he could guess, guided her eyes to scan the mosquito bites that dotted the skin on his frail body. In the silence, he felt the shame of the moment, she was the last person he wanted to see him in that state. His whole life had been about making her proud of him.

'Maami, see I topped the class.' Or, 'See Maami, I will make you happy, so happy.'

Her other visits to see him in prison went the same way. Silence. Tears. Silence. There was, however, one time that he raised his head to see what she had become. She was looking at him like a woman beholding a dead son she was hoping would rise and walk. It was that hope that now brought her to his doorstep since his return from prison, leaving him provisions and keeping on with her infrequent knocks, which was their new way of conversing. She would knock and chant his praise, struggling with the words which fell from her lips, each syllable dragging the other.

'We used to talk. Let me in.' He would wait by the door and listen to her recite his praises before she again departed.

He always wanted to run after her, just the same way he had wanted to hug her the day he left prison. Yet, he had felt a barrier between them. The visits showed their loss, and how, slowly, over the years, their laughter had receded into a vigour for other activities, like activism.

Prison showed him that life had changed between him and his mother, and it started long before his incarceration.

Was it because I decided to visit my father in the hospital? He shook his head at the thought. *I needed to know my father, I needed to know the man who birthed me. I needed to know.* He wrapped his arm around his head as the last sentence echoed in his mind, as he thought of how the hurt sat in her eyes when he insisted he wanted to be brought back to the house he inherited from his father, instead of going to hers. It was the same hurt he saw the last time she had come to see him in prison after someone smuggled her in. For the first time in a long time they had talked.

'I paid over a million to make this two-minute visit possible.'

'Why is it now difficult? Where did you get the money from?'

'Er... the government—they are killing... they killed some activists in the Niger Delta and now it's getting crazier.' She took a deep breath before she added, 'Thankfully, there are people who care about you more than you know.'

'People?'

'Yes, people who support you. They made this visit possible,' she said in a voice which vibrated through his head again and again.

'You may be placing my life in these people's hands, stop meeting people to help you see me.'

'How won't I? You're my only child.'

'I didn't ask for it. I didn't ask to be alone.'

'Don't!'

Then she stood up from the chair and walked towards the door like she was leaving but returned to the chair again. 'You won't die here. My son, you won't.'

They fell into a familiar silence as they both became lost in their thoughts. The next thing, his mother leapt up from the bench they sat on. Her eyes burnt with several emotions, and in them he identified pain, fear and anger.

'Oh! Do you think your father would have visited if he were

alive? Like he did when he abandoned you?!'

He said nothing to her, reminded of the time he had returned from school, slinging a bag filled with books down to the ground and plodded into the bedroom, his eyes unable to deny the tears which rushed down his face as he asked her what she did to his father.

'Why does he hate me this much?' He fell into her arms and they cried together. They lay like this into the night until they fell asleep; to be woken by the morning sun, entangled in each other's embrace.

Harsh knocks stirred him from his sleep now. He listened to the knock as he tried to understand what he felt; he could feel his veins throbbing and his heart beating fast, but he also felt a calmness somewhere inside of him, which wanted him to seek out company. And from the first day, when he realised it was someone else knocking and not his mother or his nosy neighbour at the door, he always rolled his fist and placed it over his mouth when the knocks persisted.

On the day he eventually opened the door to her, the knocks started from around 9.30pm. He listened to each knock. It stirred up the sound of his childhood frolics; the sound of making music with sticks on tables. He counted the beats of the knocks in his head: one, two. Three, four. Five, six... forty-four, forty-five...

As the knocking persisted, Prof stood up from the sitting room and walked down the corridor without entering the bedroom and then he returned to the chair a few minutes later. He returned to listening to the sound, which all at once stopped. He became slightly irritated when the knocking stopped. He broke free from the embrace of the chair and with his heart racing, he took quiet steps to the door and unlocked the latch, but no one was there.

'Hello? Who is that?' His disappointment made his voice lower than it typically would be. Hearing himself speak with hope of a response also surprised him. It felt as if the voice was coming from someone else.

Prof did not step out of the doorway. He looked in the direction of the stairs but could not see anyone. He was going back inside the house when he heard her steps. He opened the door wider but remained in the comfort of his dark room as she emerged from the benighted stairway and stood in front of his door, trembling. She was not what he had expected: her hair was a little dishevelled from walking about, yet she could still stand out in any crowd. Even after his years in prison, and in the dim lights, he would describe her as beautiful. In her five foot, six inch height and street-lamp thinness, her clear eyes appeared to scan everything in sight. Her eyes shone in the darkness. It was through her eyes that he sketched the rest of her. It was a slow observation, but his eyes soon got accustomed to the dim light in the corridor and he could not take them off her. She stood, legs apart, testifying to her persistence at the door; one who would not budge until answered. He knew, there was something in her to be offered and he wanted to know what it was. He said the first words that came to his head and he did not feel that they could have been inappropriate. He stood there caught in the surprise of a voice different from the ones he had heard in the past days. It begged to be listened to. He did not realise or know what he had expected to meet at the door.

Earlier that day, he could not remember doing anything different than the usual monotony his life had slipped into since he returned from prison: waking up, rolling over to a side of the bed, dragging himself to the bathroom—brush, bath, cook, eat and evening walks. He stumbled, in, out and around the kitchen for a meal, sat down in the sitting room to listen to the radio whose volume was always so low even he needed to strain his ears to hear it. The habit of straining to listen to the radio was something he learnt from his solitary days in prison. A warder used to patrol the cells with a small transistor radio, and he trained his ears to catch the sound until that warder was moved to another unit.

When she entered the room, they started with questions which circled for a long time around introduction. He did not want to scare her away, although he wanted to appear impenetrable. He waited when she spoke and she listened to him even when he coughed. He was relieved to talk to someone, and not listen to the sound of a snuffle. Her voice tinged his feelings with delight. Yet, he could not ascertain what he felt as he spoke to her; and for the first time, he realised that the ability to speak with someone whom one did not need to speak with, was itself a kind of freedom.

'We can talk on the phone sometime. You can call me,' she said.

He took a deep breath wondering if his thoughts were audible. Unsure of how to respond to her suggestion, Prof picked up the GSM phone on the table and fiddled with it. He listened to Desire's breath, which was a way of saying she was waiting for a response.

'Can I have your number?' she asked.

'I do have a GSM, is that what you call it? But I, er, you may have to check how to make this thing work yourself,' he muttered, wondering how he had not created time to understand how it worked.

She paused for a long time before she said, 'The GSM is useful, but you don't have to use it. Let's see how yours works.' Prof smiled. He respected how she volunteered to help him with the phone. He stayed silent for some time before moving from his chair with the phone in his hand and squatted beside her. As his arm brushed hers, they both pulled away in a reflex then apologised in synchrony, 'Sorry'. By the time he returned to his seat he laughed so hard that he fell into it.

And again, he felt ashamed of what he felt. The emotions that were rising inside of him were not familiar to him any more.

It was only when the clock chimed at 12 that she expressed her intention to leave. He knew she must return, and he said it as best as he could to hide his fears of her not returning, 'See you tomorrow?'

Prof leaned on the door and listened to Desire's footsteps until they faded. He could not stop the tingling which ran up and down his spine when he finally moved away from the door. He felt relief as she left. It felt like watching himself being pulled from himself, but what he would always remember about that first visit was how he stumbled and fell over a stool in the kitchen thrice in one day of opening the door to a stranger. He felt relieved. It felt like slow, unhurried sex that begged for intensity after long years of abstinence. He felt ashamed but at the same time, he felt unwound.

11

'Prof's light is never on. Do you think there could be some reason—some scientific reason for him putting the lights off?' Desire asked with a yawn.

'Let's talk common sense. You mean you've been meeting someone in a dark room, day in day out, doing what? And you're looking for science? Are you alright?'

'We just talk. We talk about books, politics, everything,' Desire said in a low voice.

'Just talk? Books?' Remilekun chuckled and winked before standing up to place the empty bowl in her hand on a table.

'Yes, just talk,' she replied with a straight face, recalling her time alone with Prof, and how the grandfather clock always signalled a departure once it struck 12. Prof would stop talking at the chime of the clock. He would clear his voice, change into the drawl of a bored, underpaid actor who forgot his cue.

'Eh... I think you should be on your way, uhn?' he would say, and she would walk towards the door.

Remilekun stood up from her side of the bedroom and came to sit on Desire's bed. She placed her hand on Desire's left shoulder.

'I was here last night waiting for you until I fell asleep, just like it has been some six or seven nights now, and you are here talking nonsense. Don't you think there's a problem here?' Her voice was now lower than when she had started out.

'I think it's... it's... it's...' But even then, words failed her. She could not describe what it was.

Remilekun finished the description. 'It is a fetish. You have dark-room fetish. That's all. It is man-in-the-dark-room fetish.

Haven't you heard that some people are attracted to shit?' She paused to exhale, and then added, 'Your visit to see that mad Prof in the dark is the same. It is like shit-fetish. I don't know who is mad, you or him. I am certain of one thing though; there is madness between you two.'

'Attraction to shit is called coprophilia! And it's an entirely different thing. Anyway, you can't understand.'

'I can't understand what? See, if you people want to fuck, just do it. No need for all this darkroom preparations. Okay, okay. Some people like sex in the dark though.' she laughed, 'Oh, please, take candles the next time and pretend it's romantic.'

Desire shook her head and Remilekun squalled, flapping her legs.

Desire thought of her last visit. She recalled how she had walked down the stairs listening to the jangling of metal as he fastened the locks and retreated into the dark. She wanted to tell Remilekun how she always felt a strong urge to light up the room and look into his face and speak the first words that entered her head when her stomach would turn. Instead, she would move her childlike frame to the edge of the chair, fold her hands below her abdomen and lean forward to press them down. These were the times she swung herself back and forth and let his voice bounce off around the room, imagining them as echoes in an empty hall; and if he changed his position so that there was a slight and brief brush of his skin against hers, her heart flipped and the silence that prevailed in the room became almost suffocating until he exhaled.

Desire reclined on the bed, moving her hands about as if she was again in Prof's room, feeling for the wooden arms of the chair. She could again feel him bent beside her as he handed her his phone, the tepid air escaping his nostrils to tickle her skin, until capsules of sweat hurried down her armpits and teased forks down her back.

'You sit in the dark with a man, and you tell me you're just talking. Talking about what? The size of his prison-wilted penis?' Remilekun stood up from the bed to remove a towel from the hanger and walked towards the bathroom laughing,

'Let me go and shower, I will return to this.'

Desire tossed and turned on the bed, the thoughts in her head flirting between Prof and the assignments she was yet to do, and suddenly, she remembered Ireti. She had not seen much of him campaigning around school lately.

Remilekun stepped out of the bathroom cutting into her thoughts, and picked up the conversation as though there had been no break.

'Hear yourself, Desire, you just talk with a man who has stayed in the prison for how many years without seeing a woman... just talk?'

'Yes, just talk.'

'It is okay if you don't want to tell me you met this *bobo* who is shagging you every night. But, if it's really that psycho man you're going to meet, please, stop. It is madness!' Remilekun threw her hands in the air, before she turned to Desire, jutting her chin forward. She took a deep breath and dabbed some perfume behind her ears; yelping and contorting her face as the alcohol waters stung broken skin. 'See, you're the one who is always asking for scientific proof, but I have it as an unreliable scientific proof. Here it is; when men stay too long in prison without sex, they develop a wilted penis syndrome. They may leave their before-prison wife to marry one with no knowledge of their sexual performance and some just never have sex with a woman again. They claim asexuality or spirituality. You get?'

Now dressed, Remilekun walked to the door, then swung around suddenly and said, 'I'll greet Mumsie for you. See you tomorrow.'

'Are you sure you're going to your mother's house, the way you're *pancaking* your face with this much powder?'

'And where else would I go?' Remilekun went to the curtain and the sun's light swept the room with brightness.

Desire smiled and looked up, so they faced one another directly, 'Okay, greet your mum.' She then sat up on the bed and turned to the cupboard that housed everything they were ashamed to leave about the room or felt too lazy to pack properly.

Remilekun took the half-used toilet roll in the cupboard and made a display of pushing it into an already full handbag. Seeing that as an opportunity to get back at her, Desire, asked, 'Are you stopping over at a shitting or semen wiping competition?'

Without looking up from the bag, Remilekun concentrated on the task of pushing the tissue into the bag. In the process an object popped out and dropped from the bag.

'What's that? Are you sick?'

'It's multivitamins!' Remilekun snapped and picked up the pack of pills in a hurry. She tucked it into her bag

'Hmmm. The doctor!' Desire said. 'I think someone is going h-o-m-e,' Desire said with a giggle.

'I am going home, okay?'

'Yes, you're going home.'

Remilekun muttered a few inaudible words at her and Desire laughed at the way her upper lip formed a spear.

From the way her friend's nerves jumped at every word, she knew the visit was to see Mr. America; a name she used for a lover who she operated a "you-see-me-you-see-me-not" relationship with.

Mr. America shuttled between Ghana and Kenya, yet returned to Nigeria, speaking in muddled American slang and British cuss words, interjecting every sentence with, 'In abroad—' He travelled out of the country for a few months and when he returned, he phoned Remilekun for nights out. 'Be careful,' Desire then raised her voice a notch higher, 'at home.'

Desire had made it plain to her friend several times that she didn't like Mr. America. But Remilekun appeared to follow the logic of a popular Fuji artist who sang that, "The one whom I was ridiculed for is the one I will eventually marry."

Mr. America was a man who loved to have a good time but Remilekun took him too seriously. He once told Remilekun on their first date that if she ever got pregnant by him, he would punch out the foetus, or if she succeeded in giving birth to the baby, he would cut it up and sell it for blood ritual, as he needed to find out if indeed people made charms from the body parts of a baby. He then told her it was a joke.

In the course of their relationship, Remilekun had gotten pregnant by him but never told him. She had cried on Desire's shoulder every night until she asked if Desire could accompany her to a clinic "to remove it."

As Remilekun stepped out of the house, she looked back and said, 'Should my mum call, spin a story.'

Indeed, the day after Remilekun left the house, Mama T sent someone to the house at noon. She wanted to know why Remilekun had not come home in two months, especially with the lecturers ready to strike. Desire lied, saying Remilekun was involved in scientific research that involved turning phones off on campus.

'Actually, she has been sleeping in school now for some days.'

The lies came so easily, and the errand lady went on about how much Mama T always talked about how Desire had changed Remilekun's life and how God would repay her and bless her with a big future.

'I'll kill this girl for making me lie to Mama T,' Desire swore under her breath.

And then the thought of what could happen if Remilekun failed to return came to mind. Remilekun had never slept at her boyfriend's houses before. Perhaps, a little late night, now and then, but with Mr. America she sometimes packed like she was going on a holiday. Desire wondered how she would explain Remilekun's disappearance if she became a victim of the kidnapping which was becoming rampant in the city, or became involved in some accident along the expressway. As the thought crossed her mind again, Desire dialled the phone number Remilekun asked her to call if there was an emergency. She could not get through. She wondered if she should call Mama T. Despite Remilekun's request, the thought niggled at her.

She tapped three digits on her phone and stopped. She remembered how Remilekun had returned to the door long after she had said goodbye, popped only her head into the room and said, 'You don't have to call my mother.' She repeated this three times. Desire had nodded in response. There was some sort of unspoken rule between them. When it was time, Remilekun would return to recount the night's adventures, such as an ex she ran into and who she went to this-and-that-place with, between laughs and excited screams. It wasn't the first time this sort of thing would happen. She always returned.

12

Prof stood up from the chair he sat in waiting for Desire to knock. He paced back and forth. In his head, he rehearsed the words to say to her for keeping him waiting, and then he tried to think of the books he would discuss with her, but both were impossible to do. All he could think of was why she was yet to arrive at a few minutes to ten. He went to the window. His eyes roamed the street, trying to pick her out from the people walking past. The smell of burning wood jarred his nostrils and he closed the shutter. The clock chimed. 11pm, and then 12am. Desire had not come.

Prof moved back to the chair. He sat down on its edge and imagined Desire in the room and how she would stand up and move towards the door when she was ready to leave, dragging her feet like she was signalling that he could change her mind to stay much longer if he asked her to do so.

'I can't make you stay longer. It is already late—perhaps too late for you to walk by yourself this night,' he said to the empty room. The words he always wanted to say when she acted this way. He never asked her to stay longer or stay overnight as that would already imply something other than the friendship she gave, which he was now soaked in. He also did not want her to stay longer, as he still felt the need to be alone; yet each time she stood up and announced her departure, his head swirled, and his heart took on a rapid gong beat. He drew his legs up into the chair and recalled one of her visits, when he started out reciting Niyi Osundare's *Not My Business* and she joined in from the second stanza. They called out each word in a chorus, slowing down or speeding up to speak the words in synchrony.

They picked Akanni up one morning
Beat him soft like clay
And stuffed him down the belly
Of a waiting jeep.

What business of mine is it
So long they don't take the yam
From my savouring mouth?

They came one night
Booted the whole house awake
And dragged Danladi out,
Then off to a lengthy absence.

What business of mine is it
So long they don't take the yam
From my savouring mouth?

Chinwe went to work one day
Only to find her job was gone:
No query, no warning, no probe—
Just one neat sack for a stainless record.

What business of mine is it
So long they don't take the yam
From my savouring mouth?

And then one evening
As I sat down to eat my yam
A knock on the door froze my hungry hand.

The jeep was waiting on my bewildered lawn
Waiting, waiting in its usual silence.

He listened to the memory of her voice and her laughter
rose into his head like the approach of a distant train. His

body drooped, and when the thought of her never coming back crept into his mind, he trembled. Since her visits began, he had denied himself the company of Desanya, his loyal companion. He tried to bring her into his presence now,   but he could not will her into a conversation the way he had always been able to. For the first time in a long time, he picked up the phone and called Kayo.

The knocking came thrice. There was no rhythm to it, yet he hurried to the door only to unlock it with restraint. He stepped back waiting for Desire to come inside and apologise, even if it was not their usual meeting time. He was thinking of how to chide her for coming at a time other than agreed to, but it was his mother's voice that slipped through the door.

'Your food is by the door,' she said. He listened to the sound of her feet, her small pleas for him to please open the door and the surprised gasp at the slight creak of the door when she leaned against it. She staggered into the room upon realising that the door was unlocked, and he wondered if she would think about whether it was probably never locked the previous times, when she came to deliver his provisions. Prof stretched out his right arm to keep her from falling. His mother fell into his arms, her body rigid, more from surprise than anything else. She froze in his arms and began to cry. Once she finished crying, she stood up straight to face him.

'Eni, Kayo said you called him last night?' she asked. He did not say a word. He freed himself from her grasp; she steadied herself and scanned the room from the door.

When she failed to step further into the house after a long time, Prof said, 'Enter.' This was the only word he said to her. He returned to his seat, and she found a chair and they sat together in the darkness, savouring the moment of being together in the room. The moment of his opening the door to her since the first day she brought him from prison with Kayo. Since his decision to start to live alone and without lights.

Despite this, all he could think of was Desire and her

absence. *Why did she miss last night's visit?*

'You need someone around you, maybe a woman,' she said. 'Have you heard anything?'

'I don't understand.'

Prof sighed and then became silent.

'You know, you raise a child and offer them all you think is the best. And then you push them and say, "I want a grandchild; child, you need a wife," and we talk about how these are the fruit of our labour.' She laughed, 'These are things many parents pray for—a grandchild, a wife for their son—until they find out they are about to lose their child.'

She moved to the window and looked outside, adjusting the curtains as she returned to sit down in the chair.

'Life is better now. Seeing you walk out alive from that prison made life brighter,' she gave a short laugh, 'But now, you have made me alive. You need to live. You are not a shadow.' She stood from where she sat, the place Desire sat when she visited and walked about the room, muttering under her breath. Prof caught a single word, "Blessing."

Prof raised his head to look at her; he said nothing, but his mind remembered all he wanted to forget.

Blessing, with the mole on the left part of her upper lip. His secretary. She made his life as a university professor and an activist almost too easy, always keeping the appointments apart and making sure he was abreast of issues in the country. He was so fond of her ways that she earned the nickname, "Compu", a shortening of Computer, from him. She was one of the people he tried to forget, because he always felt she was an interlude that was supposed to be an episode in his life.

Her skin was the colour of a ripe mango, contrasted with dark lips raised into an insolent sneer. These were things he only noticed later as he was always too engrossed in his work to notice anything else, and her efficiency and dedication to the job endeared him to her. He finally noticed her as a beauty by his side when one of his colleagues' attempt at a compliment turned sour.

'How do you carry all of this beautiful institution behind you on this small frame?' the colleague moved towards Blessing and attempted to brush her buttocks. Blessing slapped him. As Prof intervened that day, he noticed how her five foot eight frame sat well on her. She became something more than a secretary from then on.

Before that day, Prof was aware that fellow comrades and friendly faculty members cleared their throats and threw jibes at him whenever he and Blessing walked together. Although he assured them that nothing amorous existed between them, no one believed him. He tried to continue to see her for what she was hired to be, his secretary, who would help with the work before him, but his feelings controlled him. He didn't want to hurt her. From watching his mother's struggle, he had made up his mind, as a child, never to marry. Seeing his mother's plight, he feared he would only be another villain in the life of a woman of promise. He was also too passionate, too deep in his love for the people to give out a part of himself to a woman.

He once warned Blessing, 'I could torture you as a husband.' That day, she had come to him and asked, 'What about us, Prof? Where are we headed?' It was obvious she was thinking of marriage, as she believed their relationship was gathering attention and had become the subject of speculation by family and friends. She would wait for him after his lectures and struggle for his bag, along with admiring students. She brought food to his flat in the mornings and watched him eat. He didn't want to accept these meals, but being tired and hungry, he was always too glad to be fed. He also knew she was not being herself. She was trying hard to fit into the role expected of her from family, who she once told him asked her "to act like a woman" when she decided she wanted a child and not a man.

'Then don't get married.'

'It would kill my mother.'

'Balderdash! If your decision makes you happy and brings

no bodily harm to anyone, do it. Or else, you're on your way to the grave. It is also called slow death.'

'Prof, don't talk like that. My family... I would like a *proper* wedding, then children. Not a born-by-mistake.'

'You create your own universe, sing your song.'

'Okay, Prof, but you know I may get pregnant. We should use protection,' she said in exasperation and he suddenly declared that the next time she repeated that statement, he would not only stop seeing her, he would also lay her off.

'You are a human rights activist, Prof. Did you just say that?'

Prof moved away from her and turned around, 'I didn't really mean that.'

Blessing ignored him and then started to talk, 'You should meet my people. Prof, we are so close, yet you don't even know my people. What if we decide to marry?'

'There should be more to loving than ending up as a married couple. You don't even want to get married. Are you living to please yourself or others? What makes you think I'll be a good husband to you?'

'We get along. Not like—'

'See madam, marriage is not my thing. It is not your thing. And even if we want to make a baby, it is our decision. We. Decide. Not your mom. Not mine. Okay?'

Blessing turned and looked at him for a long time before taking a deep breath. She became kinder to him after this. He was the one who soon began to feel uncomfortable after his outburst as it made him ashamed afterwards, but he did not tell her he was sorry over the several months they remained together.

'I may get pregnant,' she said again one day.

'I enjoy sex better without a condom. I don't trust all these condoms they say feel like skin.'

'Professor!' she yelled. Perhaps, it was the shrillness of her voice that amused them both, but they both began laughing.

'I can just... with the thing, you know withdrawal method,' he said, seizing the change in the mood to explain himself.

'Listen to yourself, Prof,' she said, amused. 'Withdrawal method, are you in depression? Where are you withdrawing to? A whole Professor Eniolorunda!'

He spread out on the bed, his satisfied self, staring and smiling at the ceiling, breathing heavily while she lay by his side in silence for a while, before she drew a long breath and stood up from the bed, knocking off the pile of books on the bedside table in anger.

Still wearing a smile, a finger on his stomach, scratching idly, he had believed they would make up afterwards. He returned from a tour the next week to find her resignation letter on the table. He couldn't forgive himself for a long time when she disappeared. He tried to search for her, but between the activism and university work, he found little time to dedicate to finding her. Slowly, his pining to see her again faded away. The years that followed Blessing's departure were a chain of flings with women whose names he never recollected the next day. They were often university undergraduates finding a voice in activism, many of them giving themselves to him as a show of strength. To honour his time with Blessing, he offered protection to every woman whose body he would take. It was their body, it was their decision to do whatever they wanted with it. It however continued to interest him that in prison when he thought of the possibility of dying, Blessing did not even cross his mind.

His mother was the second person that week who reminded him of Blessing. Desire was the first. At their last meeting, she asked him if he had ever fathered a child. It was the most unlikely question that could have come up in their conversation. As they began to shed the skins of their personal lives, slowly at first, and without pain, she dropped the question.

'Do you want a child?'

He did want a child. He wanted a child when he tricked Blessing into using the withdrawal method. He however wanted it to appear like a favour if she got pregnant; like an I-told-you-before-hand, in case, he wasn't a good father. Sometimes, he wondered if there was something generational about absent paternalism in his lineage. He wasn't keen on marriage. His mother had shared similar thoughts—in moments of frustration at his infrequent visits and days of intense loneliness—on how his duty to his causes had eclipsed all else.

'You chose your father's innards and not mine! His lineage is known for abandoning loved ones, they always push those they love away! Is this what you are?' she spat out in Yoruba. Those words had stayed with him, even after his mother apologised—*You chose your father's innards and not mine!*

Rather than tell Desire what he really wanted, he turned to her and without thinking it through, gave the same response he gave to Blessing many years back, 'Do I want a child? To want a child is pure selfishness. It spells narcissism and only goes as far as to replicate man's perpetual want to transcend the ordinary. Once you become a parent, your narcissism doubles, doesn't it?' He meant for his last sentence to shock and he waited for another question, but Desire fell into a long silence. The intensity of the silence hit their thoughts, until Desire heaved a deep breath and laughed heartily.

'Are you rendering a theory, Prof? You shouldn't forget to live.'

'Look who's talking!' he said, a little peeved.

The sound of his mother clearing her throat took him away from his thoughts.

'When is this going to end?' his mother asked, 'Are you going to return to a normal life?'

'What is a normal life?' Her question pierced him like a dagger, compelling him to respond against his wishes.

'You are not a shadow. I will keep praying for you.'

The image of himself as a shadow echoed in his head long after she departed. Those words were in his mind as he stood by the window watching the traffic of people and cars moving about. He wondered if Desire didn't come because she felt he was a shadow. He did not know what to feel, which was the hardest part of it all. He knew what was happening inside of him was some form of emotion, but he was certain it was not the type of feeling his mother and other people wanted for him.

He switched on the radio and reduced the volume to the point where he strained his ear enough to listen to the boring social analysis of a radio presenter, who stuffed his poor grammatical and bad arguments in a pastiche of terrible American, British and Nigerian Englishes. Once the presenter felt he was struggling to make sense, perhaps, even to himself, he engaged in a reel of laughter at his own joke and played several pop songs, which Prof believed was meant to soothe the frustrations of listeners like himself until he fell asleep.

The radio was on when he woke up at 2am. It was louder now because of the quiet. He turned off the sentimental croon of Whitney Houston's *I Will Always Love You*. He listened to the night: night guards blowing their whistles to stagger the silence of space. He coiled into a knot on the chair and waited for sleep to return.

13

Desire ignored the chatting and laughing of the students, which seemed to increase each time she figured out a way to focus, so she could finish her assignment. She lifted her head from the materials she photocopied from the library, as a crowd of boys rushed into the class hailing a figure she could not yet see. They moved around in circles, their eyes vagabonding, their fists flashing in the air while they leapt and he entered the classroom.

Desire cursed herself for choosing to finish her assignments in the class instead of going to the library. As she raised her head from her book to catch a better glimpse of what had disrupted the class, she spotted Ireti at the door. He entered the class, dressed in a khaki safari suit with his enormous head of tousled hair. Desire sat up and adjusted herself on the seat with a smile. In the past weeks, the thought of him slipped into her mind at times and she reminded herself to find him at the student union's building, or talk to Prof about him. For one reason or another, the days had passed with no sight of him, until now.

As more students trooped into the class and formed a fence around her seat, Desire placed her hand on the desk to prevent anyone from standing on it; she needed to catch a better glimpse of him.

Ireti cleared his throat, looked around at the students with a smile playing on his lips. Some boys behind him screamed some slogans she could not catch. Ireti turned around, gestured to the boys to stop the screaming and fist-banging on desks. The noise subsided a little as he called out, 'Greatest Lasuites!'

'Great!' a body of voices responded to him.

'Greatest of the greatest of the greatest!'

The students rushed up, in and about, stomping their feet on the ground as they shouted, 'Ghandi Reloaded!'

After a round of greetings, Ireti silenced them, and the students settled to listen to him.

Desire decided it was an opportunity to learn more about the person whose resemblance to Prof had made her consider opening up a conversation on his private life in her future visits. She piled her books together and rested against the chair to listen to him as he ranted about what he would do when he became president of the student union. He moved around the class jumping form one desk to another, and talked to the students who laughed at his jokes, and a few who had booed him when he spoke from his makeshift podium. He threw his hands into the air as each word dropped from his lips, 'Greatest Lasuites! Greatest Gbi-Gbi! Greatest Gba-Gba! Greatest of the greatest of the greatest—' From the way he connected with the students, even with his salutations, she felt a part of her revisiting Prof's visit to Maroko. She packed away her assignment and sat on the desk, which gave her a better view of him.

Desire knew so much about Prof, how he was an only son and was not married, but there were rumours of some of his women and the possibilities of children—she read not just newspaper articles or reports, but columns in soft sell magazines like *Fame* and *Encomium*. She studied library references, research articles and interviews on Prof as if she was preparing for a law examination. She observed how he changed in the pictures; the days of his full afro hair and those days he carried rough hair that was not as full but tangled like Ireti's own.

Desire looked around the class, at the bustling students whose voices were soon raised into a shrill of 'Aluta Continua, Victoria Ascerta,' and then at Ireti. It amazed her once more that in her two years at the university she had never met this young man who was a photocopy of Prof. His voice bounced around the walls of the classroom as he spoke.

'I need your votes. Together we can say, "No to school fee increase! No to the management of student politics! We say nooooo!"' The chants spread from the classroom to the many corners of the campus, rushing off into the ears of passers-by, as far as they could reach. Ireti spoke to the students. His arms flailed as he threw long words into the air. At a point, he jumped down from the desk onto the floor; his campaign entourage and some other admirers quickly swarmed around him, so that she could not see him any more.

Her size proved an advantage again as she squeezed herself through the throng of students. At eight years old, which was a year before she met Prof, her neighbours and friends stopped calling her Desire, they called her, "cockroach". This was because a neighbour had said she could easily pass off as an underfed five-year-old, and because she ate so little, the name stuck. There were also those who addressed her by comparing her head to a tennis ball or her limbs to dried sticks. She was so used to it, that when she heard shouts like, 'Tell that stick-hand girl to tell her mother "Thank you,"' or 'Hey! Tennis-ball-head, come and buy food for me,' she ran towards the caller. There was perhaps something about the way she was called that it never occurred to her that the words, in a different context, were hurtful.

There was also a time in her childhood when the older boys used to ask her to dance like a baby *wain-wain*. It was not difficult, and she enjoyed acting like a marionette whose strings were being pulled into movement. She enjoyed how people gathered around her as she flayed her stick hands in the air and freed herself to the rhythm of their clapping while laughter jumped from their mouths into the air. She entertained them until they all dispersed, most times leaving a naira note for her and her friends to buy some coconut candy.

As she pushed her way through the students, placed her books

in her bag and smuggled her way out of the multitude, she
tried to get Ireti's attention without making it too obvious. His
face jolted her, as it carried the same intense expression that
had spoken to her in her childhood. In that fleeting moment,
she was caught up in amazement at how nature could replicate
itself, this déjà vu, before she attempted to once again escape
from the human barricade that made leaving the classroom
difficult. He was rounding off his speech as she struggled to
move out of the room and soon found herself literally being
swept off her feet until she got close to the door and the crowd
let her down. Sandwiched between the door, a wall and the
buxom student whose hair attachment pricked her neck, she
turned around one last time, only to find him so close that the
breath from his mouth rushed over her face. His entourage
engaged in a din of emotional solidarity, singing songs of
victory, pressing on and lifting the students from the social
oppression forced upon them.

She squirmed, inadvertently hitting Ireti and causing him to
let out a low moan. Seeing the awkwardness of the situation,
she muttered quickly, 'Sorry.'

They were the only ones aware of this shared discomfort at
that moment.

She began to press on to escape the tension when Ireti
tapped her on the shoulder and told her, 'I'll clear the way.'

He then spoke in muted tones to one of his allies and they
began to make a way for her to pass through the human traffic;
while some of his friends were cooing words and jokes into his
ears, laughing and backslapping, he fixed his look on her. She
felt it burrowing through her neck. He acted jolly, and when
the people were not moving fast enough, he created space by
shooting his buttocks backwards and forcing some people to
the back. They laughed at his playfulness. He winked at her
and she giggled. In that moment, she decided that she wanted
to sleep with him.

When he got to the door, she placed her mouth next to his
ear and softly, said, 'Thanks.'

'Uhn?'

'I-I said, thanks.' His attention was now no longer with her, and she had enjoyed it despite its brevity. She then gushed, 'I'm good in bed. Try me.' She said it quietly, but she knew he heard. His eyes bulged. His mouth was half-open, and his eyes roved around for an audience. It was as if he was looking for someone, anyone to confirm that he had heard her correctly. She expected him to laugh it off, but even as his friends tugged at his shirt collar, he continued to look at her, gulping her down with his eyes.

Desire fuelled the curiosity she saw in his eyes by eyeing his crotch defiantly, and turning like she was ready to walk away, assured that this would make a good joke for her and Remilekun later that night. Yet, she found herself standing outside the class like she was waiting for him, watching as he attended to his friends. She studied him. She recognised his unsettled eyes shifting about like he was in search of someone.

Desire did not go to the library. She stayed by the window until the small crowd of students had dispersed one after the other and the few that remained stood by the door throwing around banter and laughing out loud. Finally, when she felt he would not come to her, she walked towards him and resisted the attempt by his friends to block her from getting closer. He waved off their attempt and they allowed her through. She stepped away, pulling him to the side. Once with him, she repeated her previous words more audibly than the first time, only to him, 'I would like to sleep with you.'

Ireti's eyes darted from left to right and he folded and unfolded his arms. Finally, he said, 'Like, sleep...you mean sleep-sleep?' Ireti's voice stirred her. He was obviously taking her in with his eyes again to determine if she was indeed serious. She wondered what he was thinking. Remilekun once told her she looked like a nun with lips that begged to be kissed. 'You turn heads. Don't you know?' Remilekun had said. She had never considered it, but it came to mind as Ireti stared at her and she could not figure out what he was thinking.

When she didn't respond, he tried again. 'Are you a Nigerian? Are you not from this country?'

She did not get a chance to reply before his supporters, oblivious of the drama going on between them, screamed, 'Ghandi!'

Desire looked at him intently, and Ireti cocked his head and smiled slowly.

'What do you think?'

'What Nigerian girl that looks like you would say... I've never seen this kind of thing-o.'

His friends called out, 'Ghandi? How far?' while Desire wondered what kind of Nigerian girl she looked like.

'I dey come,' he turned his attention back to her as he waved for them to be patient, before he leaned towards her, moving in close.

'You're serious?' The bristles of his beard brushed against her shoulder.

She stiffened and said in a high pitch, 'I like the way you do your own politics. Maybe, we can talk politics, or something, later?'

He smiled at her. His nose twitched a little as he said in a low voice, 'Tell me your name?'

'Desire,' she said staring through him.

'Desire? Your name is Desire?' he repeated. His shoulders dropped. 'Uhn-Uhn! Tease,' he huffed. He buried his hands in his hair, and she glimpsed distrust in his pupils.

'My name is Desire Babangida Jones'.

'Hmm, interesting name.' Ireti smiled at her, placed a hand on the small of her back and muttered in her ear, 'I stay at number 12, Ibrahim Compound, Balewa Street, Ojo. Come.' He stepped back and stared at her face for a long time before he nodded, and turned to walk away. She remained on the spot, as he glided towards his friends. She took note of how his bum filled his trousers and made waves as he moved. Yet, she felt little that was sensual. She could, in that moment, understand what it meant to be an artist painting or sculpting a nude woman.

14

Ojo was an area of narrow streets that crossed each other's path forming a crucifix wherever they met. Many of these streets were lined with cars and the spaces between were filled with traders and their wares. The place was a vibrant open market where you never knew what you could find. Brown, rusted, caved-in roofs of the igloo-like houses filled the landscape like giant art installations. It was in this area that Desire walked in search of Ireti, looking at every street name until she found "Balewa Street" on a black signpost with white lettering. It was a blind alley with several houses, whose landlords, she learnt, were descendants of a settler. Desire stopped at a chemist two houses from the one she would later discover was Ireti's. A girl of about 13, with a mole on her lower lip, was in the shop watching a black-and-white 12-inch Sony television.

'Condom,' her voice was low. She felt unsure, but she looked straight at the girl's face to keep up her act of defiance.

'Na you wan use am?' the girl asked with her focus on the television screen.

Desire scanned the scanty shelf of medicine in the shop and replied with a lilt in her voice, 'Yes-o. Bring two packs.'

'How many?'

'Two packs,' Desire made a V sign with her fingers to indicate two and then slipped them into her bag as the girl returned to watching the drama on TV.

Ireti's house was also an old rectangular bungalow with walls that wore a navy-blue paint. She walked straight through the door, and down the passage of rows of opposite rooms in the house, moving past buckets of water placed at doorsteps, kerosene stoves on wooden tables and raffia brooms leaning against the walls. When she reached the second to last door, she knocked. She didn't know which of the rooms was his, but she concluded that being a university politician, he would not rent a room at the entrance of any place, for his own security. 'Who be dat?' That was not his voice, and sure enough, the door of the room was swung open by a man in underpants.

'Wetin happen?'

'Good evening, sir. Is Ireti in?'

'Ireti? Who be Ireti?'

'He is a LASU student...'

'Na him tell you say dis na him room? Waka from hia!' He eyed her with sleep-burdened eyes that were swollen and *mtssshed* at her. His mouth remained in a pout and a bulb of spit hung from the middle of his lower lip.

'You wan make I woz you.' He tightened his fist, folded it under his armpits and spread his legs apart, observing her till she sensed that he wouldn't budge unless she left his doorstep. As she walked away from him, she felt him still standing there with lasting disdain. She didn't turn to look, even when his door slammed shut. Unsure of which door to try next, she returned to the front of the house to see if she would find any clue or someone who could help.

There was a woman with a baby strapped on her back with *aso oke* cloth, sitting on the porch. 'Well done ma.'

'Wehdone.'

'I am looking for a friend. He is in LASU.'

The woman took a long look at her, and broke into a smile that disappeared just as quickly as it had appeared on her lips. 'You for greet when you dey enter? You studen-shildren *sef*. You no know say when you enta house, you go greet? Anyhow, that man no well like dat.'

There was a soft note in her voice which was not pity. The woman looked up at Desire, and asked, 'Who you say you dey find again?'

'Ghandi Reloaded,' she said, and then thinking they may not know him by that name added, 'Ireti. Student, LASU.'

'De Presido? Ha, na dat room,' she stood up, pointed in

the direction of the room and turned back in an instant to her chore of picking beans on a tray Desire had not noticed. Desire thanked the woman and walked to the door, catching her breath before she knocked like she was stroking a beloved's skin. There was a poster, bearing "**GHANDI RELOADED FOR PRESIDENT**", and a picture of Ireti in a suit and tie, pasted on the door. She had missed it earlier.

Desire stopped to listen. She heard more than one voice inside the room. She considered turning back and stood by the door in deep thought.

'You sure say na Ireti you come see?'

Desire did not turn to the woman, yet she knew she stared, so she called out and didn't knock, 'Ireti. Are you in?'

'Yes? Come in.'

She opened the door and faced three men turning to look at her. A small fluorescent scattered its light over everything in the room. She recognised two of them from the classroom incident.

'O-baby!' the one she didn't know greeted her with so much familiarity she nearly asked if they had met somewhere before then. He stood up and met her by the door. With one hand holding one of her shoulders and the other grabbing her hand for a handshake, he said, 'Hope you didn't have trouble locating this place.'

'I found it, that's what matters,' she said with a shrug.

'Ireti has not been able to sleep or eat or drink-o,' he laughed as he spoke in small bits, so that it seemed that he was holding back something more thunderous. This made it possible for him to speak as he laughed, 'So, do you want to drink, tell me and I will provide it for you. Ireti means a lot to me, and I am ready to give you anything you want.'

'Hmm.'

'Hmm what? I say anything? Meanwhile, are you campaigning for us among your friends?'

The more he talked, the more Desire wondered how long she could keep up being polite enough not to wipe off some of the spit he sprayed on her face as he spoke to her. He was one of those people who gathered saliva in their mouth when they spoke, so that every time he opened his mouth it flew about and settled on whatever was closest to him. He also turned out to be the one who talked the most of the lot.

Desire stood in front of him, but stared at Ireti with intensity, hoping that he would say something that would make him stop talking. The small talk on school politics continued, until Ireti's feigned coughing and the dragging of her feet on the floor, signified to his friends that they needed to leave the room.

The spittle-mouthed friend dropped his hand from Desire's shoulder and said, 'We'll see you again. It was nice talking to you.'

'Mmm,' she nodded and he gave her a full smile before leaving with the others who made excuses about how they needed to rush off to finish one thing or the other.

'How're you doing?' Ireti asked as the last of his friends left the room.

'Fine! Fine!' She surveyed the room, then its floor which was covered with a flower-patterned linoleum carpet. The mattress was on the floor, covering a part of the exposed cement floor. A few metres from the bed, a Tiger fan blew from a corner of the room where the unruly wires of several rechargeable lamps were plugged into an adaptor. The 14-inch Sony television on the carpet carried a CD player. There were some old newspapers on the floor. The sub-headline of the one on top caught her attention: "FREE AT LAST".

Desire didn't need to read the rest. It was a story on Prof's release from prison. She wondered why Ireti would be interested in his story. So many people had lost interest in Prof.

'Come and sit here,' Ireti patted a spot on the bed for her. His eyes had remained on her all this time. She stirred from inspecting the room and moved to his side of the bed. She waited for him to touch her and twice she lifted her eyes with the hope that she would catch him staring, but his eyes remained fixed on the floor. The one time she kept eye contact, he was watching her with something close to pity.

Desire stood up and began to strip until the only piece of clothing on her was her cotton panties. She leaned against him and raised his head to meet hers, but he turned his face away. She shook her head and walked to the other end of the room.

'I'm ready,' she said, folding her arm over her breasts.

It took some seconds again before Ireti walked across the room to her. It was just a few metres wide, but his heavy breathing and the friction of his feet on the rubber carpet made the room seem like many kilometres from end to end. 'Come,' Desire felt like she was watching herself speak, and she wanted to see to the end of what this other version of her was up to.

Ireti stood before her, his eyes fixed on what she thought was her groin—only to discover it was her navel.

'That's a neat cut. It's like a button.' He then looked away and stared again at his feet. Desire walked over to the mattress and lay on it. She faced upward, turning sometimes to look at his fluttering eyes, which he continued to avert from her as he struggled out of his clothes. He took off everything except his boxers.

'Won't you remove that one?' she attempted a giggle, but her voice got caught in her throat.

He stood in front of her again and cast a sheepish look at her. She could feel goose pimples rise on her arms.

'What is it?' she stammered.

He said nothing and tugged at the boxers but did not remove them. She didn't know what it was, but she could see he was fastened to the spot by fear, and just as suddenly, like someone who had received a quick reproach, he headed for the door. Desire sat on the bed. She felt nervous and waited for him to return. When he did not, after a few minutes, she considered going after him. Just then, he trudged into the room, the smell of cigarettes following him. He sat on the carpet.

'What?' this time Desire made sure her voice was firmer than earlier on. Ireti shook his head so uncontrollably that she sat up on the bed in haste.

'What is it?'

He just kept shaking his head and after a while he said in a voice that sounded like a father calming a troubled daughter, 'You remind me of—' He followed this with a long sigh, staring at her navel, 'Stand up. Dress up.'

Desire saw how he looked away anytime she tried to look into his eyes. She wondered if this timidity was genuine or just an act. She looked at him, now standing limp against the wall. His boxers had slipped down his waist a little and his hands were placed over his groin. He looked like a shy, young boy trying to hide his erection from the glare of girls. There was fear in his eyes.

He started in a voice that came like a car failing to start, 'I can't do it to you,' he looked into her eyes as he spoke, but kept his hands over his penis. She saw him struggling to hold back the tears. Desire clasped his hands within hers.

'Why? It won't stand, or point, or what?' She stared at his lower abdomen to assure herself that what she saw was an erection, where his hands still covered his penis.

'Are you afraid? Is it that you can't do it with a woman, is it me, or what?' She searched her mind for things she had read on impotence in men.

He smiled. 'You want to play doctor now, right?'

Desire pressed on, 'Do you feel guilty that you're cheating on your girlfriend?'

'I am a politician, I am part of the student parliament. I can be with anyone I want, but...'

Their eyes met, and he realised that his words seemed banal and tangential.

They stood watching each other as their breathing became heavier.

'Oh! You're gay, and you think I'll...'

'I think you'll what?' he raised a brow. He angled his head

and she felt his eyes settle on her. She felt there was more undressing to be done beyond her naked state. She lowered her head and her lips twitched.

'Are you...' she stopped talking and looked down at the mattress. She looked at his hands over his boxers and realised that he was hiding his inability to be aroused.

'Not now.'

'Why is it not now?' Desire did not look up when she said this to him. 'Not even an erection. Is it that bad? Am I—'

Ireti was silent but placed a middle finger on her lip to keep her from saying more. 'It's not you.' He placed his right hand over a birthmark which was right under her navel. It was a scrap of lumpy flesh, as big as a peanut. For some reason, she thought of her mother's birthmark. Desire turned her eyes away from the birthmark to a soiled piece of a rag wrapped around the cupboard at the extreme end of the room. She could not understand what was happening at that moment. He had acted so much like a playboy and was now playing an altar boy checking his actions before the priest.

Desire looked up at Ireti's face and said, 'I thought you wanted it.' She stopped as her voice shook when she spoke. The first feeling of shame came over her as she began to feel the weight of her actions.

'You don't want me, Desire.'

'What does that mean?'

'Get dressed, *oya*—next time.' Something in his eyes told her there was never going to be a next time.

She sighed and sank to the ground, picking up her clothes, one after the other. Her shame multiplied and she regretted the words she had spoken to him in the class. She thought of Prof in that moment and felt shame descend on her all over again.

Desire dressed and sat on the bed. She wished she had not come to see him. She tried to talk, but found she could not. 'I'm alright. I came to you, right? I'm not sick, okay? I just want you to take me.' Her voice sounded distant to her.

Ireti sat by her side on the bed, scratched his head and faced the floor, 'I don't feel right about this.'

She swayed from side to side. She had never done something like this in her life and the more she was rejected, the more she wanted the ground to swallow her. He was the first man she had undressed in front of, for sex. She had seen men unclothe her with their eyes many times and did not understand why this one was dressing her up with his.

'Well. You know—' he lifted his eyes from the floor and put on a T-shirt over his boxers.

'I think it's time to go home,' he rubbed his hands together, trying to break up the moment.

'There's got to be some reason. Tell me something,' she said, and then she felt more self-loathing and changed tack. 'It is past seven.'

'Or you can sleep here tonight. My friends and I would look for somewhere else to sleep.'

'Seven is late? I think I should just go,' she said quietly.

'Do you want to talk? Just talk. We can undress and hold ourselves and just talk.'

She looked at him and shook her head, slowly at first and then vigorously, his words irritating her more as she considered them. She covered her face with her hands and promptly pulled on her trousers, 'I'll leave now.'

Before they stepped outside the room, he stopped her by the door and said, 'I'm sorry.'

Desire shook her head and as she felt the bile rise up her throat she asked, 'Just like that? Who does that?'

'Please...'

Desire sighed, 'You're sorry?' She turned towards the door and he changed the subject like they hadn't seen each other naked just a few minutes earlier.

'Why do you live so far away from school? It is like living in the dark. You never get to hear anything until you are in school the next day. So, is it, eh... independence? Solitude? Or circumstance?'

Desire looked up at his face and shook her head but said nothing.

'Talk to me. You know why I gave you my address? You didn't look like the words you spoke. I just feel something about you, and as you undressed, I saw it wasn't sex.'

'*Mtssssh,*' she kissed her teeth and added, 'Seer!'

'I don't want us to start with sex. I feel like something is about to be sacrificed.' He stopped and laughed, 'You know another girl won't pass through this room without a whip from my big man here.' He looked down at his groin as he spoke and laughed, 'I don't know, but I just...'

'You just... feel sorry?' Something in her gave as she spoke.

She stayed silent until they got to where his friends sat outside, playing a game of draughts. Mr. Spittle-mouth was the first to notice them, 'Now-now-now? You people have finished?' he said with a laugh and added, 'Babeee! Stay over now,' he pleaded.

'I live in Jakande Estate, in Abesan.'

'Where's Abesan?'

'In Ipaja.'

'Ipaja?'

'I need to go. My roommate will be expecting me,' she said to them.

'*Na wa-o*! Why would you go to a far-far place like that to get accommodation?'

Ireti took Desire's arm from where it lay idly by her side and tucked it into his. Desire caught another friend wink at him and follow it with a shout of, 'Ireti baba! Ghandiiiii! Ghandiiii Reloaded!'

'Come visit soon,' one of them said to her and the others fell about laughing.

She removed her arm from his and walked swiftly ahead.

At the bus stop, he said to her, 'You'll be fine. Sex is itself an anxiety. Sex cannot cure nervousness. It's like trying to end your woes over a bottle of beer.'

'Are you also a psychologist?' She smiled, and trying to push away her shame she said, 'I saw newspaper cut-outs of Prof Eni, the activist, in your room. Do you know him?'

He ignored her question and pointed, 'See that bike man wants to kill himself, who drives like that?'

'What has that got to do with the question I asked you?'

He tried to respond but he stammered for a while, before he said, 'Well, it is a piece of paper.'

'You look a lot like him. I was just wondering if you—'

He interjected before she concluded her question, 'You know why I didn't... do it?'

'Why?' She tried to sound quite unconcerned.

But she felt her anxiety must have shown as he lowered his voice further when he said, 'My mum did not finish her university because she was impregnated in her second year, and it all appeared like history was about to repeat itself.'

'I got some condoms!' She lowered her voice as a passer-by looked at them. A car passed and she saw the deep hurt as its lights flashed from his face and tried to figure out what she saw in his eyes.

'Well, that has passed now. Maybe another time. Meanwhile, you really think I look like Prof? People say I should meet him. I heard he is out of prison now. I don't know how to. Everyone always says I look like him,' and with a brief pause he said, 'I'm just trying to put his life together. You know... find out what made him who he is and all that what-not.'

'Is that all?' she said, not fully convinced, but glad that he finally answered her question.

'I keep staring at his picture all the time, trying to find the resemblance. Anyway, it's good to look like him, you know, he is known for his integrity. I just want to know more, at least about the man I look like.' He laughed, turning to face Desire and asked, 'Seriously, how do you go to a man who never knew you all his life and say—"Hello, I'm the result of a one-night-stand you had years back"?'

He became still and looked up at her face with both relief and a plea on his face. This was how she realised it was not something he wanted to say. Ireti turned away. Desire stared at him with her mouth wide open.

'Is he?'

'Please,' he whispered. 'You... Please,' he said again, and she watched his face and the way it seemed as if his cheek was being pulled apart, yet he still managed a glint in his eyes as he spoke. 'Please, don't tell anyone. I don't even know if I want to meet him—I want to, but then I don't want to. You know that tired saying, of letting sleeping dogs lie. I want to heed it.'

'Does he know?'

'Please, don't talk about it.'

'Should we go back to the house and talk about it?'

'No! I was just talking nonsense,' he snapped.

She turned away, a little disappointed at his words because in her head she was already thinking of sharing the news with Prof, wondering about his reaction and if it would end his decision to live in a dark room, or cause him to stop her from seeing him. With these thoughts in her head, she spotted an *okada* man making a sign to her asking if she wanted his services. She flagged him down and jumped onto the back of the motorcycle. Before the machine roared off into the night, she beckoned for Ireti to come closer. She left him with the words, 'I will see to your father.'

She tapped the *okada* man lightly on the shoulder, indicating he should move. She did not turn to see what Ireti's face looked like, to say goodbye or see him wave, if he did. When she arrived at the estate, it was almost 11pm. She could not go to see Prof.

15

'Good to see you,' Prof said as he opened the door for Desire. He tried to hide his excitement but found himself trembling. He spent the next few minutes thinking of how to steady his voice and make it tender, even though he wanted to scream at her for not coming to see him the previous night. He also felt like embracing her for coming back. Instead, he said to her, 'It's a little stuffy in here today, right?'

He wanted to ask her why she stayed away, yet he said, 'You don't have to keep coming here, you know.' He stepped aside so she could come into the house, and he inhaled deeply as she glided quietly to her now regular chair. She sank into it with a thud and let out a deep breath.

The silence between them seemed different. The air was stiffened with something unsaid, waiting to be spoken of. Prof began to hum Prince Nico Mbarga's *Sweet Mother* and then faded into silence.

'You must miss your mother.'

There was a lot to say about her statement, but he decided not to respond.

'I need to tell you something. I don't know how you will take it, but it is important news.'

A shriek from one of the flats split their conversation and Prof leapt up, then fell back into the chair.

'*Be calm,*' Desanya said to him.

'I am being calm,' he turned and whispered into the air, 'you should not be here now.' He looked towards Desire to see how she handled the noise but the darkness hid her expressions well.

'Are you talking to me, Prof?'

He grunted. He didn't like how Desanya came around when

Desire came to see him. The room became silent for a few minutes again and he decided that he needed to break it.

'I don't know but I think I have some crazy neighbours. I mean, every other night there is a scream or a cry or a shout or some sound that I can't even place. I think this is close to someone's bedroom.'

'Hmmm.'

Prof took this as assent. 'I feel I need to remain here forever. To bury myself in this darkness and live here forever,' he could hear his own voice, struggling to offer the right emotions. He wanted both Desire and Desanya to share his exact feelings of confusion as he spoke, but he realised he did not even know what they were as he talked. He stood up from the chair, paced the room up and down, his voice rising and falling as he felt like he was back in his past.

'I feel there is something which brings me here to you—maybe to help you find the light again,' she said with a chuckle.

'You shouldn't make the mistake of thinking darkness is bad. Sometimes having light is the problem. Darkness is a cypher. Things, potentials, are created in darkness—think of that Bible story in Genesis; the total darkness that engulfed the earth brought light. What brings darkness? Darkness welcomes light all the time. We can see in darkness, only if we let our eyes master the dark.'

Prof stopped talking, stopped walking around the room, and moved to sit on the edge of the chair she was in. The heat of her body warmed him, and he sensed how she stiffened in the chair. Every part of his body stirred into a readiness he had not known for a long time, and he placed his right hand on his groin and stroked the stirring gently. He stayed this way for a long time and when he felt her silence was lengthening indefinitely, he stood up and walked back to his own chair with his hands between his thighs, his teeth clenched. When he could no longer take the way his body shuddered, and the way the blood pumping in his heart rushed down between his legs, he said to her, 'I want to use the toilet.'

Desire thought of the many stories of Prof that she had heard. Many people talked about how his mother wielded a strong influence in his life. There was the widespread tale of how his mother dipped him in a pot of magic herbs as a child so that no harm would come to him. They said she carried more mystery than that of Anini, the notorious Benin armed robber who some romantically compared to Robin Hood, but who had more magic than flair. Anini stole from the rich and on the busiest of days, when the sweat of everyday people mingled with their tears, he would stand at the roundabout junction in Benin City to share money with those he saw as less fortunate. No one could tell how the stories started, but soon, one person told another; it became a legend passed on from one generation to another: how Anini had the power to disappear or become invisible anytime the police raided an area where he was carrying out a criminal operation. And so, Anini reigned as a myth for the seven years in which he was never caught. When he was eventually killed, the rumour mill also exonerated him. It explained that the charm he got from his powerful medicine man had not been recharged the previous night. For it to work, he needed to practice disappearing on a prostitute's lap a day before he went on his mission—the charm would only work if the woman was a prostitute. Unfortunately, he could not rehearse that night because policemen were assigned to every prostitute joint in every hotel in Benin to trail his movements. Anini died with no word on his lips. He died smiling. And so is the legend told till this day.

Prof returned to the room, picking up the conversation as he took a seat on the arm of her chair.

'I heard gunshots on your last visit, some few minutes after you left.'

Though he did not want his inquiry to feel abrupt, he could sense that it jolted her from whatever daydream she seemed caught up in, when she let out a startled 'Oh!'

He waited, wanting to know if there was anything that

indicated he had crossed the line by coming to sit close to her, before he said, 'Now, you see why I think you shouldn't come here... if you don't want to.'

Desire's thoughts were still on urban legends. 'What do you think of Anini and women?'

He paused, 'Anini and women?'

'Yes, Anini and women. You know they say he loved women and they were his saviour?'

'So, I talk of gunshots and you think of Anini.'

'Yes, yes, yes.'

'Male armed robbers have always loved women. Female armed robbers are usually wiser.'

'So, you think, women don't spend on men?'

Prof guffawed. It warmed the conversation and he was glad it made her sit up in the chair.

'Well, we have women armed robbers, but women have been rather wise about being an unnecessary celebrity like Anini. Actually, I think he didn't like women. He loved the wisdom of spending his short life with women. He was not a woman wrapper—he wrapped himself around women and the strength they offered his timidity. A man who decides to rob others of their possessions already lives in the fear of lack, women are the only ones who can absolve fear.'

'You don't seem too interested in him.'

'Why should I be? Oyenusi, you know, was not just an armed robber. He was a philosopher in that trade. You know what he said: "The bullet has no power". The wisdom in that is everything. It is a regal statement on the powerlessness of the army that disrupted the root of this country for many years.' His voice had risen as he spoke.

Not convinced she said, 'You know that much about women and yet you have none around you.'

He sighed and tried to understand the comment in the context of his life, the one he believed she understood and the one he knew of himself.

'Women are a source of strength, you know. If anyone

decides not to keep that source of strength around them, it's an acceptance of one's weakness,' he paused, 'I was raised by my mother, you know. Solely by her.'

'How do you mean source of strength? Keep them? Are women artefacts?' and then she chuckled, 'Or maybe they are, in the context of your generalisation.'

'I just wanted to—' Prof paused, 'I wanted to explain how much support women give to men.'

'There is a way you make one feel that women are meant to be kept for their strength-oozing power.'

'What is it about women that makes you want so desperately to deemphasise the idea of their becoming as an unbecoming?'

'On whose standard is a woman judged? How does she become? What does she become? Prof, listen, womanhood is a process. We have never even been allowed to begin a journey to become. Whatever you have, or think we emphasise is that we are ensuring a presence that will make us become.'

'Hmm. That should be profound, but I have no word to say now,' Prof said and then sank into a long silence.

'Your mum had...' she started, and seeing that there was no way to frame the question right, gave up.

Prof knew her struggle: how do you ask a man like him if his mother was indeed a witch, and if it had in any way made him invincible, until he broke his vows to her and fell out of her favour? She did not appear to believe it herself. Or rather, he wanted to believe she did not think the things he thought.

'My mum...' he stopped, and moved back into that earlier melancholia she noticed when she first came in.

'My mum is fine,' he said, adding quickly, 'You never talk about yourself.' He was so abrupt with his answer that she did not even have time to think again, to determine if she wanted to ask him anything else.

Prof stood from his spot on the arm of her chair and remarked, 'It is one of those rather personal days, mmm?'

Desire did not know how to respond at first. Her visits to Ireti these past days played in her head.

The last time, she went to see him with pictures of Prof and they spoke for almost two hours in his office, as she no longer visited him at home after their no-sex episode. They talked for so long, he ended up missing his class. When she asked if he had ever tried to see Prof, all he said was, 'The chance to do so never occurred. He was in prison all the time that I was growing up—you know, when I realised I needed a father.'

'Would you want to meet him now if you had the chance?'

'I don't know.'

'When people say they don't know they mean they do want it.'

'How would you say that?'

'I say I don't know all of the time when I'm afraid to examine my feelings. I'm afraid to accept that I've made a choice.'

'See, Desire, I really do not know if I want to see him. My life is—' he paused, 'My life has a whole lot of its own problems at this time and I don't want to add to it.'

'Is there something you want to talk about? I might help, you know. I have things I can dig into,' Prof laughed.

'Nothing exactly, there is so much to learn from you. I'm just thinking on some of our debates,' Desire said.

'Really? You've been quieter than the typical days. Except of course when you went on a woman-theorising presentation,' Prof laughed, his voice renting the tension in the room into shreds. She relaxed into the chair.

'We should call this session, "Learning at the Master's Feet" then.'

Despite the way they laughed and shared small talk, the air in the room still felt heavy.

'How does it feel?'

'How does what feel?'

'Being out of prison. Staying here all alone by yourself. You know, we have a democracy with Obasanjo on his second term. Don't you feel you want to meet and talk to people, your friends, about what they think about him?'

Prof did not respond. Desire did not know how to pick up the conversation again and she waited, hoping that he would break the tension.

He started to talk when she was lost in thought and certain they were going to spend the rest of the night in silence, 'They took me away. I am not the one in this body any more. They took me away.' His voice became crusty and he tried to speak slowly so the words wouldn't bear the weight of him crumbling with the pain of those past years.

Desire did not know how to help him gather his emotions. She had assumed that his prison stories were under his control.

'There would be a time when a man loses his body...'

'It's okay,' she said, finally.

He sighed, and like he was not the same person who spoke earlier, he said, 'Let's say, I feel like a lighter without a flame. It's time,' he added in a low voice. 'Yes, we should talk about something else.'

'Like what?'

'Your name. You know you never told me why you are called Desire?'

She sighed. He continued, 'Usually, it is our relatives from the south-south that make a history lesson of their children's names. The Yoruba and Igbo on their part are typically mundane philosophers,' he said with a laugh. 'I once met an Ijaw man called Government. So, tell me, what's the story behind your name?'

'Should there be a story behind every name?'

'I have a feeling yours is not just any name and it has a story.'

'Well, my mother told me my father wanted a boy desperately and when he didn't have one, he gave me the name "The Undesirable Element", after a Pacesetters series novel my mother said she was reading at the time.' Prof chuckled. 'My birth certificate carries the name Undesired. My mother renamed me Desire, like it was the shortened version of the name.'

'Hmmm, I'm called "The one God created"—Eniolorunda, but my many imperfections offer doubt to that name.' He cleared his voice after a small laugh, and followed it with a question, 'You should tell me more about your family, your father, your mother—'

She switched the topic and using the tangent of his question, she said, 'You never talk about anything except old politics and maybe your mother dropping off food now and then.'

They both became silent. She realised that this was the first time they would introspect their lives without giving attention to politics. This time, she felt naked.

There appeared to be some mystique—created or assumed, that brought them together, yet it was apparent they were yet to find it. Suddenly, she found that she did not want to ignore the noise of the outside—it was there when she first stepped into the room. It existed as she sat in the room listening to him as he talked, but with the weight of the unspoken lingering around, she listened more to the humming of the generator and distant traffic, like that was what she needed to converse with.

'You don't want to go into the past, right?' She did not respond.

'Right?' he asked one more time, and she responded with a grunt.

The clock chimed.

'I hope to see you tomorrow,' he said as he locked the door to the lightless room.

16

Ireti sat on a wooden bench in front of a kiosk painted the cherry-red of Coca-Cola. There was a young girl on Ireti's lap whose cheeks were rounded like she stored sweets in them. He and the girl appeared like effigies, facing the street. Desire walked towards him with a frown. Her muscles tightened as she drew closer to him. From that distance, she could not tell if noticing her facial expression was what caused him to jump from the seat and drop the girl on the bench, or something else. Ireti walked towards her smiling, with open arms.

'The madam herself. Coming to see me in this hot sun,' he laughed. It felt forced, and he suddenly turned sombre, 'Thanks for coming to see me.'

Desire was angry. She walked ahead of him towards his house, stomping her feet on the ground. She wanted to turn to see what his eyes looked like as he inspected her walking before him. As she reached the main door of the house, she stopped and turned to face him, 'Your friends are shadowing me all over the campus.'

He frowned, deep gullies forming on his forehead.

'Can you imagine? The four of them just stood by the window of the classroom looking like people who want to steal a fish from the fishmonger?'

Desire couldn't find the words to describe the intense choreographed look that had kept her neck stiff and straight all throughout class, while she fought to listen to the whispers passed around the classroom about who the boys were there to "shadow". She felt some point at her with their quick glances— although she did not catch anyone looking directly at her.

The professor continued to teach. He behaved as if he was unaware of the situation, although everyone could see how he also stammered and fidgeted as the boys fiddled with their hands in their pockets and coughed to be noticed—either by her or by the lecturer, or perhaps as a warning to any boy who might be interested in her. At a time when cultism was rife across Nigerian universities, only a few university lecturers would have dared to play Superman when a performance like this was enacted.

As the class ended, and one of the boys came up to her, calling 'Our wife', she clenched her jaw. Quivering with rising rage, she hurried to the student union block to talk to Ireti and didn't stop even when they called out to her. She felt irritated. The more she thought of the Ireti she was left alone with in the bedroom, the one whose penis followed the direction of his eyes, downwards, and the one whom these boys here were displaying machismo on behalf of, the more she felt a deep growl forming within her.

'He's at home,' a teenage boy with a cackle for a voice told her at the student union building. She rushed off to see him, her anger boiling. She planned to attack him with a barrage of questions about what rights he had to monitor her around the school, but this went up in smoke.

Once they were in his room, Ireti leaned on her and his high-pitched cry had her stuttering, 'Are you okay? What happened?'

The next few minutes were spent consoling him while she remained baffled, until he finally uttered the words that cleared the air, 'I lost my mum this morning.'

'Your mum?'

'Yes. That's why I was trying to reach you. I sent my boys. I only asked them to tell you I needed to see you.' He unhinged his arms from around her neck and moved to sit on the mattress.

'You could have sent a text message or called! Ireti, we have spoken almost every day since we met. You talk to me about your day and I tell you about mine.' Then she paused to think, 'Well, maybe not too well in the last two days because I have had to complete some course projects.'

Ireti attempted a smile.

Desire stared at him in annoyance. His swift change of mood from the carefree tenant sitting outside chit-chatting with the round-cheeked girl, to this whimpering man inside the room, irritated her. Desire's throat bobbed as she swallowed. She was still irritated by "the boys" and their ways. She placed her hand on her waist and made sure their eyes met, before she asked, 'Why didn't any of them think of asking permission to speak to me outside and say something like, "I think Ireti needs to see you urgently"? Why would they act like idiots?'

'I'm sorry, Desire. I have been so busy with this campaign thing and when I tried to call you these last two evenings your phone was off.'

'I was busy!' she snapped.

The more she thought of their actions, the more she concluded it was not her problem that his mother died. She raised her eyes to look at him. The sight of his head thrown forward with grief made her feel a touch of guilt at her coldness. She moved closer to him, lifted her hand and placed it on his shoulder, caressing it gently before tightening her hands around his shoulder blade.

'I sometimes wonder if my mother wanted me to meet my father,' he said.

Desire squirmed in the chair. She could feel his muscles stiffen under the surface of his skin.

'Would I offend her spirit if I meet a man who I bet wouldn't care about me? How do I even know where he is?' he threw his head back and sighed, puffing his cheeks. 'I mean, I know he's out of prison, but where do I go looking for him? Does he even know I exist?'

It seemed rather strange at that point, that this boy she had met only a few weeks before could trust her with his pain. As she watched Ireti, and thoughts of Prof crossed her mind, her eyes watered and she let the tears run. She slipped her hand down from his neck and slowly stroked his back.

'How long have you known about him?' That didn't sound quite right, so she asked again, 'How did you know?'

Grief was not enough to make him less of a storyteller. Ireti varied his tone of voice to capture the different emotions that he felt at each phase of the life he described.

'For a long time, I didn't know who my father was because it was something that I learnt early never to discuss. As I grew, I observed that once the news came on, and Prof was on screen, my mum's mood changed immediately, and she always walked out or switched off the TV. When she returned, I could tell she had been crying.'

As each word fell from his lips, he appeared to grow smaller: he was a boy, lost in the city, looking for direction. She listened to him, waiting for a time to come in, to intervene and help him find his way as he told her of how he moved from Benin to Lagos because his mum kept hoping that his father would find her.

'Did she leave when she found out she was pregnant?'

'I'm not sure. She only always said, she left because it was the best decision. And considering that many years since that day, he never married or fathered a child—at least from what we hear... She left, perhaps, when she realised she could be pregnant—I really don't know.'

'At least you are not an orphan. You still have a father.'

'He fathered me. It's better not to have a father, or to have one that disowned you, rather than a father who doesn't know you exist. How do I go to a man fresh out of prison and ask him to claim paternity?'

'Maybe, it's not that hard. Maybe it is. One has to try,' she bit her lower lip as she struggled not to tell him that the reason her phone was switched off every night was because she was with his father.

'You know, the name on my birth certificate reads: Eniolorunda Iretioluwa. I was Eni all through my secondary school, I changed to Ireti when I was admitted into the university. Some people still comment about the resemblance, but I always shrug it off as happenstance.'

'It is uncanny,' Desire said. 'Don't you want to meet him now? At least you could use your mother as an excuse. You may want to break the news of her death—'

She looked at Ireti and seeing how he couldn't meet her eyes as he spoke, she looked at the floor.

'My mum always said my destiny was in my hands. Meeting or not meeting my father wouldn't change the fact that I can be whatever I want to be. Instead, it can affect the course of my life.'

'These things depend, you know,' Desire said.

'When I came out top in my exams, my mother woke me up in the early morning. She does—did—sorry.' His lips shook, but he continued, 'She always woke me up in the early morning when she wanted to tell me something important, or at least, she felt was important. She said, "Even when one doesn't have an arm, he devises a way to put food into his mouth." She told me that my father's absence should never be an excuse for truancy or underachievement.'

Desire listened to him as he spoke of how Prof being in prison for the most part of his growing life, did not make it easy to even brag that he was his father, even if he wanted to do so. It was as though his mother's death had given him permission to unearth his long-suppressed impulse to talk about his father.

'That morning, as we sat in an embrace, she cried and told me that my father never wanted a baby. She didn't let him know she was pregnant because he always said he didn't want a child. I happened by mistake, Desire. I was a born-by-mistake,' he laughed.

'You know, I didn't like the way she said it that day, but she's my mum. She's that kind of person. She always just spoke her mind like someone who had not given much thought to what she had to say. She'd say, "Eni, you're a born-by-mistake, but it's not the end of the world."'

Ireti explained how it was a phrase his friends used in school for describing someone without a father, or whose mother was rumoured to be promiscuous. None of them called him a born-by-mistake to his face because of his popularity in school, but there were times he wondered if they talked about him behind his back. This was the reason that he did everything he could to uphold that place of likeability among his friends. He was the one who did things the others could not do. He asked them to dare him to go and pour shit on the principal's doorstep. He did this for a couple of nights, praying to God that no one should catch or see him. He also asked his secondary school friends to dare him to have sex with the head teacher's daughter and they did. He asked the girl out but never slept with her. She was one of those whose parents had told her repeatedly that if she so much as touched a man she would get pregnant. And each time they met, she sat a few inches from him smiling and hugging herself. On his part, he knew he was still trying to figure out what a real vagina looked like, outside of the ones he saw in X-rated movies. The day he took the bet on her with his friends, he explained to her, as he walked her to his house, that she must groan like someone in pain because some people wanted to hurt her, and he was trying to protect her from them. He would deal with them himself, and this was why she must cooperate with anything he said. For some reason, she believed him. She believed anything he said. He was the popular one who continued to have good grades despite his pranks. His friends came around to the house, it was all planned. They were outside, listening to their activities.

'I told her to scream: "Haaaaaaaa. Don't hurt me. Don't hurt me please. It hurts. Haaaaaaa!" And I said, "Just wait. Next time, you'll know your daddy. Am I your mate?" I tried to say all the things I felt should be said when having sex.'

He stepped out of the house, with a bare chest, smiling at his friends, who gave him the thumbs up and left before the girl came out. The following day, he told his friends, 'She was just crying like a baby. She is a *vir*-gin! She kept screaming as I was just going inside and out.'

His friends loved him more, except for one. He was the eldest and he just looked at him, laughed and said, 'Fool!'

Desire laughed softly as he narrated the story of his escapades to her.

'See, I'm in the university now. You know things are different. I stand up for students' rights and I can walk into the Vice-Chancellor's office and tell the man the "pain of being a Nigerian student". Things are different now for me. But, I am still the born-by-mistake.'

'So what if you're born-by-mistake?' Desire asked.

Ireti stayed quiet and didn't respond to her question, instead he said, 'Since I met you, I have woken up in the middle of the night playing our first meeting in my head.'

'Why? Do I scare you?' She felt she could see through him. 'No. You give me courage. I'm afraid I may go looking for this father with my mum now dead, and no longer there to give me those long calls on why I should continue aiming high. You know, the last time, before the message came that she died in her sleep, I told her I was thinking of meeting my father. And she replied, "Have I been less than a mother and a father to you?" You know, she said it in that tone that required me to ask no further question.'

'It's the pain. The pain is the only thing she remembers. And, you know, we all turn towards imaginative questions, questions that empower us, so we can bury those stories that we won't give words to because they've corrupted our memory,' Desire said in a small voice.

Ireti raised his head, 'Is that a quote from someone I can read?'

'No. It's me just thinking. I've always considered how some stories will never get told. It's the way it is, Ireti. Silence is where we go to listen to those stories. Sit in silence and listen. Silence tells stories too, you know.'

'I don't want silence. I want those stories she did not think should be told. I really want them, Desire. I want them.'

17

Desire slipped into bed without removing her shoes. She covered her face with the *ankara* material which served as a duvet and ignored Remilekun's griping on how she was becoming more of a stranger with each passing day.

'I'm going out. Not coming home tonight,' Remilekun said and began to whistle Onyeka Onwenu's *You and I* song like she did not care whether Desire responded or not.

'Okay, stay well. Can you please put off the lights on your way out,' Desire said, her thoughts full of how she would arrange a meeting between Ireti and Prof.

Remilekun left and shut the door. Desire plumped the pillow, placed it in the middle of the bed and lay prone on it. Her nose dug into the mattress, taking in the smell of her own stale sweat. After several tries at falling asleep, her eyes remained wide open. She stood up, turned the lights on and began to organise the room. She moved the curtain to see what it was like outside. It was as dark as soot with only amber bulbs sprinkling light that fell into sparse corners of the area. A stray dog howled on the street, and then, the distant hoot of a night guard's whistle made her jump. She was reminded of how a man lost his life while peeping out of his window at night.

The night it happened, she was returning from Prof's house and she heard the gunshots. She walked home briskly only to hear the next morning that a man in the neighbourhood had died from a gunshot wound because the armed robbers who came to the neighbourhood thought he was spying on them from his window. Sadder still, was that a woman who was returning from a visit to friends was hit by a stray bullet from night guards who had shot into the air to scare off the thieves. They said the bullet lodged straight in her skull. The question many in the area were asking was why anyone would wake up in the middle of the night to look out of their window, especially after hearing shots being fired? Why can't anyone look out of their window in the middle of the night, to enjoy the feel of night, that velvet black where things bounced about, and shadows became the mystery waiting to be discovered?

What was wrong with looking out of the window at the skies? Was the world no longer ours? Was the world ever ours? Desire wondered what would have happened if she were the one who died that night. Were she to die, by some ill luck, would similar questions arise? Who would mourn her for looking out of the window as shots rang out, when others were sleeping? Maybe Remilekun and her Mama T. Desire would be mourned for some time, and then she'd be forgotten.

Desire returned to sit on the edge of the bed. She stared into the darkness until she had formed a mental picture of Prof being there with her. It occurred to her that the moment she began to visit him the little details of him she had carried for many years were becoming blurry. She sometimes needed to look at the newspaper cuttings to remind herself of the man she met in her childhood. She tried to think of him in the same way as this man she met in the dark. The one in the dark was the one without a definite face and who remained a silhouette, but could talk and make her body react. The one in the paper was different, he sat in her head like a father's final admonition before dying.

In one of the newspaper cuttings of him, which she kept in her purse, he was bald. His scalp gleamed from the lights of the photographer's camera. She wished more than ever these days to get one chance to put on the lights during one of their meetings. She wondered if light would still fall on his scalp. She wanted to see if his face twitched when she recounted her story of this old acquaintance she knew from a long time ago. The one whose photo she took with her every day. The face she had memorised since she was a child. She would tell him they met in a place that no longer existed, and he might have laughed and said, 'Eldorado?'

And she might have laughed, and said, 'Kind of. For some of us, imagination is our reality.'

She thought of telling him what she had just uncovered about his past, her past, their past. It was beyond Maroko. She felt like an unpleasant whiff. The more she thought about it, the more she wondered if it was her place to tell Prof about Ireti, or to tell Ireti about Prof. She also thought of telling Ireti about him and them about her.

Desire sat up on the bed and looked for a pen and paper to write down the dialogue she imagined could happen between herself and Prof. And then Ireti and Prof. And then herself and Ireti. She wrote on and savoured the way it sounded. The possibilities of seeing the future where all their lives would find some meaning. She finally stood up from the bed as she managed to convince herself that this was a dream she could slip deep into if she lingered any longer. At this point, what she wanted was to stick with reality. She did all the things they say can make the mind focus better; a deep breath, a concentrated stare at an object, the thought of something other than that which was disrupting her train of thought. Nothing worked. Thoughts of Ireti and Prof filled her mind like vapour in a bottle. With Prof in her head, she found herself sneaking about the room until the thought of being late for a class test slipped into her mind and snapped her back into the moment. She rushed into the bathroom, only for an empty bucket to stare her in the face. She kicked the bucket, sending it sprawling to the extreme corner of the bare bathroom as she realised that it was the one with a nail-tip sized hole that was barely noticeable at the bottom, which Remilekun discovered some days earlier. She stood with her hands on her waist for some time, picked up another bucket and flung open the door.

All of the estate used to have water when the blocks of flats were first built. A few years before she and Remilekun began to live in the house, a road construction was said to have resulted in major water pipes getting broken in the estate. Two years after they moved into the area, the road was rehabilitated, yet no one considered repairing the pipes even as the years ran into themselves and the taps in the bathrooms and kitchens became rusted antiques. Some houses built boreholes. Many of the neighbours eventually removed their bathtubs and placed them in front of their flats, where they served as water storage and washing bowls. Those who lived on the ground floor found it easier to get the *mai ruwa*, who fetched water for people for a fee, to supply them.

Desire lingered by her door when she saw a *mai ruwa* who sold water in metal gallons walking towards her neighbour's flat in hurried steps. Water splashed from the two tilted metal gallons in his cart. Someone must have paid him the previous night to supply water. She watched him: the poise of the cubic-shaped metal containers which hung down from a rope tied to a bar that sat on his shoulder. She wasn't ready to go to the tap to fetch water, and her pocket money from Mama T was running low, so she couldn't afford to pay the *mai ruwa*. She considered stealing water from one of the neighbours' water storage containers, like Remilekun sometimes did whenever she was broke, running late, or just too lazy to fetch water at the tap.

Desire smiled and greeted the water carrier. She watched him move towards a drum and pour the water in it. She waited for him to leave, turning left and then right to look out for any early risers. She scanned the neighbours' water containers from her doorstep without moving, so as to move quickly and precisely towards her target without arousing anyone's suspicions. She moved towards the container with the confidence of an owner, looked around once more, and set to work. She scooped one bowl at a time, quickly, so that the water furled and unfurled into the bucket until it was full, and then she hurried into their self-contained one-room flat.

For a moment, Desire considered carrying a bucket of water to Prof's doorstep as an excuse to see him in the day, before remembering that his flat was in one of the buildings that did not have water issues like hers.

She moved from the window to the bed, pushing away Remilekun's washed bra, which limped down from a nail above her. Her friendship with Remilekun had taught her that being estranged from one's relatives was not enough to hate them. Remilekun was the 54th child of a man with the skin of a shrunken banana. Yet, she spoke with so much affection of aunties and uncles, brothers and sisters, and of her father, a man who she had to make an appointment to see every three months. Although Mama T had not seen her husband in many years, she made sure that Remilekun visited her father every year, to celebrate Sallah.

Desire reflected on how society placed so much emphasis on family, yet there was more dysfunction than normality. Before her death, her mother told her of how Babangida's relatives visited her after he died and "took care of their kinsman's belongings."

Her father's family came early one morning while the world was still asleep. They sat her mother down and told her they would exempt her from the required rites as she was not a properly married wife.

'However, we must recover the things our son worked for as he is still owing the family for the money we used to send him to school.'

She said there was nothing to argue or struggle over, considering that he left nothing. She made a visit to the police to claim gratuity, and she was told Babangida had several uncleared loans for which they would need to do some deductions. A few more visits and she was told there was nothing to take home as gratuity.

Desire would always remember how she could feel the fire burning in her mother's eyes as she told the story. She

could still remember the way her mother's voice held a laugh
between the stories. Her face, however, carried the disdain
and pain and anxieties of those years.

'I turned to the black and white Sony television and told
them that was what he left behind, and then I stood up and
went inside to sleep beside you. I left them sitting down in the
parlour.'

That was the day she spoke the proverb that Desire always
repeated when she was faced with a situation that made her
feel shame for herself, '*You know when a big shame pushes you
down, even a small one would want to dance on top of you.*'

'You know, they carried the TV,' her mother said, laughing
as she went on to describe how they then returned for the
refrigerator she sold iced water from the following day. It
was as if they held a family meeting to return to the house a
week later, to claim things that her mother thought were her
security each time Babangida maltreated her. They claimed
the only piece of land he owned in the village, four old suits,
and even two ashtrays with marks from cigarette stubs. On
their way out, they offered to give Desire and her mother a
50 naira monthly upkeep allowance, but they were expected
to come to the village to collect it. The bus fare to the village
was 80 naira at the time. It was sheer luck that these relatives
did not know about the land in Maroko, which was bought a
year after Babangida met her mother, and while their love was
still on fire.

Alone in a house stripped of everything in it—bed, refrigerator,
television and clothes—the landlord reminded them of the
couple of months' rent they owed. Desire remembered him
leaning against the door smacking his lips. She later learnt,
when her mother was not in one of her ghost states, that he
had offered to marry her and take care of Desire by making
her his eighth wife.

Years later, when they were both thrown out at Maroko,
Desire always remembered this drama because her mother
acted it out once madness began to settle on her. Those times,

when there was no food in the house, Desire wondered if her mother had made the right decision. How much can a woman, dressed in shame, bargain for her pride?

Desire did remember, in those faded snippets of memory through which the past visited the mind, being strapped onto her mother's back as she walked away from the broken-toothed landlord, stomping her foot, cursing and tapping her fingers and turning them in a gyre over her head, before repeating over and over how a union between her and the landlord would be over her dead body.

As the days lengthened and it became apparent they would not be able to pay their rent, their landlord would deride them, or lock the room, until other tenants begged him to please let them sleep one more night, at least for Desire's own sake—who was a little girl at that time. The night when she and her mother slept outside the house, and rain beat them until their skins glistened like they were oiled, was when Desire's mother considered the land, with the uncompleted building, in Maroko could make a home.

Maroko was the promised land for Desire and her mother. Once the landlord sent them away, her mother became certain her husband foresaw it all.

'A man can know the right thing but own a wrong mind. A man's mind is formed by the people around him. The wrong set of people is equal to a wrong mind. Knowledge is not enough to do the right thing. The right people is equal to a right mind,' she said about her late husband.

Desire listened as her mother recounted how she and Babangida used to lay on a small mattress, dreaming of owning their own house in Lagos. Of how their children would have a room of their own and they would travel back home, so that people could see that they had not wasted their lives as predicted. They laid the foundation of the house, before Babangida's attitude changed towards her. Desire's mother never told her what the changes were, but she knew that he was far from whatever aspiration he started off with.

'The moment we were married, he took me to this man who was his friend in Maroko, and a son of the soil and said, "This is my wife, we are buying our first land together."'

He was Baba Ondo, a retired police officer who had lost an eye in the line of duty. When Desire and her mother arrived in Maroko, she traced him, as he luckily still lived in the same house. She introduced herself as Babangida's wife, 'the only one who could take or claim the land if anything happened to him.' Baba Ondo was kind enough to show her mother the land, offered her a stall to sell food, and the first raw materials for a make-shift house. He helped them to settle down in Maroko, where the actual meaning of childhood, for Desire, was shaped. She was beginning to believe she would have a father-figure in Baba Ondo, when he was lynched to death by boys who wanted to snatch his bag, a few months after their arrival in Maroko.

18

Desire woke up the following day, amused that she slept through the heaviness in her mind. She hurried through the normal things that readied her for campus, locking the door in a flurry of activity: slipped on her sandals, ensured the lock on the door keyed in, said goodbye to neighbours who greeted and then rushed down the stairs.

Outside, the harmattan haze courted dried mud on the stretch of untarred road and when vehicles sped past, it formed clouds of dust that painted houses, signposts and billboards in a rusty, red hue. Desire walked fast despite the dry harmattan wind lashing at her face, and the burden of the secret that she bore. She tried to make her strides longer but ended up stepping in potholes. She drew close to the retail market road with her bag hanging loosely over her left arm and three hardback notebooks in the fold of her right arm. At first, she walked hurriedly towards the junction; approaching the stalls and branded tarpaulin umbrellas studded by the roadside. There was a canteen just after the road junction which led onto the main road. Her nostrils picked up the smell of fried plantain set against the stinging odour of stale piss in the open drain.

She suffered the visual fuss of faded paint, coated and bright colours contrasted on the low cost government houses, dust drifting from the dried clay by the side of a recently open drain which was now swamped with garbage; nylon sachets and broken plastic. This was mixed with the Ipaja smell of the fetid roadside take-outs bragging for recognition; that coalescence of fried plantain and yam, prepared over mobile kitchens that stood over drains harbouring faeces and urine, which meant that many seconds usually passed before a breath of fresh air. This smell was not permanent, it floated from one end of the area to the other, hopeful. A few steps away, smoke filtered into her nose from a burning bush. Above her, the colours of the sky mingled with the unsettled ashes drifting in the wind like a condensed swarm of fleas. Under this sky, the sun wandered across like a lord.

The temperature was rising, and what should have come as the eager bustle of morning risers, expectant workers and school children, could be compared to workers returning home at night after hectic traffic. Desire turned around to check how far she had come, and as she turned, her first step landed in an unobserved pothole.

'Hey!' the scream of the man in front of her and the struggle not to fall shook her. The lanky man, whose foul breath almost knocked her over when he drew closer, helped her up and she staggered backwards to escape the odour coming from his mouth.

'Sorry-o. De road too bad. Even we wey dey waka, our leg no even free from dis potholes.'

The man picked up and handed back a copy of a newspaper cut-out which had fallen from between her books. It was the picture of Prof. The one she had carried in her bra for many years. She had only moved it to her purse recently. The picture, if it could talk, would tell the maturity of her areolae. It was a miracle that she had never developed some horrible breast rash or infection during those teenage years. It was only recently, when her visits to Prof began, that she stopped slipping it into her bra. Instead, she made copies of the cut-outs and put them between the pages of diaries, books and in purses. She felt a sudden shame as the man picked up the paper and handed it to her. She did not raise her eyes to acknowledge the man's own, as he held out what she considered her major secret—which even Remilekun did not know about—to her. How would anyone understand why she had carried the same picture of one man for about fifteen years?

'Thank you, sir,' she mumbled to him without smiling. In this

state of walking in and out of the stench in Ipaja, she arrived at
the block with Prof's flat. She stopped a few metres away and
stared. She was oblivious to the people setting up their shops,
the feet hurrying past her and the honking cars that slowed
down as they approached the potholes on the road. Around
the three-storey building were wood stalls, covered with rusted
zinc roofing sheets which leaned against heaps of garbage in
jute bags. She wondered if it would make any difference if
all these people knew she came to see him at nine and left at
midnight.

The longer she stood in front of the building, the odder it
felt being there. Prof's windows were shut, yet she felt like
she was being watched. She wondered if he would be able
to recognise her outside the room—would he be confused by
her features and guess endlessly as he looked out from the
window?

Like many other buildings in the neighbourhood, his had
sash windows, and a net. The other flats, with louvres, had
their curtains tied up in a bunch forming the letter M. His flat
was the only one in a building of twelve flats with its louvres
closed. From where she stood, one could almost assume it
was a single slab of glass. She looked at his window; just a
calm row of shut slabs. This reminded her of the stuffiness
and silence that reigned each time the laughter stopped, and
silence settled between her and Prof.

*Are the walls painted blue, or green or even grey? Is it a room
without paint or one with wallpapers with patterns of flowers
on them?* she wondered, remembering that the walls felt glossy
when she leaned against them. The walls were painted, she
concluded.

As she stood in front of his block, she longed to go and see
him that instant, so much that a hunger stretched the muscles
in her chest that she felt she could tell what it was like to be
in the early stages of cardiac arrest. Those nights when she
would stop herself from going to see him and she would end
up nestled on the bed did not count. There was something she

assured herself of—she was not in love. She was inquisitive. Desirous to see a man who was from her past and whom she now felt a duty to connect to his long lost son. Once she was done, she would move on, she thought to herself. Perhaps, she may consider Ireti's unprofessed attraction. She wanted to believe he was attracted to her. Perhaps.

Desire sighed and made a quiet vow to keep Prof out of her thoughts until evening, when she would insist that the room must be lit, to tell him about Ireti. She felt that once she saw his face, she would not feel this weight of curiosity. First, his face in the light needed to be unveiled. Then she needed to persuade Ireti to come and see him.

She moved a few steps away from the building, and although the thought of being late for her class bothered her again, she found herself stopping once more. It was the first time she had come close to his house during the day since she began to visit him. She watched a little girl bathing by herself in front of the house, splashing water on two boys her age who were laughing gaily, only for her to hurry off as a man who could be her father approached her swiftly. Desire did not know if she was the one making assumptions, but the fear in the girl's eyes as the man approached mirrored the one she felt for her father as a child, those days in Oshodi, before she and her mother moved to Maroko.

She walked towards the house thinking of how there was no better way to preserve a landscape than in the agonies of a childhood suffering. Just how the memories of Oshodi rested in her head like dew settled in the early morning on leaves. In a way, it was different from Maroko, where she experienced what it was to be homeless. Oshodi, the place she was born in, was soaked in a terror which was beyond the pictures of a street with a panorama of dilapidated tenements, clinging side by side and running into bends.

On Mosafejo Street in Oshodi, when they lived there, there were no recreational parks. The children created their own entertainment. They carved out playing spaces from abandoned sites, or streets with lesser traffic, where they kicked makeshift balls made from rags and broken condoms found on the road. In the mornings, the edges of the open drains were filled with naked children bending over to scoop water with plastic vessels to bathe themselves. They stood against gutters with brackish water flowing with stale food, shit, and urine; with all the odours hanging in the airlessness. Between this, hordes of food sellers hawked past, with the still-naked children running after them, sometimes with soapy heads, and shouting at them to stop and sell. The sellers walked towards them, placed their wares on the ground, close to the drains, and waited for the children to go in and bring bowls for the food, after which their mothers—clad in inches of cotton *ankara*—brought them money.

The sandwich of houses faced an improvised bus terminus which left the narrow streets perpetually rammed on most days, so that screaming voices of bus conductors called out for passengers going to different areas in Lagos at every hour of the day. Close by, there was the popular Lion Junction, where area boys continued their conversations between puffs of cigarettes and rolls of *gbana*. She could not forget the screams of women whose bags had been snatched, howling and running with legs scattered like chickens being pursued by dogs. Considering how young she was when they moved, it always amazed her that she remembered names and people and even faces—once or twice, she met people they had lived with in Oshodi—but they rarely ever remembered who she was.

Her eyes moved about and landed on a policeman scratching his crotch with one hand and shouting orders to a motorcyclist with his baton pointed at him. The posture and faded black uniform soiled her thoughts. She and Prof shared one thing in common: they hated Nigerian policemen. Her father was a policeman, Prof suffered torture at their hands, and Remilekun was indecisive about them.

'Who cares? A bad man is a bad man. A bad man in a uniform is just a consistent badass man,' a drunken Remilekun had said, in a voice filled with laughter. 'As long as they fuck, they can be fucked, and they respond to fucking, they must mean some-fucking-thing to somebody.'

19

Against a faded signpost, Desire watched as young boys and girls sold bread, sachet yogurt, biscuits and other sweets about the streets, while men in suits and women in high-heels rushed everywhere. There were also streams of school students fooling around and chatting in twos and threes, while the lonesome ones dragged along looking lost. The electric poles had their cables twined like wire meshes; one pole had fallen onto the road and was causing heavy traffic. Car honks belted out a incongruous tune that travelled into her eardrums, beating the sanity from her head.

Desire jumped as an *okada* rider trying to wriggle his motorcycle from the traffic screamed at her. She leapt across the open gutter and struggled to keep her balance on the kerb. She tottered. All the exercise books she held to her bosom fell into the drain. As she raised her head to scream an insult at the man, he drove off laughing. Desire stooped lower, until her buttocks sat on her hind legs, and she stretched her hand to pick up the books from the dry drain.

On the other side of the kerb, a stray dog with ears half-eaten by fleas stood in the middle of the road, sniffing at a black polythene bag. She watched as the dog ran from motorcycles as they headed straight towards it. Each time, it howled, running away, only to return to nibble on what, on a closer look, she found to be a dead rat.

Her phone rang at the bus stop and she was thankful that it broke up her increasingly revolting observations.

'I can't sleep,' Ireti started in that voice that sounded drowsy. There was a chuckle accompanying his words. 'What happened?'

'You know you keep me awake.'

She laughed, as she continued to walk towards the bus stop, ignoring a few heads that turned towards her, 'Be serious.'

'I just want to know if I can come to your house this weekend. You are avoiding me—this idea of switching off your phone at night from 9pm. Why is your phone always off by this time?' There was a long pause, which carried an anxiety she was eager to ease.

'We need to talk. New things about my father.'

She felt her heart jump. The way he directed the statement at her, made her uneasy.

'Why are you telling me this?'

He ignored her question. 'Will you come and visit me?'

'Maybe.'

'Where are you? It's noisy.'

'I'm at the bus stop. Waiting for a bus to take me to the campus.'

He stopped talking, and then said with a note of finality, 'Come, and let's meet on campus. I have to see my father.'

'*Hehn?*' she asked. Her voice was lower and her heartbeat increased. She wondered if he knew that she met with Prof every night. Or maybe Prof had contacted him and they talked about her. There was nothing about Prof that indicated this when they met in the evenings, but since she had not visited in a while, she could not tell if something had happened within the days of her absence.

'Desire, are you there?'

'Yes. I just need to know why I have to see you.'

She waited and when he said nothing, she switched off the phone and joined the bus in front of her.

Desire walked through the giant arch at the gate which carried the inscription: Lagos State University. She turned to the right to face the temporary bus park where only three of the yellow and black striped danfo buses were parked.

'Iyana-Ipaja, Iyana-Ipaja! One more *yansh*!' each conductor shouted, coaxing the undecided students to join their different buses. A scar-faced conductor held Desire by the hand and she pulled herself out of his grip. She pushed away his hand when he tried to grab her again and walked away, as she considered buying pure water for her parched throat from one of the string of hawkers lined by the curb. She handed a five-naira note to a teenage girl whose eyes were almost as round as the tray of oranges which sat next to her bowl of pure water. The orange seller, a heavy breasted woman, squatting on a small wooden bench besides the girl gaped at Desire with a smile on her face. At first, the gawking seemed like one of those sudden moments of interest, but when it persisted, Desire returned the woman's stare, eyeball for eyeball, ignoring the scar-faced bus conductor who returned to squall 'Iyana-Ipajaaaaaaaaa' close to her ears, like he was being pinched with a pincer, before turning towards other students strolling past the bus stop.

'*Hehn!*' The suddenness of the words were met by the spring of the orange seller who jumped from her squatting position to house her in a tight embrace, while beaming at Desire's face with a Mr. Bean smile. Desire pulled back, until a rush of spittle bearing the words, 'Desire. Na Basira,' splattered across her face.

'It is me now! Basira-*oke*,' the orange seller said, holding her in a tight hug and dragging her in an embrace to the side of the road to escape colliding with students rushing out from the campus. All this time, Desire was racking her head to remember where she knew the podgy woman, with breasts that navigated northwards, from. Then she saw the rabbit ears. Desire remembered in an instant: the long hours of sitting together exchanging neighbourhood gossip, sharing knowledge of contraceptives and family planning while stroking those ears that she joked connected her to every titbit in the neighbourhood. Basira, who with the suffix '*oke*', became the Mountain; because boys swore to voyage and conquer the world through her breasts. The one whose laughter sounded like thunder when she said she did not want to have ten children like her mother did. The disappointment in Basira's eyes switched to pride as Desire greeted, responding with a laughter that wrinkled the corners of her eyes.

Basira turned Desire around, touching her cheeks and smiling,

'*Two re o!* See your baby-face! You have not changed!'

Desire nodded at Basira's inspection. She could not help but respond with, 'You have changed-o—you're like a balloon!' She stood before her childhood friend, smiling until her cheeks were sore, watching Basira, the girl who started wearing a bra before any of the other girls. She was also the one who became a mother at 15.

There had been a group of six friends on the beach: Desire, Basira, Chioma, Sikira, Kemi and Funmi. Like all the girls there, their first admiration for boys fell on the teen bus conductors, who had been hand-picked as "forward-looking", for renting half-lit one-room flats, as opposed to sleeping under the bridge drinking *paraga* or building their own shack on the beach. The boys with their own rooms invited teen girls to watch Indian and Yoruba films on video players, and perhaps, even enjoy meat pie and soft drink, usually Coca-Cola or Goldspot from an eat-out restaurant. Love, if that was what happened to them, seemed simple in those years. It was all about springing a breast, finding a boy who played films in the one-room flats and figuring out sex there if you were being pruned for wifehood; and if you weren't, it was many days of sprightly fondling lemon-sized breasts behind make-shift stalls and on danfo buses.

It was Basira's breasts that disrobed the five friends of their naivety, once they began showing under her T-shirts and she spent the first days walking with her chest withdrawn, like that could suck in what for her then, were lumps. Basira's shoulders still took on that perpetual arch from trying to draw in her chest. Her shoulders adapted to this posture as those "lumps" grew bigger and manifested into breasts—much bigger than those of some of the women in the neighbourhood.

Basira offered herself to her friends as an experience, the experiment, on how to live when their breasts began to form. First, she told them, for the ache the two painful swellings would cause, sleep facing up and wear loose blouses and dresses.

'*Wo!* Let me tell you. It is painful, very painful when your cloth is touching the *koko*,' she pointed to the small buds on her chest.

She also told them a fitted T-shirt would only increase attention from boys, because some would even touch them and run off. Secondly, as the steady growths formed, here is how to wear a bra—cup the breasts, hang the straps over your angled shoulders and strap right and tight. Or else, your breasts would fall off and become slippers like grandmama's own. Lastly, when Desire's breast failed to grow at 14, Basira advised her to put an antlion on it.

'See, if you put the *kuluso* on the nipple to bite you, your breast will be big well-well. If you want even original, correct breast, just sing: *Kuluso! Kuluso abiamo feyin so*, seven times, after it bite you finish. O-girl, you will have correct breast.'

'Why do I have to sing the song?'

'Han-han, don't you know the meaning of the song is the prayer for yourself? So as you are praising the *kuluso* for acting as good mother that carry baby, you too will born and carry baby when you have correct breast.'

'I don't want to have a baby now.'

'Ha! You will have baby for future now. And your breast will call man. Big breast, correct man-o.'

Desire wasn't worried about her flat chest. She was curious about the efficacy of the insect to grow breasts, so she tried it. She went around looking for sunken areas in dry sands, so she could find a *kuluso* that would bite her nipple. She eventually found one and scooped it up by the conic area into a milk tin.

She placed the antlion on her chest every night before she slept, singing in a low tone *'Kuluso! Kuluso abiyamo feyin,'* and after two weeks of no results, she threw the can away with the insect.

'How's your mother?' Desire said, observing how on a closer look, Basira was turning into her mother—the woman who handed them puff-puff, with a smile in her eyes, as they returned from school.

'She has die-o. Last two years. She die in her sleep after coming from mosque. To die inside sleep is very good death.' Desire nodded and Basira released her hold on her, laughing gaily while the other hawkers watched between smiles and awe. Basira's smile was like a half-moon, as she talked, making sure her voice became louder each time she explained, 'Those days we are—were young children playing in the sand until we old to born baby, then we go different part,' so that the pure water girl and the other hawkers could hear. But they were only interested in dragging customers from the throng of students coming out of the campus.

'Selling has closed, today,' Basira said, huddling the oranges into a raffia basket, before lifting it onto her head. Once it was steadied, she held it with her left hand and dragged Desire with the right. In a few seconds, they were on the other side of the road, away from the hawkers lined by the school gate. Desire watched Basira's eyes as they scanned her and rested on Funso Aiyejina's *A Letter to Lynda, and Other Poems* and Odia Ofeimun's *The Poet Lied.*

'You still carry books. I am no surprised at all to see you here. You like book since we are a child. You like to read in that err—pubic library,' Basira said, patting Desire's face again and again, like she needed to assure herself she was not hallucinating.

'Public library,' Desire said with a smile. 'Pubic means *obo.*'

'Ha! I didn't mean that one-o,' Basira laughed. 'How's your mummy? How's her body now?' she asked, avoiding Desire's eyes.

Desire nodded, staring into the stretch of road before she said, 'She's dead too,' with a note of finality which Basira didn't prod. Everyone in their neighbourhood had known her mother had mental issues, but never publicly discussed it. The interlude of noise from the traffic, blaring music, and background babble of the confluence of voices around them doused what could have been awkwardness.

'God give her Al Jannah,' Basira said, before she went on to explain that she was now a mother of three, living in the Idi-Oro area in Mushin. 'The place is a very okay place,' her eyes fluttered as she spoke. 'The landlord didn't have any wahala. The place is room-and-parlour self-contained house. My husband is a Benz mechanic. Everybody knows him in Mushin for car repairing,' she said with pride. And with a smile still lingering on her face she added, 'I have no surprised to see you inside LASU. You're always used to be a book person.' She laughed, 'See now, you are even now speaking in English like the NTA people.'

'How about Kemi, Sikira, Funmi and Chioma, how are they?'

'Everybody waka. But Sikira die now—remember? She die before we begin to waka? That time you have start working inside market?'

'Yes, yes. I remember. May her soul rest in peace,' she said, although she didn't remember.

Desire had been the smallest in the group, but she was the one they consulted as they laughed over boyfriends and their parents' dated advice on how to handle sex and boys. She owed her love for reading to Prof—the same Prof she now visited every night, except for the last three. The Prof, who she knew would not remember the little girl he carried at a spontaneous rally.

She had kept Prof in her imagination as the father she wanted to have, after she dreamt of him telling her he would take care of her and never let her suffer. She owned the dream. She loved the kindness in his voice and how it calmed her. It became the voice that calmed her fears and anxieties. So, each day, she walked to the library, imagining one dream after another. One night, she dreamt she was walking on the beach alone at night. The whole seashore was littered with books of every kind but whenever she reached for a book, it disappeared and she was soon rushing about in a frenzy trying to grasp and hold on to one—any book. When all the books were gone, she fell to her knees, sobbing uncontrollably. After a while, she heard a voice, like it was calling unto her from the night sky—it was Prof's! But this time, it wasn't kind and calming, but angry and loud. She wanted to ask him, 'Where have all the books gone?' But before she could speak, Prof began to chide her for keeping late nights, hanging out with strange boys and not reading to change her future. And the longer he spoke, the angrier and louder he became. Angrier. Louder. Angrier. Louder... then, she woke up in a sweaty fright.

There were times she wondered if she did not first receive the words "Books would make a difference," from the morning assembly mantra spoken by her headmaster whose beard was so bushy the pupils called him Father Christmas, who repeated the sentence ten times every morning at the assembly ground, or from Prof in that dream.

The following afternoon, after her strange dream, she walked around the garbage dumps in her area, picking up books and any printed materials to read—torn Physics textbook, newspaper cut-outs, family planning manuals, ledgers and invoices which became notebooks and many other bits and pieces. Later, when she discovered the library at Isale Eko, she learned to read fiction and history books. Each day, after school at 1pm, she walked from the beach where she lived with her mother to the USIS library on Broad Street on foot. She returned at night, to explain the ideas she read in the book to him, while imagining that her mother's dysregulated speech was his response. There were times her mother would awaken to catch her replying to her imagined Prof, and Desire would offer the explanation of revising her school work. The Local Government Library was her refuge. She read all sorts of books there; from philosophy to religion to fiction to biology—where her special interest was reproduction, when her friends began to ask her to find out what the books said about preventing pregnancy. She left the five of them: Kemi, Sikira, Funmi, Chioma and Basira in different spheres of life, gaining unread experience – as a sex worker, a ghost, a thug, a traveller, and a young mother.

'So, you are going to be a doctor, or lawyer, or engineer?' Basira asked, intruding on her thoughts.

'No. I'm studying Political Science,' Desire said in Yoruba, too.

'You want to do politician? Maybe even president...' Basira switched to English.

'I want—' Desire started in Yoruba, and seeing the disappointment in her friend's eyes, started to speak in English, 'My sister, make God help us *jare*.'

They alighted from the bus as it stopped at Mushin Olosha and walked into the street, passing women who sold peppers arranged in layered boulders on plastic plates by the roadside, and moved into a street with shops displaying provisions for sale; between them were those selling eat-as-you-go foods like *akara*, buns, apples, *dodo*, fried yam and so forth. Basira mentioned how she was planning to own a stall in the market, which, like the rest of Lagos' open markets, transformed into hope for traders, who waited for night dreamers; with their tin oil lamps and *aso-ofi* tightly wrapped to protect themselves from the chill that came in the evenings, while their young children, also covered, like small bundles on pieces of cardboard by their feet as the teenaged ones helped out.

'I for don start, but I just dey recover from miscarry.'

'I'm sorry about that, Basira.' Desire was going to commiserate further when Basira stopped walking.

'This is the house,' Basira said. They crossed a wooden bridge placed over the gutter, greeting an old woman shelling melon seeds in front of a bungalow bullied into physical

irrelevance by the two multi-storeys on its sides. The walls of
the house, with its flaked off paint, carried a roof which was
lowered to cover the main door. Anyone taller than five foot
eight would have to bend to enter, before straightening up to
behold the stretch of wood that supported a dotted hip roof
which covered a number of face-to-face rooms. In front of
every room was a bench with a kerosene stove on it.

Basira's room was a square box that accommodated a
standard double bed and a cupboard as its major furniture.
There were extras like a 14-inch television and a video recorder
that were placed on a sideboard. Focusing on the map-like
water mark on the near-white ceiling, Desire listened to Basira
as she pointed to three children smiling in a photograph,
two of them open-mouthed, with their two incisors missing,
to the camera: 'Jadesola, Jenrola, Jokotola.' They were on a
sofa with a brown pattern, the same as everything else in the
room. 'This is the three children I have born now. They are
in school; one girl, one boy, one girl. God is good.'

She looked up to see Desire's face, and she smiled, 'I hav'
tell ma'guy from the beginning, say we go do family planning,
and he agree.' She raised her eyebrow, 'You remember him?
He is the same boy that im-pregnant me that time.'

'Oh! You're still together?' Desire asked, sincerely glad for
her friend, but unable to resist goading Basira. 'You didn't
forget all those my talks about having children one can cater
for, *abi?*'

'Yes-o! Na only me and my husband get children in private
school for this compound. We have cut our coat inside the
size?'

'Cut your coat according to your size,' Desire said shaking
her head and laughing. '*Wo*, don't break my head with this
your English-o, speak Yoruba,' she added with a long ring
of laughter that sounded like a duplicate of a childhood with
Basira.

She thought of their years together. Those years they left
for school from the shelter of rusted corrugated sheets and

tarpaulin banners, dressed in school uniform with holes akin to polka-dotted fabrics and no sandals on their feet. She was in touch with Basira who dropped out of school for a while, until she left the area to start work as a porter in Isale Eko.

'*Oshisko*, Professor and Dr Madam, I will talk the English I can talk-o,' Basira sneered.

'You seem happy,' she said.

Basira shrugged, avoiding Desire's gaze and said, 'Happiness is from God. He gives you a good man that allows you to stay, *abi?*'

Desire took a deep breath, stood up and hugged Basira, who held her close and squeezed her shoulder.

'I need to go,' she said.

'I no even offer you anything,' Basira said releasing her grasp on Desire.

'*Ma binu*, time has gone. I will come back to visit,' she said, turning to see that there was now a strain of tears on Basira's eyelids.

'Desire. Please, come back. I no get original true friend again.'

20

Kayo didn't stop knocking on his door begging to be let in. He never forced his way through. Kayo spoke of the times they shared and how they needed to talk yet he never elaborated on what the talk was about. He went on about his family and how it would be nice for Prof to meet them. He described how he told his wife of their escapades as children.

'You know, she won't believe that I once used to dress like a woman when I was a teenager. I told her I dressed and danced at the market to raise money for our Friday hang-outs.' His laughter trailed off when Prof did not join in.

'I have to leave now. I have to pick up my wife from her friend's place where she is making her hair. I'll come again, okay?'

Prof did not respond. It took a while before he heard the sound of his feet fade from the corridor. It was the way Kayo was; hopeful that things could change, playful and receptive of life's inadequacies. Yet, even he could see that something was different about his friend. He spoke between philosophies. He spoke with a deliberateness which made it seem like he was weighing each thought before it was spoken.

Kayo looked out for him. Kayo never told him, but he sometimes wondered if his friend became a cult member. He had this feeling of being watched over all through his days in the university as a prominent student union member, and then a student union president, before he was ousted by a group the government bribed. He never encountered problems with the cult groups. The student union president before him was hacked down in front of the university gate by cultists, and another one became a cult member and ensured calm in the school. Kayo protected him in a way he never understood. He only remembered that whenever Kayo came to his university, he always used the excuse of seeing his friends in the evenings, tucking a blue beret he never wore elsewhere into his pocket. Even now when he spoke, he would slip into that carefree way of his younger days, 'Once you can settle people's needs—there is always one need—you'll be fine. Everyone, everything, wants something. If it is money, give it to them.'

Kayo always knew what was going on. He was the one who rushed into his house one day, before he went to prison, to warn against granting an interview to *Tell Magazine* and *Tempo Newspaper*.

'You can't. We all know that Abacha is looking for a simple mistake from you.'

'I will do what I want. I have to let the people know they can fight.'

'Fight who?'

'See, I have already spoken to others at the NADECO meeting, and Baba Fawehinmi...' And Prof thought over what he was going to say, changed his mind and said instead, 'I can't say what your exact fears are, but with over twenty of our people in exile and a similar number held under detention, everyone says I'm lucky and should be more careful.'

'Exactly!'

'But Kayo, when you have a cause, a cause that grips your heart morning and night, you don't become careful. You jump in and do all that needs to be done.' He smiled and looked at his friend, 'The CLO is organising a march today, will you join us?'

'Just remember your mother. You're not even thirty!'

Prof leaned against the door as his mind filtered in the days before prison. He shook his head and wondered how he might have introduced Desire to Kayo if things were different. He wondered how Kayo would have reacted, perhaps a little bashful remark on how he needed to "corner" the girl before she left him. Then he might have asked, '*Abi*, you're still on that priest level? Are you still abstaining?'

But this Kayo was different. He chose his words. Sometimes too carefully.

When it was evening, Desire didn't visit. Day two, she didn't either. On day three of her absence, he began to feel his body split, like the hairs on his skin were ready to search for hers. He thought of the times she visited. His hairs stood erect when she swept past him towards her seat in the darkness. He started to inquire and argue with himself over whether he should not have opened the door to her when she first came knocking. He replayed her breathing, her sighs and the way her legs shook when she sat on the chair, the little laughs and small silences. Prof realised that just like the way a shattered mirror reflects our many parts, a broken individual captures how we are—he felt like Desire was himself. He relived his past and tried to think of what life was before her visit. And then, he thought of that first day when she didn't visit. That inconsistency discomfited him.

Before prison, Prof's hair was cropped low and the strands curled into themselves like worn wool on an old towel, which gave the impression of him balding. His thin eyes sliced into the edges of his face with webs at the corner indicating a perpetual laugh in his eyes. It gave him the look of an excited schoolboy, so that when he was actually agitated or excited, he looked like a baby who was about to cry. This boyish look was the reason he left the whisker-like hair on his chin and attempted to grow a beard in secondary school, yet it only made people tell his mother he would end up a heartbreaker. Girls hung around him like flies around an open sore. In the early days, his mother took the time to warn him about how he might drop out of school to have to fend for his child and its mother if he impregnated anyone. So, from his secondary school days through university, he tried to keep his relationships with girls as mere trifles—once his friendship with a girl became dependent, he broke it off. This earned him the nickname, *oniranu*. They saw him as a lover boy and player—which was contrary to what he intended.

There was however an exception to his constant girl-dumping relationships. Victoria was the first girl Prof almost broke the rule for. He was 16. He couldn't remember how old she had been, perhaps a few years older. He could never forget the days of lying in wait for her to return from her mother's stall and the demure return of his advances. Kayo found a way to convince her on his behalf but her first visit to his house was not a successful rendezvous. Just as he was becoming comfortable with his guest, his mother walked into the house. He could still remember how he avoided saying anything about Victoria, whose hands were tucked between her thighs, waiting patiently for him to introduce her to his mother, who flopped onto the sofa, shaking her legs while her eyes remained fixated on the door. As Victoria stood before her, trying to find the best way to appear respectful and in love and shy and scared at the same time, Prof felt his mother's words springing out—although they were unspoken—to haunt him: 'Don't impregnate anybody-o. At least, wait until we can eat well.'

Prof tugged at Victoria's hand and dragged her with him, pulling her through the streets without stopping, towards Kayo's house. Through all of this, she complained about his strange behaviour, and he mumbled something about wanting to see Kayo urgently. The truth was that he never prepared for his mother's appearance when they planned on bringing Victoria to the house. His mother, however, decided to fall sick that day.

Years later, his mother would be the one begging him to find a woman to be with.

'Your mates have three children now, and you're going about living like a lifetime bachelor.' For his mother, a man needed to be married and with children—that was success.

He was 27 when he stopped having sex. This was after Blessing,

and the numerous girls who came after her unveiled his years
of suppressed emotion. So, he stopped having sex. He woke
up one morning and convinced himself that he could access
self-denial. He was not doing this because he wanted to be like
Sigmund Freud who, perhaps, sought to write great books.
Perhaps, Prof's hope was that his abstention would generate
ideas on how to win the war of ignominy he fought for *his*
people. There was so much he tried to explain to Kayo, who
was the only one he told about his abstinence at the time. He
was the one who also told him, 'Are you mad? Sex is life,
man!'

He didn't respond. The thought in his mind was simply
that nobody feels sensual when they feel cornered and
trapped. For one, he could never understand how anyone
with a conscience, who had travelled the world and seen the
potentials of the country, could still feel sexually aroused, with
all the pain the people went through. The pain which was
trapped in their eyes, which begged him to fight for them—the
tired, hungry mouths which were like locked lips deprived of
drinking water. He compared them to lamps burning without
oil. He walked the streets, each time convinced he was born
to save the people from suffering.

Once his decision to abstain from sex came, he would
excuse himself after the caucus meetings he held with other
comrades—which usually led to sexcapades with other
activists—to go and think. He left many of the men and women,
who had fed each other with looks lingering for greetings and
the exchanging of room numbers. He witnessed some hold
hands and tickle palms as affirmation of their sexual hunger.
Sometimes, when they insisted he should stay around after
the meetings, he would mutter something about being too
tired or deep in some documents which must be understood
before "the next congress".

At first, Prof reasoned his abstinence on his rising anger over
the state of the nation. He told everyone who cared to listen
that the mind was where pleasure and pain lived and one

of these emotions would sometimes supersede. His friends joked about how they who were married "cut side shows", and he was always quick to explain that what they thought was a stifling of heat between the loins of people who were not sexually active, was simply wet coal. For a stove was not hot until lit with fire: you become what you think about. It had already been over ten years of anger taking the place of his sexual desires, pushing his needs down to the dark places, which he now felt were being erupted by a woman whose name sounded like an aphrodisiac.

21

In her sleep, Desire heard loud curses and as she turned to move closer to the voice, she opened her eyes to the sporadic thuds against the wall by her bed. This was when she realised that she was not dreaming. She sat up on the bed with her hands cupping her bowed head and listened to the violent exchange between Baba Bolaji and his wife.

'One day, you will realise I am the man in this house.'

'The bastard man, of course.'

'See her, bearer of an evil head.'

'Owner of rags and worms.'

'It is your maggot-infested father and mother that didn't give you home training that you're talking to.'

Earlier in the day Desire had watched their son, Bolaji, as he played with two of his friends, all between the age of five and seven, by her doorstep. They ranted about their favourite cartoon characters, who was taller, and the different contortions they could make with their faces to scare younger children. Their conversations were in the background of other noises in the neighbourhood as she locked her door on her way to the campus, until one of them told the others, 'My father has bigger wickedness than your father.' He hopped about with excitement and made faces at the others. Desire turned to look at the boy to compare the enormity of his words with his frame. There was nothing significant about him, no special features, just one of several children in the neighbourhood who, out of many, would not be singled out. He was typical.

'It is a lie! If my father beat you with his cane, you'll be asking to drink water,' Bolaji, with a head that reminded one of a yam tuber, said, reeling to the ground.

'Yes now, men are stronger than women,' the boy who started the conversation said.

'Who told you that? I don't even know who is stronger in my daddy and my mummy. My daddy can beat, but my mother would beat you so much you won't talk for many days. Let me show you how she punches my father in the eyes.' He stopped to demonstrate the punch by wheeling his right-hand several times before he continued.

The other two boys laughed. Desire fiddled with the door but tried not to interrupt their conversation.

Bolaji continued, 'My mummy would then give him blow in his eyes so that it can swell up like watermelon.'

'It is a lie *joor*! Your daddy told my mummy he was in a car accident when she asked him about his swollen eyes. Your mummy cannot tell lies. Is she not the one who is always saying, "Love you" to your daddy, and she even buys sweet for all the children?' the other paused and faced each one in turn, as if checking for a contradiction.

'Your mummy is nice. Yesterday, I saw her hugging Temi's daddy in her shop, and he was crying, while she was saying "Stop it. Stop it."'

'My mummy is strong, and see—'

Desire locked the door and walked towards the boys, who stopped talking and muttered greetings as she reached them. She took some time to look at Bolaji and saw a noticeable resemblance between him and his father. It was the same kind of uncanny resemblance they said she had with Babangida, but for her complexion.

It was also interesting that Bolaji's parents were known for the legendary length of their sex bouts, as their noises could be heard in the passages some afternoons, when she returned early. Sometimes, it was difficult to know if they were engaged in a fight or sex. When they fought, Bolaji's mother, being one not to forget the scars on her, fought back like her life depended on it, and most times it did. Theirs was not the relationship where one person beat the other. They fought, and each day, a new winner emerged.

'I am a real woman, not road-side, walk-past-her-woman. If you show me one, I will show you one to ten!'

And then there were those days, predawn, when Desire would hear moans and screams which were always loud enough to wake her. Screaming, '*Ma pa mi*—okay, kill me. Just kill me and let me know I am dead.' It took a while for her to realise that this was only make-up or till-death-do-us-part sex and not one of their fights. The days when they had sex, one would see them the following morning, wearing each other's arms around their necks on the balcony, shouting endearing words loudly for the benefit of anyone who gave them attention, 'Love you so much, baby! Mwwwah!'

When they first started to live in the neighbourhood, Desire once told Remilekun that she feared she might break down their door and kill them because of what they made her remember, her parents. It was however not the same. The difference between Bolaji's family and hers was that her father beat her mother. He beat her anytime he returned home drunk. Her own mother waited to be beaten. Desire's mother was nothing like Bolaji's mother, whose screams alerted the neighbours that they were about to fight. Once Desire heard, 'I am battle-ready for you today. I am a woman! I am a woman and I can stand on my own,' she knew that a fight was ready to begin between the husband and wife.

Desire's mother was not ready for anything but hope that her husband would change and love her again. Desire remembered those mornings when she woke up to Babangida beating her mother until she was arranged like a torn puppet on the floor. The room filled with the smell of weed soaked in *kai kai*, the local gin.

'He is not my daddy. My real daddy is in the village,' she remembered telling one of the other children.

She told this story so often to the children she played with, and they saw her and her mother as victims of a wicked stranger. And he was a stranger.

She went to Oshodi after she gained admission to the university and tried to locate the house she had lived in with her parents. It was no longer there. The place had been replaced with a fleet of small shops where traders sold lace fabric. Desire stood in front of the shops that day trying to remember the smelly gutters and her father on the balcony, smoking. She saw him trampling over her head on the mat as he entered the sitting room and then stumbling into the bedroom, with the lingering smell of alcohol following him as he went past her to the toilet.

Her mother remembered him differently. 'Tall man, and very handsome. You have his face,' she said to her, on one of those nights she reminisced about their earlier days. Before she started talking to her shadow.

'I don't look like a gorilla!'

Her mother stood up from the mat she was on and opened an old purse she kept photographs in.

'See. That is Babangida and Sarjee, your father's friend. That man—'

'That man what?' Desire asked, watching her mother take a deep breath without saying a word.

The friend—Sarjee, a corrupted form of Sergeant, was one of the few whose names she surprisingly remembered. The picture had not been among the others she originally kept in the purse. She found it stuck between the pages of an old exercise book with names of those who owed her money in Oshodi.

For the first time, her mother spoke up. 'That man was a bad influence on your father,' her mother finally said. Her index finger touched the tip of her tongue, and she raised it to the skies.

'True.' Desire kept the old photograph for a long time but lost it on her matriculation day in university.

Sarjee was Babangida's sidekick, or, perhaps it was the other way around. They were always together for as long as Desire could remember. She could not remember seeing a relative coming around to the house, or visits to see grandparents anywhere. Sarjee was the one who came around to visit, and considering that he slept in the house sometimes, he was not only almost like a relative, but literally a part of the house's furniture.

He was unforgettable for many reasons to Desire, but there was first his physique; his body was a signpost of human oddities. This made him quite memorable. His body carried a form that was difficult to miss: a big head, a blackened lower lip that drooped like an overwatered cocoyam leaf, a nose that reminded you of rat holes and his stained incisor teeth that were shaped like shovel pans. His friend, Babaginda, the man whom Desire insisted she would never call Father, was a big contrast, his features were forgettable. Although people sometimes commented on him being a handsome man who destroyed his looks with his excesses, Desire always struggled to remember the things that were striking about him, and found it quite difficult to recall even moments spent with him that were not marred by his alcohol induced anger. Little things like lounging in the sitting room with her on his lap, sharing fatherly moments, seemed to have never existed. Whenever she thought of Babangida, she recalled flashes of him relaxing on a wooden stool with a bottle of dry gin and a chewing stick at the side of his mouth in the mornings: sometimes sharing truck-horn laughter with Sarjee, or alone, passing comments on neighbours who hurried past him.

In Oshodi, in place of a park, the streets or compounds became the playground for the children. There were those who pushed and chased after abandoned tyres with sticks, like they were driving cattle. Some bent low over tops, throwing them to cemented grounds. There were those who played football on the streets, creating goal posts with stones or sticks. Of all these, what Desire loved most was playing with rubber bands, although they never allowed her to join in because she was too young. She still stuck around, because she noticed that some of the players were her age mates. She learnt to ignore the other children who showed that they had been warned by their parents to stay away from the policeman's daughter. She stayed close enough to see what they were doing, but at a slight distance, to avoid getting humiliated. She smiled and laughed at the fun while never really understanding what the game was about, other than it involving looping rubber bands onto signed marks on the ground. She also tried to believe that she could not join in because she was not old enough to join them. She learnt to ignore those ones that told her, 'Please we don't want your father's trouble now.' But as they were always in need of rubber bands, she developed the habit of gathering the objects—begging for them, seeking for them, stealing them, and then offering them to the friendliest of the older children who courted her friendship. At other times, she wore the rubber bands on her wrist like bangles— sometimes she doubled them on her wrist and they were so tight, that her veins stuck out and her skin darkened around this region. Her mother did not like this, and always warned her against it. Sometimes, she threatened not to give her food, or even report her to Babangida, but at these times, Desire would laugh and run away.

So, on one of those days that Babangida was in a bad mood, he called out, 'Mama Undee—' as he would typically call out to her, and she, according to him "counted his voice, and waited for him to call more than once." As Desire's mother moved close to him, his hand bound into the air, landed on her face, and returned to his side. Just as she was going to ask what she did, he lifted his hand in a fist and landed it on different parts of her body, like a hammer driving a nail into wood. Babangida staggered about throwing his punches on a woman who waited for the blows to descend on her, so she could move on to other things. He screamed, 'Bringer of bad luck and a lack of promotion at work!'

Desire also already knew the landlord would not come to rescue her mother. Some of the tenants rushed about, seemingly more busily, to start their day. Not one stopped or offered to stop the beating because they were used to seeing this happen. Desire watched it all from a corner of the house, her hand in her mouth to choke the cries that wanted to come out. Over time, she had practised stuffing her mouth with a handkerchief. She moved to the wall, and pressed herself against it, trembling as she listened to Babangida's friend,

Sarjee, who held a roll of marijuana between his fingers, laughing like a bad car spurting, screaming, 'I will help you drop her down from the balcony. *Sebi*, you want to kill the woman?'

'Gerrout! Bag of bad luck!' Babangida screamed at his wife, then turned to Sarjee, who was going about the compound in his typical manner, neighing and saluting the neighbours who condoned his jokes in amusement. He walked down the corridor of the tenement building like he owned the house, and when he felt he had greeted every person, he moved towards the gate. The people mimicked the police salutation in response, 'Ah-ten-shun, sir!' He laughed and responded to everyone the same way, followed by, 'How *bodi?* How life?'

The scent of the *gbana*, which he smoked openly, diffused into different rooms as he walked to sit on a raised platform on the veranda. That distinct smell of weed: deep rust, was familiar to her, as it always indicated that Sarjee was getting ready to go home. Once the show had ended, the children gathered to resume their play. Desire walked briskly to join them. She dangled the rubber bands on her wrist like bangles, so the other children would see them and try to gain her favour. Instead, it was Babangida who turned to her and shouted at her as he walked to meet his friend by the gate, 'You better go and throw away that rubber nonsense in your hand.'

Desire walked away with the intention to obey him, but when she saw he was no longer watching her, she picked up the rubber bands again and wore them on her wrist. She soon joined the children who gathered around Sarjee, and clapped excitedly over how the puff of smoke from his nostrils formed a cloud as he smoked his *gbana*.

While Sarjee entertained the children with the smoke, their parents shuffled around; only a few were bold enough to drag their wards away from him, except a few who screamed for their children to come away from the group. Sarjee puffed long and blew into the air so that the children named an object that they thought the smoke resembled, 'Ball! Car! Man!' He puffed again, they shouted, 'Boat!' This was how the smoke moved from the abstract and became concrete objects.

Desire, in later years, never met anyone whose whiffs of smoke came out like cotton solids and floated slowly into the air until they formed different objects like his. Sometimes, when she saw someone smoking, she would look out for objects, and usually, there were none.

Babangida sat at a distance and smoked without the distraction his friend enjoyed. Desire was losing interest in the smoke game and stooped to pick a rubber band from the floor when she felt a strong hand on her arm. Sarjee sprung from the raised platform he sat on with Babangida and grabbed her hand. Desire was so shocked she did not know whether to cry or laugh. The other children ran away. It was, however, the next thing that Sarjee said, that made her scream. This brought her mother rushing out from the room.

'Na today, I go marry you. Good, good, yes-yes that is her mother coming.'

She could not remember the expression on her father's face, but it appeared laced with gratitude. She watched with shock as her mother, who had been an object of pity only a few minutes earlier, took sides with Sarjee. Desire begged her with her eyes as she approached the two friends. She struggled to release herself from Sarjee's hold.

'You remember that we said, it is the day she wears a rubber band on her wrist, that we will marry her off to Sarjee.

'Yes. Today is the day,' she said gladly.

Desire screamed louder, so that even the landlord came rushing down and he was told about the event. He joined in the fray, asking his youngest daughter to go and prepare a room for Sarjee and Desire. It was a joke that was apparently open to everyone, but she did not find it funny at the time. She was to be married off as a seven-year-old girl. She tried to shrug Sarjee's hand off her shoulder. She fixed her eyes on Sarjee's mouth, which reeked of *gbana* mixed with bad breath. Despite the sharp smell of weed, he drew her close and kissed her lightly on the cheek. Her father clapped. Some tenants from the tenement house were laughing, and one of them promised to give her a portmanteau to carry her things in. Another said his village would be good for "honeymoon". She looked at the faces of all the adults around her with confusion, and those of the children, filled with emotions between pity and amusement. Her face was covered in snot and tears, and her mother stood at a distance, smiling. It was while the celebration was being "planned" that she started to remove the rubber bands from her hand, stretching the ones that were too tight until they snapped.

'Ha! You have cut our wedding band,' Sarjee expressed, like he was truly shocked. Her child's mind had believed it. She hurriedly removed the rubber bands, seeing what she thought was alarm on his face.

Desire, realising that something appeared to have gone wrong, dropped the snapped rubber bands on the floor and stepped on them. She looked defiantly at her supposed husband, who now had his hands over his head. He even let out a pretend cry.

'See what my wife has done now. Ha! See, me I don't have wife again-o!'

As every other person, except Desire, was in on the game, they pretended to be sad. Some even approached her and asked why she did something like that. It was only Babangida who asked that Sarjee, stop his "cry".

'Don't worry, Sarjee, she always wears a rubber band. Anytime you see that she is wearing one on her wrist, carry her home as a wife.'

Desire ran into the toilet and, mindless of the layers of faeces that settled in the broken WC like overcooked porridge, remained there until Sarjee left the house. Her mother was the one who found her there, asleep and standing in a puddle of stagnant water.

22

Prof was thinking of going to bed when he heard a knock at the door. He unlocked the latch and returned to his chair, leaving Desire to slither into the house with the smoothness of a snake. She moved towards the chair muttering, 'I am s-s-sorry, sir,' before she added, 'good evening, sir.'

The silence in the room was bold. Desire waited for him to talk, or at least respond to her greeting.

Prof stayed quiet. Only the fleeting sound of voices and traffic which came as a scream, a cry or a glass-shattering honk from outside, broke the quiet between them. He decided he was not going to say a word until she explained her absence. The silence, however, began to irritate him. He sighed, exhaled out loud and coughed. She did not say a word.

'One, two, three, four, five, six, seven...'

Desire clenched her teeth as her fury grew, listening to him recite the numbers. She was getting angry at herself for coming to see him, only to be entertained by his silence, and now counting. She felt like a piece of furniture. She wanted to say, 'Are you counting down to my exit?' Instead she asked, 'Do you want to live in this darkness forever?' He stopped counting, but had no answer for her. 'Do you want to turn on the lights?'

Rather than answer her question, he stood up from the chair and said to her, 'You should start heading home. It's late.' The clock chimed 12, as if to confirm his words, and she stood up and walked to the door. He thought of Desanya, his constant companion who always appeared when he called on her. He had abandoned her since Desire began to visit, now he felt she was a better companion who didn't bring him anxiety.

'You came in late today, anyway,' he said. Then, he did what could have made her jump out of the window if she was close to it. He moved towards her for the second time since she had started to visit him, found her hands in the darkness and tucked them into his, tightened his grip and in a low voice said, 'You should stop asking about the lights.' Desire could hardly hear him over her pounding heart, like the sound of a horse's hoof stamping the ground.

Her head swirled and she stiffened to steady her feet. She wanted to think of something other than him at that moment, but with her head spinning so much, she knew it would be too difficult for any thought to stay in her head. She knew she needed to do something to put a stop to the way she was feeling and the way he was trying to make her feel, so she announced, 'I met your son, Prof. His name is Ireti and he wants to meet you.'

She found his eyes and looked straight into them. She felt his hands go slightly limp against hers. She rushed out of the door. It was the first time she left without hearing him say, 'See you tomorrow.'

Prof sat in the dark after Desire left and started to replay her visit in his head. *A son?* The idea that he was a father to someone calmed him for a few seconds and then his heart raced until he stood up and started to jump. Prof wished she was still with him in the room, so they could talk about everything, but not *his son*. He wanted to tell her about how he screamed in the prison when the warders came to pick him for the usual routine. He would have loved to tell her how he decided light was not for him. The more he thought of it, the more he could feel his head lengthening. He held his head in his hands and shook it, screaming, 'Maami!' He calmed down, breathing heavily and fell in a swoop on the ground in loud tears.

Prof hoped that one day he would tell Desire of his time in prison. He bore the early days. Those days when he thought the worst thing was complaining and planning with other prisoners over the prison food; soups that lacked condiments: just water, a sprinkle of dry pepper and salt. He was strong for the first year. He yelled at the warder and proclaimed how the country would become a better place because the people would fight back soon. They came for him. The warders took him into rooms where he was beaten until his bruised body and broken bones made him walk with a bend.

In the second year, the routine of his punishment changed. The warders came to him in the mornings, in the full glare of a hot northern Nigerian sun where he stood outside the prison walls with fellow prisoners and waited for the warders' directives. The warders made them stand completely naked in the sun, like wet clothes being hung out to dry. The sun licked every part of his skin and scorched it with its rays until he felt his skin crackle in the heat. This was when he fell to the ground, shrieking, 'Maami' until the warders picked him up and threw him into a solitary cell. He picked a corner of the cell and shivered on the ground trying to make his body his once again.

In the evenings, a new set of warders came to interrogate him, 'Tell us, who are you working with? Is it the US government? Who is funding your activism?'

He stayed quiet. They shone flood lamps in his eyes until he fell down calling out what was now a regular cry to them, 'Maami!' As he always failed to talk or give them the information they wanted, they would cover his head with a hood for many days. He always lost count of time and how it flew. Sometimes, they took him into a room where his hands and legs were shackled. They then forced him to endure strobe lights while screeching Fuji music blasted from the loudspeaker. His body hardened.

The warders then laughed at him and said, 'Professor! March now-now. Change the world. Change the country.' They lifted him from the ground, put a veil over his head and took him to his matchbox prison cell. Once they veiled him, he knew the strobe lights were over. He began to find pleasure in how the warders veiled him.

This was the routine until the head of state who threw him in jail died and another military government came to power. The strobe light routine ended. There was no longer any need for the warders to put the hood over his head. Yet, in the five years of having his face concealed, he had enjoyed the way it sealed the darkness and enclosed him in his own thoughts. His body grew rigid when they brought lights to his cell. It made him shut his eyes until they ached. He devised a way of dealing with the lights by wearing his cloth over his head like a veil.

23

The past is always a place to look for directions for tomorrow.
This was Prof's thought when he requested to see Kayo. He
picked up the phone his mother had left for him and called
the only number on it.

'I want to see Kayo,' his voice was steady, and he did not say
more as he held onto the GSM. His mother's silence made
him fidget. He listened to her deep breaths on the other side
and then she cut off the call. He tried to call her again, but the
line wouldn't go through. He tried throughout the day. He did
not go for his usual nightly stroll.

The next day Kayo sat in front of him. There seemed to be
so much to say but it was evident they both felt there was no
adequate way to start. Prof wanted to start by apologising but
he did not know where to begin or what to apologise for. So
instead he said, 'How's your family?'

Kayo did not answer him and he repeated the question. 'My
wife died in an accident on the day you went to prison, with
our only child.' His voice dropped so that Prof needed to
strain to hear.

'I didn't know that.'

'Yes. That's not the type of news you offer a man in prison
or on the day of his return.' He knew that Kayo was trying
to bring up the way he was treated by Prof when he returned
from prison.

'I am sorry.'

He bowed his head and thought of Kayo living without
his wife. She was one of those women who never seemed
bothered by anything, and Kayo always seemed like a school
boy around her. She was his student, and one of the brightest
minds he had ever met. She came to his office on one of

those days that Kayo visited him on campus, and he did not introduce them. So, it was almost a shock, later, when Kayo said he was ready to marry, and she turned out to be the bride-to-be. Even all that time, Kayo was the one who was excited by the idea of marriage, she just wanted to live in the house with him.

'So Kanmi is dead,' Prof murmured to himself.

'Yes. She died in an accident. But it's a long time ago now.' Kayo said. He leaned forward and asked, in a voice filled with anxiety, 'I have a new woman now. How are you?'

'Good.' Prof said, surprised that his voice was stuck in his throat as he tried to make it louder. He could not look Kayo in the eye any more.

Then he turned to Kayo, 'Kanmi is really dead?'

'Yes.'

He nodded and said, 'A lot happened in my absence. Anyway. I'm glad you are...I mean, that we can talk again, after a long time.'

'You're talking strange, man. You are my man.'

Prof ignored him and stood up from the chair. 'Do you want some water?' he asked as he reached the door.

'I'm fine. I want light,' he paused before he added, 'I want to see your face when I talk to you.'

'Power is off in this house,' Prof said and moved into the kitchen to get water.

He returned silently and the quiet between them grew slow and stately, until it rested on them so much it expanded into a vacuous state of mind. Not knowing where to start his conversation, he said, 'Do you think I have a son?'

Kayo, at first, held a long pause, which was spat into a spurting, loud laugh.

'How would I know that?' There was a slight irritation in Kayo's voice.

'I need to know if one of those girls from the past had a son for me.'

'What's with this sudden search for a child? You who choose

to stay in the dark?' he said with a sneer.

Prof ignored the lowered voice that followed the second statement, or the snigger which he could hear behind it.

'Do you know where Blessing is?'

'Blessing?'

'My secretary, the one you said I should marry. She was also a student then, but she worked for me.'

'Oh, that nice lady? No.' There was a silence which left room for more words, and Kayo filled this with, 'Why are you asking me this now?'

'Why? Something happened, but I don't think that is what I want to dwell on now.'

'Okay. If you say so.'

Kayo knew him, as much of him as the girls he slept with before he began his abstinence. They talked about the most likely person to have given him a child, Blessing, his secretary.

'I don't know but they said she has a partner, but was yet to have a baby.'

'She is the only one that will keep my baby, or what do you think?'

'She left angry,' he said. 'Consider you activist people slept with each other a lot.'

'I never—'

He then remembered one night in his final year in the university.

He was at a congress meeting with leading activists from different parts of the country. All of the comrades who mattered in Nigeria were at the Obafemi Awolowo University to strategise on how best to weaken the obsessive, oppressive nature of the then military government to cut the academia down to size. He was the representative of student leaders across the country.

'Every semester, not less than four or five student leaders go missing or die from accidental discharge. These students are the future of this country. Many of them are learning to become the enemy's spy. They will rather sleep with the enemy than lose their lives. We need to fight against the corruption of the future of this country...' Prof was the youngest at the meeting, but they listened to him. He gained respect for his introspection on issues. Many of them always forgot that he was not even out of the university yet at the time. They always treated him like he was already a professor. He was leaving the staff club of OAU, where the meeting was held, when he noticed her. She stood with legs astride, biting her fingers and this disgusted him in an instant.

'Beautiful woman like you eating your nails as if it is sugarcane.'

'And how is the biting of my nails of more concern than the sorry state of our country?' Her tone made him feel as small as he had felt that night—standing right in front of a man like Prof Soyinka, whose feet he worshipped at as a student union leader. He stood there for a while. Finding no immediate words to respond to her, he found himself laughing.

'Comrade, oh, have you met—' He didn't pick up her name and throughout the night, he called her "Fire", which she giggled at, because he did not want her to realise that he could not remember her name or had not listened when they were being introduced.

After her sharp response, she offered to help him with his books to his guest house room, and after a back and forth of 'Not necessary' and 'Prof, it's not a bother,' he let her follow him.

She sat on the edge of his bed before she was offered a seat and then she started a conversation. At first, he wanted to tell her he was tired and needed to get as much sleep as possible, but she wove one interesting topic into another, and it amazed him that a mind that intelligent and beautiful, could also say some of the craziest things with a straight face.

'You think stopping coups and military rule in Africa will change our lives,' she said.

'It is one step towards it. I know that these leaders, change from military to civilian and remain in power...'

'You have answered yourself. See, Prof. It is the West calling us to join their train and that we "need" to fall into the democracy league.'

'You don't think democracy works.'

'I don't believe in democracy, Prof. We never had democracy.'

'The Igbos were a democratic...'

'Prof! You shouldn't be saying this. We have categorised the Igbo form of rulership into democracy based on the structure expected of us. While I do not have a name for it, it was certainly not democracy. Not like America's.'

'I'm trying to understand you. You want this military rule to continue or what?'

'Prof, I don't care. See, coups and military rules may no longer be in fashion, but the dehumanisation of human beings is dateless. It never goes archaic.'

She moved on to dissecting global politics and just as he was thinking that they would spend the whole night talking, she jumped up on the bed and threw a pillow at him. It thawed the tension of the past hour they had spent in intense argument. She laughed like a child being tickled. She dissolved into a familiarity that amazed him into believing such a moment of intensity, following introductions that were made barely four hours before, could exist. The more she talked, the more he realised that "Fire" was what was meant when people talked about how a beautiful mind washed out all forms of physical beauty. Were it not for the university rounds they were to go on the following day, he would have asked her to stay in the guest house with him, so they could talk and laugh and talk and top it off again with sex. Prof lost interest in what she looked like and even after that experience, which he described to Kayo—the only one he told of how he would not have minded bringing her to Lagos sometime for some more intimacy—he could not describe her.

He gave her Kayo's landline number and the best time she

could reach him. Kayo was already working while he was in school. Most times, Prof went to his office to wait for calls on the rotary dial telephone whose ring was always so sudden, he jumped. The first few days after their meeting, his body felt giddy whenever he remembered the moments he spent with Fire. He wondered if she would call or seek him out. He wondered if she would dislike him if she discovered he was not a young professor but just a student union leader, who was well liked by the older activists.

It was in December, during a meeting to call off the strike action of teachers across the country, that one of the more senior comrades who was at Ife told him of how she had just disappeared from the campus and no one could trace her.

'Disappeared? What do you mean disappeared?'

'She stopped coming and friends went to check her at home but they could not find her. You know, no one knew where she came from... she was playful, yet seemed to carry so many secrets.'

The first few days after he heard this, he felt like someone who lost the chance to adorn a prized jewel. The years that followed were filled with activity and a simmering on the political landscape, and exceptional moments of sex and good conversation in the archives of several others.

Many years later when he began his abstinence, Prof remembered those days he went around universities and how on a few of those nights, he might have been careless with women who were introduced as comrade-this or comrade-that, and who lingered in the rooms until the heat in their bodies made sex a vent. These were women, who over bottles of beer offered his obstinate will a weakness with their intellectual debates, which usually led to him trying to break down their mystique into an intense, unforgettable night of submission through sex. As it turned out, these girls broke down his ego. As he woke up most times, he wanted to be under the sheets, as their "conquered" smile and hot breath teased him into quiet.

'Prof, Prof,' the girl might hail with a chuckle escaping her lips.

Among these many girls, he always hoped that one could be like Fire. None met her standard. He sometimes felt it was the youthfulness of his mind and his imagination that made her grander in thought than she might have been. Once he realised none of the girls was ever going to be like Fire, it was easy for him to lay claim to an abstinence that gathered the collective anger of the people in his veins.

There were so many years of sworn secrecy between him and Kayo, and Prof knew that he was the best person to discuss his new speculations of a child with.

'So, what am I supposed to do about this new information?' Kayo asked.

'To help me find out of if I have a son.'

'And what if you have a son, do you want to meet him in the dark?'

'That's not the point. I—'

'What's the point? You really can't live like this.' Prof felt the anger in Kayo's voice.

'I. Can. Live. How. I. Want. Kayo, I really just wanted us to talk, to catch up.'

'So why don't you switch on the lights?'

'Why should switching on the lights become the problem or the answer to my questions?'

The pitch of their voices had increased. Kayo stood up, pacing from one end of the room to the other.

'We waited all of these years for you to return. We carried our own pain. Do you know what I went through? Trying to have a family and keeping your mother alive so you could meet her when you return. Do you know what it has been like? No one would give me a job because I was your friend!' Kayo breathed heavily. 'They were scared the military boys would come for them,' Kayo's voice broke and Prof wanted to stand up and give him a hug. He, however, did not. He remained in the chair and listened to his friend.

Finally, Prof screamed, 'I—I—I just want to talk!' It calmed the air for a few minutes and then Kayo started all over again.

'You don't think I want to talk. It is always about you! You think you're better than me, because you went to prison. You've always believed you're better, the good one.'

'Kayo, stop it!'

Kayo was now at the point where his anger dug into him and reached for any word that could hurt. It was no longer about the discussion at hand. It was about years of feeling like a side-kick, of feeling that he was unappreciated, of a need to spill out whatever tension was inside of him that needed to be expunged.

'You are the holier than thou! Pretending like you didn't know you had a son somewhere. You have not left this house since you returned, how do you suddenly think of a son? Hahaha, you don't want to feel irresponsible like your father?' Prof stood up, holding his head. Kayo's last words echoed in his head. Desanya, who he had tried to bring back for some time leapt into his head and started crying, *'No one should tell you that. No one. No one.'*

'Get out!' Prof screamed. His eyes were wet, and he felt he was going to fall as all he could hear was, *irresponsible like your father*. He felt many voices in his head telling him what to do. He could not distinguish which one was Kayo's from the others.

Kayo stood up from the chair laughing, 'You really need help, and you need help fast.' He walked towards the door and spat on the ground, 'Die alone.'

'That's your best friend leaving you.' Desanya said. She just came in, when he least expected.

'Who asked you to come here?' he turned his head to face her, where he sensed she would be in the room. And then, as if he was reminded he was yet to respond to Kayo's invective, he screamed, 'You'll die first! Who knows if you killed your wife? Bloody cultist!' He didn't mean to say the words as they came, but once they were out, he looked around, ashamed of everything.

24

There was a time Desire could keep her thoughts in her head, unbothered about wanting to speak to anyone. Now, she was used to sharing her deepest concerns with Remilekun, who now spent most of her days with Mr. America. Desire, for a second, thought of calling Basira and asking her about the miscarriage she spoke of and maybe discussing Prof and Ireti. She pushed the thought from her mind and walked into the street, although people were around her, she was oblivious to them.

A young man in a suit and an unknotted tie jumped in front of her. His shirt was unbuttoned.

'Have a great day,' he said. She was startled.

'Smile. The day is bright.' He placed his hand on his waist and said, 'Smile, I'm waiting.'

As much as she hated how the young man laughed at her cheerily and with some familiarity, it all felt like a dream. Still, she wanted to tell him to get away from her because the day was not bright. She wanted to tell him to look up at the sky where the sun stayed behind the clouds and gave a dull ambience to the environment. Instead, she took two hurried steps away from him.

He ran up to her, 'I won't leave you until you smile for me.'

'Smile for you?' Desire was going to say something else, but there was this distant brightness in his eyes. She tried to force a smile, but she could not. She hurried ahead and crossed to the other side of the road, when she heard a sharp scream from the same man who had just greeted her. He was screaming as he pulled off all his clothing. He pulled down his boxers and wriggled his waist at any woman who walked past him. Desire found herself unable to look away, while his suit, shirt, singlet, trousers and boxers lay on the ground, not far from where he now stood, laughing and pointing at the skies. He turned towards Desire and she saw the dry chest and pancake abdomen, which were a contrast to an unusually long penis that swung like the pendulum of a clock as he flounced onward with his briefcase. Desire slowed down as the man reached her and walked past, without recognising their earlier encounter. She looked at him as he flashed that impersonal smile which he was offering everyone who stared at him, like he knew something they did not. She stood on the spot with her mouth agape, her legs wobbling, and her heart beating like rain against a corrugated roof. It was one of those moments when words seemed inadequate to question the absurdity of such things. She was trying to understand what could have happened in those few minutes. Would her smile have saved him from whatever made him pull off his clothes? She thought of her mother and she felt a little fear creep up on her. Desire hurried to board the bus that arrived at the bus stop. She jumped on and it was only when she was seated that she asked where it was going.

On the bus, there was a talkative man who sat two seats away from her, who started a discussion on how bad the road was and how one day the potholes would become so big they would become gaps that would swallow them.

'See, see, everywhere...' The other passengers on the bus ignored him. It seemed there was a mutual agreement that it was too early in the day to join in bus conversations, until he declared, 'I just want all of us to wake up one day and die.'

At first, there was silence, and then a rising murmur with one noticeably loud voice—a woman who responded, '*Abi*, this one has gone mad?'

As the woman mentioned the word 'mad' Desire felt her head swirl. She wanted to scream at the man to stop talking. Instead, she simply hoped that her eyes conveyed her irritation. He turned to her, 'Aunty, you look like a learned somebody. The way you are looking at me, I see you understand my talk.'

He smiled, '*Se*, you are getting me?'

Desire looked up at the man. She wondered how to tell him how his tanned afro and the folded flesh around his cheeks made her angry. She sighed, dipped her hand in her bag and brought out a book. She bent over it, flipped to a page and pretended to read.

25

Prof heard a light movement outside the door and knew his mother had come to drop off his provisions. Desire and his mother came at different times of the day, but he also recognised his mother's arrival in the way she lingered at the door, not her knocking. Her presence was carried by her long, intermittent sighs and heavy breath. She would knock. Slow and steady until it became an earworm.

These days, she stayed at his door waiting for him to open for her. Before then, she would knock, then drop his provisions after a performance of his panegyric. But since that time she found herself inside the house, she always shuffled her feet at the door until he opened. The practice was for him to open the door to her and follow behind her as she quietly went to a chair. He then returned to his seat with a grunt. Sometimes he responded to her greeting and followed it with a long silence; the awkwardness of many years of unspoken bitterness, underlined by a devotion based on knowing they both had no one else but each other.

This time as she sat down, he wanted to talk. He wanted to tell her about Ireti. He wanted to tell her about Desire too, but he thought of Ireti more.

Maami, do you think I can father a child? No. He thought of another way to ask the question. Did any woman ever come to you saying that I fathered her child? No. He tried to think of another way to frame the question and he could find no better way to explain to her that he felt he might have fathered a child.

Prof sat in the room with his mother; the breathing between them became a dialogue of their worries, until he coughed while getting up to use the bathroom. He returned to the seat with the hope that Kayo might have hinted at the issue of him being a father to someone, to her.

There were stories to be told and explanations to be made and the silence was lingering too long. The pain was becoming unbearable. He also realised that he no longer felt angry about the past, he only felt that the anger in his past needed to be understood and that was why he heaved and sighed when she brought him food, hoping she would talk about his father. This visit though, what he wanted to talk about was his son— the son.

'You can't go on like this. You need to come back to yourself.'

Prof raised his head in the direction of her seat. He wanted to laugh at the idea of him coming back to himself. He thought of prison and the feeling of himself floating up to the skies. When was he ever himself? How did deciding to live in the dark become the criteria for judging the total life of a man?

'So, you stay here all day and all night with no visitor?' There was something about the question that seemed based on an assumption of the contrary happening. Yet, he did not say a word in response. He saw it as bait and it pricked his thoughts at first mention.

'I've tried to understand you since your release and I know you're going through so much, but I can only help you if—'

'There's nothing to understand. I just need to do some thinking — and you can start by telling me who my father is.' He felt this could be a good way to divert the conversation to Ireti.

'Is that a question that deserves an answer?'

The silence that followed was laden with more heavy breathing. He felt a searing guilt and did not know how to ask what could have happened between her and his father that he hated them so much. Why was she without family or friends around her? He could not remember seeing anyone, besides his mother's colleagues from the market, rally around her. He had always felt guilty each time he attempted independence, and he told her that once. Her response birthed a bitterness in him, when she said, 'Independence is not about being on your own, it is not freedom from influence. You are truly free when you become the influence of your own life. Sometimes, we are our own problem.'

He waited for her to say something about his father but she did not. She picked herself up from the chair and sniffed—that was when he realised that she had been crying.

'I was your father, I was your mother, what more do you want?'

'A child has a right to know his father, does he not?'

'A child has a right to know he was taken care of, stood up for, and protected by someone who didn't throw him to the dogs. Of course, you met your father, and even on his dying bed, how much of a father was he to you?'

He thought about Ireti again and wondered if bringing him up at that point was a good idea.

'Are you really my mother?'

'Eni, I don't understand what is happening to you. But I have paid my dues, years of working as a farm labourer so you could feed, and I could become a typist that could afford us better feeding, and you ask me that question?'

'Is sacrifice all it takes to be a mother? Look at me, Maami, I'm 45 and I feel like...'

She stood up and paced around for some time. And then she laughed, slow and small, and faded off into a sigh.

'Tell me, what's bothering you?'

Prof stretched and sat erect in his chair when she said that. He watched her outline swimming back and forth in the room. For a few, very brief seconds, he relived a time when he was a 15-year-old desperate to get an answer from her about who his father was.

He had entered her room with a knife in his hands, and with his muscles vibrating. He ran towards her.

'You have to tell me who my father is today or I will kill you,' he said between tears, still shaking, with sweat rushing down from the centre of his head. 'That man can't be my father. He hates me so much.'

She had looked at him hard and said with a calmness he had never seen her display, 'Tell me, what's bothering you? Is being called a bastard the worst thing in the world? What would you do if you were called a thief or a murderer—*you* should decide what you are, what you want to be. See, if you leave the world to name you, all of your life would be in the hands of strangers. If you let people determine who you are, by the time you need to be someone and it matters that you are, you'll realise you're a nobody.' And then, she stretched out her hand and said, 'Put the knife on the table, go into the room and stare at the face of your father's photo on the table— and you should make sure you are far from it, in behaviour— and promise never to be an idiot.' She then walked out of the room, unafraid that he could stab or kill her from the back.

Prof was not holding a knife in his hand this time, and even though he had met his father before his death, he still felt a perverse desire to make his mother feel guilty for his father's absence in his life.

'Talk to me, is this question about your father related to something bothering you? Talk to me, my son.'

He did not wait for her to destabilise him with her analysis, so he asked, 'My father denied me until his death, and when I thought I was accepted, I felt even more shame. Don't I have a right to know?'

He waited for her, but all she did was take a deep breath before she returned to sit on the chair.

'Your father—see, how do I tell you this story? You're 45, forget.'

'Is it possible to forget what one does not know?'

'There are no reasons why marriages dissolve—infidelity, anger, pain, bitterness—it just has to be tied to something, but if we could forget, there really are no reasons for breakups. For instance, was there a reason for your father to leave?'

'You tell me. I still want to know.'

'He was convinced I slept with his boss and he threw my things out.'

A silence that was lengthier than whatever had existed between them before, climbed on board.

'Did you do it?'

'Your father asked me to, and I said no, I wouldn't, and he cried, saying it was his only way of getting a promotion. The man requested I come. Anyway, I went there, thinking I could persuade him somehow, and I returned home, smiling and eager to tell your father nothing happened between his boss and me. Yet, my crime was accepting to go to see the man. Your father said I must have been unfaithful to him before then, that was the reason I accepted the offer to go without thinking twice. What was I to do? You should have seen the way he was rolling all over the floor begging me, that his life depended on it, our future would be better for it. This one and that one...And so I went to his boss that day feeling like a barter. It was the most horrible feeling in world. From that day, your father started to beat me. One day, when I could not take it any longer, I took a ladle and hit him on his penis, making sure he felt the pain many years after.'

'What do you mean?'

'Your father was told he would never have a child after the blow. So, you see, you're actually your father's only child, in a way. I discovered I was pregnant after the supposed plan for me to sleep with his *oga*, and he couldn't—you know...So, he believed you were not his.'

'But I saw his children that time I went to his house, when I ran away from Ilese to Lagos, to see him.'

'Only he and I know he can no longer have a child. His wife—the new wife knows too. Perhaps she discovered. I don't know how she did it, but those children are bastards. But which Nigerian man, especially one like your father, who suddenly finds some social standing wants it known that he can't father a child? Those are not his children.'

'But, am I really his?'

'What do you think?'

She walked towards the door and stopped, not opening it, 'I gave birth to you, and I showed you your father. He denies you and humiliates you, even in death. You should believe what you think makes you happy.'

He felt every part of his body singe, as he could not understand why she was being calm while he brimmed with anxieties.

He shook in his chair and thought of how every fight in his primary school resulted in a song, 'Show us your father.' How everyone got to know he didn't have a father always baffled him and it was that anger in him that he transferred to fighting bullies; that he soon became known as a saviour of soft boys. And then, he read, and read, and read, and found himself believing he was made to fight for the causes of the oppressed. Even Kayo became his friend because he had stood up for him when a teacher called him 'a blockhead who could never make it in life.' He stood up and narrated how his mother and himself carried heavy baskets of cocoa from the farm to the market, before she became a typist. He told them how it appeared like he would never sleep on a bed when they slept on a mat, 'My mother could barely read when she decided to become a primary school teacher. Ma'am, if my mother could do it, why can't Kayo?'

He was the eight-year-old who wanted the world in his hands at the time. It was also an open secret that Kayo was a scoundrel who could be found on every wrong side of the law. On that day, Kayo stood head straight, his eyes turned to him in full gratitude. Their friendship began. Even though Kayo continued to do things which made the adults throw curses at him; looking at women taking their baths in the stream and rushing off with their wrappers or inviting other young boys to peep at adults as they made love. Kayo was everything a parent wouldn't want in a child, or a friend a mother wouldn't encourage her son to keep. Yet, their friendship endured—until he went to prison.

'Eni, I—we suffered. Your father decided his path, and when I look back, I wish I never listened to his plea to go to his boss, so he could get a promotion. Even though I never slept with the man, my crime was that I agreed to his request. How could I have known I was not to accept? How could I have known that he would turn into a beast? He threw me out of the house at just a few minutes to 3am.'

'Why didn't you tell me this earlier—45 years, and now? How do I authenticate this, this—fable? Do you know how I struggled to know him—the little of him I knew? Do you know what it means to—what do I know? I've never even met your relations.'

There was a tear in her voice when she said, 'But you know I am an orphan. I was raised in the Methodist Church.'

'Yes. You're so good at stories. Who are you really?'

'I'm leaving. It is better to leave now.' There was not only a note of finality in her voice, her voice shook, and though he couldn't see her, he was certain she trembled as well. At that moment, he was past caring.

'Leave! Leave and never come back again. Ever! I've known more sorrow in years. I see why you always wanted me near you like a loincloth tied around your waist. I see why I could never find a reason to settle down...you are a—' Not finding the words, he said, 'Leave!'

'Eni...' her voice was calmer now.

'Leave! I don't want you in my life any more. Ever. If you come to this house, I don't know what I'm capable of, if you return,' he said. And in a voice meant to hit her in the hardest of way, he said, 'Why do you keep coming to me? Why do you hold on to me if you don't have an agenda?'

'I'm your mother, Eni. You're my son. A good mother won't give up on her child, even when they choose darkness over light.'

She sighed, and he imagined her shaking her head as well.

Standing by the door, he saw how desperate he was to have her tell him something from her past. The few facts he knew about her were from unfinished notes in diaries, photos with dates and names behind them, and addresses to places about which he spent his younger days wondering, *what happened there?*

From Ilese, when he could spell suffering back and forth with the hard life they lived there, while she went to study for her teacher training, to the move to Lagos, when he thought he was now closer to his father, and could perhaps enjoy the benefit of having one, his mother's silence remained, and the few times she spoke, it was like his life would remain a search for puzzle pieces. She always left something unsaid, something left to be found out.

Prof took a seat and contemplated how his life was surrounded by a grief that invented him again and again. Perhaps, he thought, if Desire came to see him, he would share this part of his life with her. He wondered if he should run after his mother and invite her back into the room so that he could tell her that he never felt present in his own body all those years—and his fights for people were a fight for himself. For every fight he won, he felt like someone who had surmounted a demon that reduced his identity, his achievements, and his hopes into one word: bastard. He knew she felt he did not need to feel like one, but how could she know what it was to feel what you had not carried? She was no longer outside when he checked from the door, and he went back into the house. With his lips trembling, he finally let out a muffled scream, 'Maaaaami!'

26

Remilekun returned from Mr. America wearing a gloomy face. Desire did not ask her what was wrong with her, she simply stood up from the bed and decided to take a stroll down the road. She wanted to talk to someone, someone who would listen. As she approached a bend that led into another street, she stopped by a stall whose owner was most likely home at that time, looked at the Nokia phone in her hand and mustered up some courage to call Basira. Desire had no idea what she wanted to say to Basira, but she called with the hope that she would listen.

'Basira, *bawo ni?*'

'I am fine-o. You go fit call me back,' she yawned, 'I just finish fucking.' There was a giggle in her voice.

Desire was quiet, 'I hope you're fine, now.'

'I'm fine. God give, God take. It is God that take pregnancy that spoil that will give pregnancy that will give baby. Anyway, to have baby you fuck, you lose baby you fuck,' Basira laughed. 'Pray for me, or anything you know how to do. I am starting to think I should have more children. Maybe four or five children in a house are good. I want plenty.'

'Take it easy. I thought we agreed you won't have more babies.'

'I have to do baby more-o. How person will hold man down?'

Desire paused and not pushing the discussion asked, 'How is your husband taking the news of the miscarriage?'

'He did not happy at all, but that is the way God do His thing. He give. He take.' Suddenly, Basira's voice became full of life, 'Me and my husband have accepted the thing that happen to the pregnancy... *Inna Lillahi wa ina Ilayhi raji'un.*'

As Desire listened to Basira's lively voice and the way she

appeared less bothered about the miscarriage, she felt there was no way she could initiate the conversation about Ireti and Prof, and to make it more confusing, she did not know what to say about them. She hesitated and then said a quick goodbye and cut the phone call.

She walked back to the house, and Remilekun opened the door for her and welcomed her with a gentleness that was not typical of her. She returned to her bed and said nothing more to Desire. Then, as if it suddenly occurred to Remilekun that she was too dressed up for the room, she started to take off her clothing, one item after the other. The slowness and distant look, the small smile that came and left her face scared Desire and she remembered the young man on the road and her mother at the same time.

'Remilekun, what is happening? You have been too quiet.' Remilekun sighed. She came to sit on the bed beside Desire, who now noticed the faint marks left by tears below her eyes. She watched her lips. She resisted the urge to start the conversation until Remilekun broke down crying.

'Talk to me,' Desire said, her hand cupping her shoulder.

'I am pregnant.'

'Is that why you're crying?'

It was not the first time Remilekun had been pregnant. Most times, it was after the abortion that Desire found out, when it seemed she was wearing a sanitary towel for more than five days, which was usually followed by two days at home taking Ibuprofen every few hours with condensed milk. Remilekun's pulled-in chin told her that this pregnancy was different from the rest..

'Why? Why?' Remilekun cried. She nodded in response to any questions, which made her look different from the brash Remilekun she had come to know, 'Why can't I have his baby?'

Desire said nothing to her. She knew that if the baby was Mr. America's, then it was never going to have a father. It was strange watching Remilekun become timid.

Desire's phone rang, and she picked it up from the windowsill without looking at the caller. She assumed it was Basira calling back.

'Hello.'

'Hello Des-Des, hawayu?'

There was only one person who called her by that name. She sat up on the bed immediately and making eye contact with Remilekun, indicated that it was Mama T calling.

'You fwiend's fone has been off since. Why?'

'Ha, I think her phone was spoilt and she took it to the repairer, but she is here with me, Ma.'

Desire handed Remilekun the phone and watched her friend struggle to sound normal, 'I have serious fever and if not for the test I would have come home straight... no... don't bother coming... okay Ma... alright. She's taking care of me, Ma.' She handed the phone back to Desire and forced a smile.

They both took in the moment in silence.

'I thought he would ask me to marry him this time.'

'Remilekun, we've been on this road before! What do you see in that guy?'

'What do you see in the madman you go to see every night?' Her voice was strong, yet Desire knew that the response was just a defence mechanism. Desire stood up from the bed and walked around the room for a few minutes before turning to her friend.

'I'll follow you to do it.'

'Thank you.'

'This will be the last time.'

* * *

A small signpost: Tayo Clinic, stuck out from the rooftop of one of the houses hidden inside Mushin open market. It was sandwiched between two two-storey buildings. It could have disappeared within the other houses in the area but for the colour. It was painted in saffron; the colour of Lagos' danfo buses. It was sheltered by rows of provision shops, spilling into the walkways arranged with packets of milk, cocoa drinks, cornflakes and biscuits. They were packed so high that they tilted forward, but didn't fall to the ground.

She followed Remilekun down an alley which led to a thin, spindly stairway by the right side of the building, amidst the clamour of traders shouting out as many Yoruba endearments as they could come up with, 'My sister,' 'My husband's mother,' 'Fine aunty,' 'My aunty...' before asking 'What do you want to buy?'

There were a few more attempts at drawing her attention but when they noticed her lack of interest, the traders were soon calling on other passers-by. They entered the second flat and she opened the swinging door, which had a panel painted in faint white letters: Tayo Clinic. The smell of urine and antibiotics wafted into her nostrils as she walked into the clinic's reception. They walked towards a girl in a frilled fluorescent-green blouse, sitting behind a counter with stickers of all sorts, selling medicine covered in those same labels. The girl was engrossed in a programme showing on the portable television which sat on the counter. Three empty white plastic chairs in the room were not left out of the sticker plastering. A nurse, sleeping with her mouth open, was in a reception chair.

'Good morning,' Desire and Remilekun chorused.

'Welcome, ma,' an unrecognisable accent, as if from living among people of different ethnic groups, bounced from the girl's mouth.

'I want to see a doctor.'

'Are you sick? Do you have card here?'

Desire did not reply. She watched the lady, whose eyes widened each time she spoke, with slight amusement. The lady's pencilled-in eyebrows were like two triangles without bases.

'I say are you sick?'

'I think the doctor will be the best person to know that. How much is your hospital card?' Desire asked.

'But, Doctor is not around now-o!' the receptionist stretched her hand towards the open-mouthed nurse and tapped her shoulder.

'Nurse! Aunty! Aunty! Aunty Nurse!' Exasperated by the lack of response, she tapped harder. 'Me, I don't understand how someone will be sleeping like this-o.' Three more slaps on her back and the nurse stirred, taking time to stretch out her arms in full.

'Patient is here-o. She wants to see doctor. Maybe you'll give her injection if she has malaria, before the doctor come *sha*.'

Desire looked at Remilekun as the receptionist spoke and they shared a knowing smile.

The girl took out a file from behind the counter and scribbled answers as she asked.

'Name?'

'Ayo. Ayo Obembe,' Desire gave a fake name and looked to Remilekun for confirmation.

'Sex?'

Desire said nothing to the frilled-blouse girl, who looked up expecting an answer. She realised her folly, with laughter between her teeth.

'Ha! Female.'

'Age?'

'30.'

The girl looked first at Desire and then at Remilekun. She could tell they were not under age, but they were certainly not 30.

'Occupation?'

'Teacher.'

'Family or personal card?'

'Personal.'

'Sit down there,' she changed to pidgin, 'I don finish my work with you be dat.'

The girl pointed to one of the white plastic chairs and then turned back to the television, 'That nurse wey dey sleep, maybe she don get belle *sef*, she go soon come to you.'

The nurse, who was now awake, muttered a 'Good morning,'

and got up from the chair. She stretched her arms, staggered forward and walked into an inner room. After a few minutes, she came back to the waiting room with a dash of water on her face and faced the girl on the counter, who was tuning the television set to another channel.

'You better not give people the impression that we remove pregnancy here,' she spoke in Yoruba. 'The doctor is on his—'

The girl raised her head up and exclaimed, 'Ha! Doctor is here-o!'

Desire collected the card from her and did a quick scan before she handed it to Remilekun, who looked away. She handed it to the doctor who was as thin as a javelin pole. The man stretched past the doorpost and walked with what seemed to be caution, as if he was afraid of being blown across the room.

'Have we met before?' he asked Remilekun, who looked down at the floor and would not move from the door.

He added, 'Madam, please come in,' his voice loud for his thin frame. Desire stopped at the door but Remilekun again insisted she follow her into his office, a small room partitioned with wood.

'Sit.'

Remilekun sat down on a plastic chair in front of a swivel chair that served as a table, with piles of brown files. Desire stood behind her. The second chair in the room, for visitors, had a broken leg.

'So, what can I do for you, miss?'

Desire looked at Remilekun with the hope that she would talk this time.

'My husband wants an abortion. He thinks three kids are enough.'

Remilekun placed her hand on the table, so he could see the ring on her finger. She wore it while they were on the bus, and although Desire wondered why at the time, she had not asked. 'We don't do abortion here,' he shook his head like he was confirming the truth of his lie to himself, before he added, 'Not any more—but... this one that *oga* does not want the baby, we can do it.'

The doctor asked in an English woven with the distinctive Yoruba tonality, 'Have you paid the nurse?' and then, without waiting for an answer said, 'Have you eaten food?'

'I haven't eaten anything this morning?'

'Okay then. Come. Let's do the thing quick-quick. Many patients will soon start coming.'

Desire looked around again. There were spider webs in the corners of the walls and she sniffed dust.

The doctor stood up and took her into a small room with a white-metal single bed with stirrups hanging from iron rods, sticking out of its sides. The bed took up most of the space, leaving just enough room for a doctor and one nurse. A nurse entered, she was not the same one that had attended to them earlier. This one had a lower lip that drooped like a flower petal sprinkled with too much water. The nurse stood by the door, carrying a tray from which the doctor picked all kinds of instruments.

'You have to leave the room,' the nurse said to Desire.

'She stays.' Remilekun said, with a note of finality in her voice. She looked at the doctor, and he did not appear bothered.

The nurse wrung her nose and Desire slid into the room from the little space by the door, throwing a stealthy look at the array of steel instruments in the bowl: Karman syringe; sponge-holding forceps; an instrument with a flat metal loop at the end which she suspected was the curette; sponge; and pencil-shaped dilators of different sizes. All terms her mind had stored from reading all those medical books and pamphlets she had picked up along the way. She was now studying the objects, comparing them to the shapes she remembered from the books. Reading widely made everything in the world familiar. She had a theoretical knowledge of what was to take place. She moved to Remilekun's side and held her hand in hers.

Desire observed as the doctor placed Remilekun's legs on the metal loops which were hinged with one half falling away, so that her positioning made her bum hang over the edge and her pubis was in clear view of the doctor. She took a moment to think of all the women who had lain on the bed like Remilekun, for the same purpose but with different reasons. Remilekun tried to shift into a more comfortable position.

The doctor tried to keep up a conversation as he wore his gloves. Desire looked up at the ceiling her friend would face as they performed the procedure. It was a once-white ceiling with filaments of cobwebs hanging down the cracks. A spider dangled from a strand of thread in a corner.

'Madam. Injection?'

Remilekun turned to look at him and smiled. Desire knew her friend enough to assume that she suddenly found the peanut-shaped head of the doctor amusing, if she had not earlier.

She shook her head in the negative, 'I want to see it.'

'Okay, I will give you general.'

'I don't want injection!'

'Sure?'

'No injection,' she repeated quietly, but with a tone of no-question. He looked at her for a moment, like he was waiting to see if she would change her mind. No word was spoken again between them. Desire caught the doctor signal to the nurse, who passed a syringe to him, and he punctured Remilekun's thighs quickly. They had gone ahead to inject her despite her wish.

Desire watched as the procedure started. First, he cleansed her with something she suspected was an antibacterial scrub, then he slipped in the metal dilators, and inserted the other metal object with a flat metal loop into her. Each of these objects—cold steel, all of them—slipped into her, disappearing to find the foetus.

She watched the deftness and ease with which the doctor attended to his job. Remilekun couldn't hold back the tears. Desire held her hand tighter.

'Sorry, madam. It's one of those things,' the doctor turned to the nurse, who spoke, and whispered something to her.

Desire knew it was over as the doctor pulled off his gloves and said something she didn't hear clearly about waiting for a while. The leaf-lipped nurse helped Remilekun up from the bed, with the bed spread falling to reveal a nylon-covered mattress. It was with slow steps, and her hand against the wall, that Remilekun moved to a ward to regain her strength, while Desire rubbed her back before going to meet the clerk in the reception to settle the bills.

Remilekun moved about the house like a sick dog. She stayed in bed. She was not willing to go to classes or answer phone calls for a week. She ate little and said less and Desire was becoming afraid when they heard a knock on the door.

'Could you have kept that baby, even if he didn't want it? You wanted that baby.'

'He didn't want it.'

'But you did.'

'Where is paternity without a father's acceptance?'

Desire sighed, and that appeared to have been the cue for a whisky-scented Mr. America to flounce into the room, shocking them with an unintended reminder of a door left unlocked.

'If you leave me, I would die,' Mr. America said. Desire wrinkled her nose. She looked on as Remilekun fell into his arms, and she muttered something about taking a walk.

She did not have any destination in mind, but she arrived at Prof's door.

27

Desire did not know what to expect as she knocked on his door. It was two weeks since her last visit to see Prof, the day she mentioned Ireti's name and left without any explanation. She twiddled her forefinger while waiting for him to answer. Prof opened the door, paused and then broke into a small laugh as he moved towards his chair without speaking. She followed quietly behind him, slightly irritated that he would let her in without making her feel any guilt for her absence. She sat on her usual chair and waited for him to begin. She wanted to talk but her mouth was dry. Soon, a small silence drowned their intermittent sighs, deep breaths and pounding hearts. Neither of them gave an inkling of the thoughts in their minds. After about 15 minutes, when they had both settled into their seats in the room and still had not spoken, Prof asked, 'Would you like some water?'

She ignored him.

He stood up and entered the door that led to the other rooms in the house, but he returned to the sitting room almost immediately. He sat down and returned to the silence which was there before he left.

She said, 'It is really dark in here. Is it darker? I'll switch on the lights.'

She stood up from the chair and placed her hand on the switch, unsure of whether she would flick it on or not. The thought of him springing from the chair as she did so, and perhaps strangling her, made her shudder. It was so strong an image that she gasped in reality. She shook her head and wiped her brow with her right hand.

'Don't you want to know what I look like today?'

'Would your look change the price of bread in Lagos?' he

said with a small laugh.

A speck of light slanted onto her chair from his neighbours' flat. Again, her desire was stirred; but his hawing and heavy breathing stood as a warning of an imagined doom. Desire stopped to weigh his unwillingness to see her. She rested her head against the wall. In synchrony with her thoughts, she moved her hand to the wall and her palm coasted against the coarse text-coat paint as she fingered the protruding button of a switch. Her hand lingered on it as she tried to find the courage to push it down.

'*You can do it,*' a voice in her head spat out in repetition. It was like the refrain of a song.

'You've not said very much today,' his voice shot at her. She removed her hand from the electric switch, so that it fell to her thigh. She adjusted her position in the chair and gave a deliberate and audible sigh. Then, she cleared her throat like she was about to talk but used the moment to gain courage to put the lights on.

Once she felt she was confident enough, she said to him, 'Sir, please put the lights on. This room is too dark.' She explained that she needed to tell him something and it was important that she saw his every expression as she said it. She waited only for a while before she added, 'And I have not even seen you since I started visiting. I don't know what you look like since you returned from prison. I want to see how you've changed. Please.'

Desire closed her eyes in anticipation of what a lit room would make of her. Perhaps, it was best to be a mental subject than to reveal herself to scrutiny under the lights, and this applied to him too.

When she opened her eyes, it was still dark, and she hadn't asked any questions. There was even more silence in the room and it was as if they had both stopped breathing. The humming of generators in the distance sounded like a trombone in her head. She arranged her hands over her shoulders and asked, 'Why is there never light in the room?'

He spoke slowly as if he was measuring his words, 'The colour of the room makes me nervous.'

'Change it. I'll get a painter tomorrow and I will bring you a transistor radio.' Although she didn't know how she would get one, she said the first thing that came to her.

'I don't think that's necessary. I don't need anyone.' 'Why?'

Prof became silent, his deep breaths vibrating through the room.

'I think there's value in the dark and the light would swallow it.'

'Ha! Sir, what does that one mean again?'

'Prison makes you a philosopher who sees the difference between light and dark. It brings out the sage in you,' he laughed as he said this. 'Then when you're out and alone, you become even more sagacious.'

She squeezed her face, wanting him to fill the space inside her. 'What does darkness do for you?'

'Like, does it help me wash the dishes or run errands?' he chuckled, but it sounded rather eerie to her.

'I mean, what does it do to you?'

'Well, I've come to realise that it is best to be in the dark. You could compare it to a vacuum, a space. It is like being in a place where heads are left to roam and mature into their own form, a place without external forces beating your choices into shape. You know, darkness can be the place where   one can understand existence better. Darkness... that state of assumption that brings continuity to our lives; we can hope in the dark. Don't seek to fill it—you know, the emptiness, the rest of our lives is necessary.

'Poets will disagree with you. I once had this friend, a poet. He was part of the movement then. He taught me these lines from a poem by a poet called Pablo Neruda. It is called, *There's No Forgetting*: "Why should day follow day/Why must the blackness of night time collect in our mouths?" You should read the full poem.'

'I don't know poetry, sir. But, your theory, sir, I must

disagree this once, doesn't work. Darkness is not home. And it is not gathering in my mouth. It is not home for anything. It is gathering in my—' she stopped and leaned against the chair, letting him interrupt her. His voice became a thunder in her ears, it drowned her as he spoke of how empty the world would be if there were no poets.

'You should only look around you to know that we exist for poems. Life is poetry. The dark is where you find light—this is what poetry does for us.'

Desire pressed her fingers against the arm of the chair and said to him, with a lilt to her voice that sounded like she giggled as she spoke, 'I thought you were an economist, an activist? Not a philosopher. Not a poet.'

'We lose ourselves to many things when life chances upon us, Desire. You should know that.'

She swayed, holding her head.

'And chancing on the fact that you have a son is not enough reason to want the lights on?'

'What has light got to do with the assumption that I have a child?' he said slowly and with a tone that Desire struggled to read.

Desire shook her head, closed her eyes and plotted how she would get the room lit up. *This madness must stop*, she thought to herself.

She got up from her chair and left.

* * *

'Your father never puts on the light.'

Desire snuck a glance at Ireti's face as they walked down the street. He was only half-listening. He smiled and waved to a man standing in front of the chemist where she had once bought condoms.

'I know I sound crazy and it is still really crazy to me. But do you know all the time I couldn't see you I was seeing your father at 9pm?'

Ireti stopped walking, he looked at her face, and smiled.

Then he tucked his hand into hers and said, 'Let's get a drink there.'

They walked to a shop with a roof that extended outside. On the plank holding the roof in place was written: *Comfort Eatin' Place.*

A boy who walked with a limp came up to him and asked them what they wanted. The smell of freshly made pepper soup floated about the place and Ireti ordered two plates without asking her if she wanted anything.

'Don't you want to know your father?'

Ireti looked up at her face and waited, like he was studying her features, before he said, 'No. I already met you. My sister. You know you're like my twin sister. I feel I can tell you anything.' He laughed.

'You are certainly not serious! You are friend-zoning me,' Desire said and sank into the chair again. Her heart became torn as she realised that the idea of her meeting with Prof sounded bizarre. 'It's true Ireti. I know your dad.'

Desire looked Ireti over. He seemed different, his hair bushier and uncombed.

'We need some space—for some weeks or months. I need time to think. I need space,' he said shaking his head.

Desire stood stiffly for a while, unsure of how to respond to him, and then she walked away swiftly. It was after many steps that she looked back. He was no longer there.

28

Prof's phone rang. He picked it up, 'Maami, yes... okay... I still have enough... tomorrow... it's fine... okay, okay, I'll call you. I need to go now.' As Desire's absence grew longer, he found himself calling and accepting his mother's calls more. He tried to call Kayo, too, after their last encounter, but his friend never picked up the phone. Loneliness was not something he had considered until of late. Solitude and loneliness inhabited the same space and he found how easily one could take the place of the other with a sudden shift in feeling. It had been a month since Desire last visited.

As the grandfather clock chimed 12 times, Prof realised that regardless of how much time had passed, it still felt like the first night without her company. His heart was singed as he thought of a future with her continued absence. He went to the door and stood there for almost three hours, with the hope that she would knock, with explanations of how she needed to stay home the previous night because she had been sick. Some faint sound reached his ears and Prof leaned against the door, straining to catch the footsteps he thought he heard. When he returned to the chair, he still waited for the sound of her knocking. He listened until he was certain he heard something. He leaned forward on the chair and then sank back, before getting up and walking slowly to the door. When the sound came again, but not the knocking he had hoped for, he interpreted it as a fear of being unable to knock. He had told her that he did not want her to come again, had he not? He leaned on the door and listened harder to what he assumed were descending footfalls. With sweaty palms and shaky knees he flung the door open to ask her to come in. Outside his doorstep was a tabby cat, with gleaming white eyes, scratching the wall. The animal moved its head to watch him for a while, let out a "meow" and disappeared down the stairs. Prof returned to his chair where he buried his head in his hands and sobbed.

A voice in his head urged, '*Eni, find her.*'

But before he could send messages to his limbs to move, another voice cajoled, '*And why would you want to do that? You're the one who likes it in the dark.*'

'*How would you have expected the girl to accept your darkness?*' the first voice added. '*To make matters worse, you asked her to go.*'

'*But she didn't complain. She never did.*'

'*She never did?*'

As the voices in his head conversed, Prof shook his head vigorously; a side of his head throbbed as he did this. He wrapped his arms around himself and closed his eyes. He wanted to cry but his eyelids ached.

'*Light!*' And with this prodding from the voice in his head, Prof stood up again and walked to the light switch with jittery hands. He leaned against the wall and built up the courage to push the button. His middle finger rested slack against the switch, and then it became rigid against the button. He waited till his whole hand rested against the light switch.

He pushed himself to put it on for an indefinite length of time before he slid to the floor shaking and jerking. He saw flashes of whips landing against his flesh.

'Can you hear your colleague in the other cell?' the soldier who accompanied the warder asked him. His laughter bounced about until it felt like it landed on him in the guise of a slap on his face. Blood rushed down from his nose, he wanted to plead for mercy.

'Water, water...' he said instead. The two men laughed. They dragged him up from the corner he had fixed himself into in the solitary cell, as if the wall would open up and he could go through it. The kicks came in; one, two, three... ten, he lost count. He held his pain between his teeth, except for the muffled grunts that escaped his lips when the kicks got him in the ribs. When they left the cell, he waited to count the five clicks of the torturers' heels as they walked away. This told him that his two torturers were now many cells away from him. There was silence, except for the sound of water dripping from the decking.

'No! No! No! Leave me, leave... Please, help.'

Prof pulled at his hair. He wanted his head off from his neck. He wanted to forget, so he concentrated on the pearls of water dribbling from the middle of his head to his face.

'I can't. I can't do it,' and when he felt he was becoming loud, he cried, but it sounded like chuckles, because he tried hard to suppress himself from a loud cry.

Then, from nowhere, in his head he heard, *'Ha! Put on the lights.'* It was like his mother's voice but it came with an authority he had never heard from her. He stopped his ears with his forefingers but the voices were coming from inside him and they became even louder and more confident. His breathing became laboured. He wept.

Desire, his mother and even Kayo, shouted, *'Light! Light! Light!'* He heard some other voices shouting in his head too.

The voice of the son Desire told him he had screamed *'Light!'* at him too, as if that would make up for all his indecisions, his failings, his pain.

He could not scream, so he slid down to his knees and cried in pauses, one sob at a time, until no sound came out of him. Desanya came to him once again, *'I can't stay any longer. Light! Light! Light!'*

He saw several mangled bodies laid upon themselves, soldiers flogging and kicking young boys and girls. He heard someone screaming for help, 'I don't want to die!' and he saw the rumpled body of Kayo's wife, his father's begging eyes— the images flickered through his mind and he held his head in his arms. It was just like in the early years of prison, when all that he remembered were the bad things. He recalled things that related to him and things that did not. He saw screaming as he held the *Concord Newspaper* showing the scorched body of the journalist, Dele Giwa. "They got him, they got him."

He was remembering all the bad things in his life, in the lives of those he knew, and he could not scream, but it felt as if every part of his body was shouting for help.

He stood up from his position on the ground with a sudden resolve, pressed his hand against the switch, but he still couldn't gather enough courage to push it down. He shook his head, he was beginning to feel woozy.

He thought of those days in prison; when the lights came on, he knew that only meant hot iron marks on his back, lashings, and sometimes punches that left his bones praying for a partial immobility. He thought of his father, who did not think he was worth being called a son. He thought of women he could have loved if he had tried, and he broke down on his knees. He cried thinking again of every time they beat him in prison because he shed no tears. For not standing in front of his father and his lawyer to tear up the papers for the house and bawl at how anyone could think he could be bought. He cried for Desire, for his mother. He cried to feel safe.

In the first week in prison he felt there was enough of the idea of salvation in him to save Nigerians. He carried this air of invincibility about him and a boldness from never having stayed more than three days in prison. He remained straight-backed when the head of state came to visit. He looked the Number One in the face and for a second time, spat in the president's face. The man simply asked for water to clean his face and said nothing more than, 'He hasn't learnt, has he?'

Prof hastily replied, 'No. I haven't learnt from your rubbish! Give my people what they deserve. I am the one who was made to change their lives.'

'Which people? The ones that have forgotten you? Do you know the price of *garri* in the market? Why would they think of you when you can't solve the rising price of rice?' The head of state laughed like a jackal and walked away. Two of his entourage of soldiers who were ready to act on the president's behalf were about to leap on him—one had in fact already planted a slap on his face—but the head of state shouted, 'No! No! Leave him. Be kind to his skin,' and he walked away without a backward glance.

For many weeks after that visit nothing happened, until one of the soldiers deployed to monitor him, alongside the prison warders, "caught" him reading a page from an old newspaper used for wrapping balls of *akara* that the warders had eaten. He had found the paper on the floor on one of those mornings when he was outside for the usual grass cutting duties with other prisoners sentenced to life imprisonment. He had scavenged reading material in the past and no one ever countered him for that. On this particular day, when his agony was to begin, the soldier caught him and made him realise he committed a "sin" for picking up an oil-soaked newspaper, oozing of the residue from a clod of *akara*, to read. The soldiers, drunk, it seemed, with the power the regime fed them, ran towards Prof from the spot behind where they had been observing him.

'You want us to lose our job?! *Provezor* Idiot! *Provezor* Enemy-of-progress! *Kai! Provezor* Stupid! Bloody civilian! Officer! Officer! Come. Come now and see what this bastard is reading. Paper! *Shege.* Sabotage inside prison. *Ode!* He is reading paper!' The soldier, the type that can be described as beer bottle shaped, rushed at him and kicked him in the groin with his boot. As Prof bent over in pain, clutching himself, the little boldness in him made him challenge them.

'What have I done?'

'Shut up, you! Bloody civilian! You think you have sense, *ko*?'

At first, he felt he could talk his way through and had in fact, begun throwing invectives at the soldier.

'Mr. Man? Be careful what you do to me. I was just...'

He didn't finish the sentence because a round object landed on his jaw, sending two teeth flying from his mouth. His moue dissolved from a cackle into a pang of feverish tears. Between his cries, he noticed that standing next to the beer bottle soldier was a rockier soldier whose face had scars of all sorts. He didn't do much talking but hit Prof continuously with the butt of his gun, like he was pounding seeds. It was an understanding of being sprawled on the floor, with two soldiers over him, and the warders watching the "cinema", and laughing, that made him change his arrogance to loud pleas of 'I beg you, sir! In the name of God, the Creator of heaven and earth. Forgive me. Forgive my insolence. Never again.'

It was too late. The men's displeasure had risen to their eyes and their anger was now flowing through their nerves, with their necks tightly stretched. They dragged him from his single cell, where he had books to write in, and placed him in a cell of ten people. He was chained together with the other men, so that at night when one of them wanted to turn, he would tap the man next to him and that man tapped the next... and when they were all fully alert to reposition themselves, an adjustment could be made. On those nights, he rarely slept. Two days later, before he was again taken away from the cell, a boy, who was already showing signs of dementia, died. They only took his body away four days later. Prof was later taken to another cell, where a sympathetic warder told him that the soldiers harboured a peaked hatred towards him for his insolence to their boss.

The next confinement that the beer bottle soldier took him to one morning, was a six-foot square room with no windows. In the evening, he came and removed the bulb in the cell, leaving him in the dark. That day, alone, he cried himself to sleep. He felt some peace.

And when the soldiers came in the next day, they replaced the bulb and the cell was lit. The two soldiers walked into his cell with different objects—wire, an iron bucket, a boiling ring, and an amber-coloured gas lamp, or sometimes, a fluorescent lamp, and other things he couldn't identify. What pained him the most was that he could never remember the way the soldiers looked, other than their shapes. Their faces remained unknown. Each time the lights in his cell came on, his pulse raced in readiness for the horror that was about to begin. On most days, the soldiers first put him in a stress position, where they forced him to kneel down, shackled his hands to the ground and made him lean back with a slant, for a day and a half. Sometimes, they told him to squat on the ground, making sure he stood on the balls of his feet, with his hands behind his back. If he lost his balance, he got a big slap to the back of his head. The torture methods always differed.

'I am happy today, okay?' the soldier in charge of him for the day would say. Most times, they came reeking of *burukutu*, so the alcohol always ran into their words and their actions to correct him seemed doubled. Once, they used a hot pressing-iron on him. On the days when they weren't too high, some sense of humanity crept into them as they would at least flog him without first pricking his skin with needles. Still, whenever those lights came on, his heart beat hard against his chest, like it was about to jump out. The sweat ran down his body, reaching into the corners of his groin. It was in those days that he swore against lights.

29

She was sleeping. She found herself again in a chair in his room, only this time with the added sensation that accompanied the meeting of her skin and that of Prof's. In her dream, life began to have a pattern and she became comfortable with using the first-person pronoun for him in Yoruba. The awe with which she held him, career and age wise, dissolved into moments of passionate kisses and arresting stares, which had them giggling like teenagers later on. Soon, she became more confident and she started to call him by his first name, Eni. She stopped feeling a small lump in her throat when she did; but because she still respected his past and their considerable age difference, she whispered Eni, with a fondness that unfurled an ache in her voice each time she did. Sometimes, she would whisper, 'Prof,' to herself, caring less about those around her. She woke up.

Her first urge was to see Ireti. It came strongly at her, like never before, and she stood up from the bed and went to the bus stop to go in search of him that afternoon. She knew he would not be in school because of the ongoing university lecturers' strike so she went to his house. The house was different when she got there. The co-tenants looked through her and this amplified her being a stranger in their space. She knocked on his door, remarking that the campaign poster which she had noticed on her first visit was half-torn, and elbowing it out of its former position was another poster for a concert featuring the Plantashun Boiz. She pushed the door slightly and it swung open. His friends were in the room, gathered over a bowl of rice, shirtless and laughing, until she opened the door. They were the same boys who had spied on her, laughed with—and at—her on her first visit, and now as she peered into the room, they all looked away like they had never met her.

She asked questions like someone who was trying to find the directions to a toilet in a crowded hall while trying to hide how pressed they were. They didn't even wear a smirk, they looked at her with straight faces and answered her in monosyllables until she realised there was no way for her to get anything from them, except what they wanted to let her know: he had moved from the house. She had gone to the student union office on campus a few times but he was either not around or always too busy to see her. Ireti who appeared to be present everywhere all the time, was suddenly nowhere to be found, and she could not understand why.

'Please tell him I came.'

'Okay, we will. Shut the door on your way out, to keep our sanity.'

She felt a weakness in her legs and even though she knew he might not have meant it in the literal sense, she felt he had communicated to her what she feared, that he suspected she had some connection to Prof.

When Desire got home, she rolled back and forth and sideways on her bed. She thought of Ireti and considered going to tell Prof that he had disappeared and he no longer needed to worry about paternity, but this would mean returning to him. She thought of how she had sat on his stairway and wept. She waited and hoped he would fling the door open, running and shouting into the streets, 'Desire! Desire! Wait, wait, I am sorry!' She inhaled a gulp of air knowing how fickle imagination could be.

When she left him, she had wanted so much to believe that she had misread his intent and she was being taught a valid lesson on resilience. And then when she got home, she prayed he would come to her flat the next day to find her and apologise. Her hope evaporated when she remembered that she had never told him which block she lived in.

How could she explain her return? 'I have come because I

want to give you my address, you know, in case—' She wiped her face with her hands and shook her head. It was one thing that would not come to pass. She wondered if he would pull her close and draw a line on her skin with his finger, as they sat together in the room. She pictured herself saying to him on one such occasion, 'What would people think?'

'Which people would think of us—the ones that know or the ones that don't?'

'What about Ireti?' she asked.

'What about him?'

Desire pictured herself laughing like she had not done in a long time, throwing herself into the air, leaving her weight to fall into his arms as he spoke.

The world built in her imagination, however, collapsed as a mosquito hummed in her ear. She tried to catch the insect, slapping the air.

She saw herself on Prof's stairs once again. She thought of it as the place where her dreams became even more vivid. Desire wanted to run through the door and down to his door, banging on it until he came out to see her. She wanted him to open the door and then she would fall into his arms begging for help from the dark room of torture; all she needed was access to his home. She considered asking him, 'Aren't you satisfied with being in darkness now? What is the point of a light that does not shine?' She wanted him to say he was sorry, and she would fall on his chest, and they would cry together. But more than anything, she felt she needed to run away to a place where she would not be reminded of him, or even Ireti, or anything in her life. How easy would it be to forget, was there really something called forgetting? Somewhere she did not feel like she knew the both of them—and did not care either.

30

Desire slept and woke up in the wee hours of Sunday to the frenzied screams of 'Alleluya' and dissenting voices following the shout with a gospel song. Church service at one of her neighbours' started in the middle of the night, unlike other churches. He once told her he believed in the teachings of the Seventh-day Adventists, that church day is Saturday, but also felt some validity to his being raised a Sunday church boy, so he decided to hold masses in between—and these fell in the middle of the nights.

Papa, as he was popularly known in the estate, had turned his flat into a church where he held a vigil every night. Anyone who complained of noise was cursed and accused of being a demon and an agent of darkness sent to destroy the good work of the Lord. Other than the church noise, he was a good guy who remembered to sweep beyond his vicinity and would go downstairs to clear the open drain weekly without being asked. Sometimes, he offered to pay electricity bills for those who could not immediately afford to. These were some of the reasons people forgave him and took his point that all he did was cast out generational curses from his family, and they were invited to remove theirs too. His Christian ministry was to fight demons. They were so used to it that whenever there wasn't a service, one could hear people asking him the next morning, 'Pastor, is everything okay?'

She felt like going to his room to see the curses walk away from the prayerful people. Perhaps he could reveal whether there was some supernatural curse hindering her.

'Die! Die! Die! Fall down and dieeeeee!' Then a bumble of humming would start and a song ascended to ignite the fire that Papa called to consume the curses on his generation and those of the inhabitants.

'Fireeee connn-ssssume them. You, curse of stagnancy!' he shouted and his family and other congregants responded, 'Dieeee! Die. Die. Fall down and dieeeeee.'

As the noise persisted, Desire continued to turn on her bed until her sides ached. She remained supine, counting her fingers until she became tired. She turned towards Remilekun who looked doped in sleep. After a futile attempt at trying to sleep, she left her thoughts to circle around Prof. She desperately wished to think of something else. She tried to think of how the ongoing strike would keep her years longer in school. She thought of her late mother, of Remilekun's sisterliness, of Babangida, and her mind just assumed a blur, like one getting out of a hangover. Her throat burned. She jumped from her bed and walked towards the cupboard where the utensils were stored. A jar filled with water was on it.

'You okay?' Remilekun asked with a yawn.

'Yep,' she whispered before she poured some water into a cup and gulped it down in one breath.

She had not expected Remilekun to be awake, since she always slept through Pastor's noise and whenever Desire mentioned how it kept her awake, her roommate joked that she was still weak from going to Prof's house for *the thing*.

And then Desire would ask, 'What thing?'

'The thing you always go and collect at 9pm,' Remilekun replied.

Desire felt Remilekun regarding her for some time, but when she turned to tell her to go back to sleep, she was already in a deep slumber. Unlike Remilekun, who slept so easily and wouldn't stir in any noise, Desire always found it difficult to sleep. As she lay on the bed, she placed her hand on her navel and stroked the umbilical tip. There was no place to hurry to that morning.

'You're thinking of that Prof man, right?' Remilekun said in a sleep-laced voice, surprising her.

'I thought you were asleep?' Desire took a deep breath and

returned to answer her question. 'Not exactly,' she started to say and then she changed her mind to confide, 'If I had not condoned visiting him in the darkness, would anything have changed?'

'Are you trying to say, would you guys have fucked?'

'Can you try to think straight for once? Life between a man and a woman is not all about physical attraction,' she said.

'Hear yourself,' Remilekun said and then took a turn to mimic her, animating her words in a funny voice, 'A search for the soul! What is that?'

'I needed to contact my past.'

'Ha! Why are you talking like this? Contact your past? So, because it is the past, it is best seen in the dark?'

'No, it is in lit souls.'

Remilekun became silent and then she screeched, '*Egbami ke!* God, someone help me make sense of this girl's madness! I should have known-o! You were normal before you started seeing this prison madman-o. Or I thought you were. This guy has turned your head upside down. See what nonsense you're saying. Soul! Light! Dark? Past? What is all this nonsense talk?'

Remilekun jumped down from her bed and paced about the room.

'I am now truly concerned.'

Desire noticed her voice shook as she spoke.

'I am fine. I really am,' Desire said, with her gaze on the ceiling, noticing a cobweb on the farthest corner, the insect trapped in it not struggling. She counted her fingers. Her mother used to tell her to do that when she couldn't sleep at night, back then in Maroko. And then, she leapt up from the bed as she thought of how much she wanted to talk to him, but on her own terms. She walked towards the door and clicked the lock.

'Madam, where to?' Remilekun's voice stopped her.

'I-I-I, I just want to take a walk.'

'A walk?' Remilekun jumped down from her bed and walked

towards the door. She flicked the switch on; power was back. 'Can you see what the time says?' Remilekun pointed to the wall clock. 'Well, if you don't know how to read the clock any more, here is what it says, 3.45am.' Remilekun stopped talking and they locked eyes. Desire bowed her head and placed her hands over her mouth. 'Now, I am convinced you are not okay. I am so convinced. I don't know what is happening to you-o. I don't know,' Remilekun's voice still shook as she spoke to her.

'My head is full. I need to take a stroll. Now.' Desire leaned against the wall and avoided looking at Remilekun.

'You need to go to your bed and sleep. Now! You want to go to nutty-professor's house, huh? For the sake of your dead mother, please, Desire, leave that man alone. He is mad. Everybody knows it, why don't you accept it? You have been acting strange—too strange,' Remilekun leaned against the door and exclaimed in successive spurts, 'Oh! Why did I even mention that he moved into our area? What is it about him, anyway? Are you people... is there something you are not telling me? Is it a cult thing?' Then she decided against what she intended to say, and sighed, 'Don't do what you will regret. I am afraid. That man is mad, and there's something else about him. I know—or why else are you acting this way?' She paused to swallow before continuing, 'You are sane. Remain so,' Remilekun's voice was softer this time as she spoke. For the first time, it dawned on Desire that she was losing control of herself. She closed her eyes, placed her back against the door and slipped to the ground shaking, and Remilekun covered her with her pestle-like arms, stroking her hair. In Remilekun's embrace, they cried together.

'Could this be love or what do we call this?' Desire looked up at Remilekun, who said nothing, but kneaded her shoulders like an experienced masseuse, until she felt the emotions in her dissipate.

Desire woke up sprawled on the floor. Her arm was wet

where it met the linoleum carpet which now stuck to her skin like a sticker losing its gum. Her left leg leaned against the door weakly, and the other leg was apart, seeking company on a pile of dirty clothes. She blinked to acquaint her eyes to the lights. Remilekun had not turned the lights off. She could not remember falling asleep or falling in front of a door to the floor. A left turn and she remembered her roommate had slept beside her, but was no longer there—she was nestled back in the bed. She stood up and walked towards the switch to turn it off, and the thought slipped into her mind, *Why do most people put off the lights to sleep, although many fear the dark?*

For a better sleep, of course!

How can you hope for a better sleep in your fear? People don't like the dark. She slept in the dark, because, well, that was what you did—eyes shut to welcome the dark should be enveloped in the dark. She had not found a reason to question her answers until now. Leaving the lights on, she returned to her bed and tried to sleep. She again considered getting up to go looking for Prof.

'Why didn't you turn off the lights?' Remilekun's brash voice broke into her thoughts.

'I thought you were asleep. You left me on the floor. So nice of you.'

'These days I'm scared roomie is going crazy.' Desire pretended not to hear.

Remilekun sighed, 'Put off the light. It is still sleeping hours. And babe, don't do anything crazy, like sleepwalking out of this room in search of crazy Prof, okay? I can't round up a search party.' Then she added, 'I will call my mummy-o, this is getting scary.'

Before Desire could respond, Remilekun turned her back to her, and either feigned sleep or indeed fell asleep.

'There are so many things you don't understand,' Desire said, still, mindless that her roommate was no longer listening.

She lifted the bedspread so that it could cover her body properly.

Papa's prayer session was over at this time. The building had resumed its mournful silence, until the call to prayer from a mosque close by splattered the quiet of the early morning, and slowly, the distant drone of traffic on the road rose to significance. The thought of Prof, thinking of her as she was of him, floated across her mind. She could not get her mind off his acute quietness whenever she moved towards the door to leave for home. It was as if something needed to be said, and a stillness reigned asking that they both hold a one-minute silence for the death of important discussions. Desire sat up on the bed and watched Remilekun. She watched as her body danced to the rhythm of the hum of her breathing.

When you cannot forget, is that what it means to be madc crazy—over the top? As she tried to understand herself, she lay on the bed writhing, like one with sores all over her body. She missed going to see him. She wanted to *not* go and see him. She thought of Ireti too, and how she had imagined walking with him to Prof's doorstep, saying something like, 'Here's Ireti.' Or just, 'Your son,' and then sizing each other up, learning the other in silence.

31

Prof was on the sofa when he heard a rap on the door. He stood up from the chair and walked out, looking down for a moment from the top of the staircase. There was no one there but him. He folded his hands into a crisscross over his shoulders and leaned on the banister. He wanted Desire to be there. He wanted her to be on the last railing where she could stand and look up at the landing with his face telling how much he yearned for her. She would let out a sigh, with her head lopsided and her countenance turning into something like ice about to melt, when she saw how dejected he looked. At a time, he felt she would never come, but she did. On remembering the pain she put him through in the last few days, he turned and watched her walk up the stairs with shaky legs, gripping the banister for support until she stood in front of him.

Prof went straight ahead and said, 'You.'

'You,' she replied. And they both started laughing. He turned and moved towards the door.

When he got to the door, he walked into the room ahead of her.

'There is light in the room. Please. Come in.' This was his first real invitation to her. 'There will always be light. Light, no more darkness...'

She put the tip of her index finger on his lips. 'Shhh...'

For a while, he stood patiently, as she took in the room. He watched as her eyes moved from the bookshelf with so many thick, hardback books, which faced the door directly, to the TV stand which had no television on it. A small Phillips transistor radio was plugged into a socket close to the stand. It stood on a small table a few metres from the shelf. The colour of his Persian rug was a mix of black and red. The grandfather clock stood some metres away. Their eyes met the object at the same time, and they both smiled at the memory it bore.

Prof watched her walk into the room, dazed. When she caught him staring, she looked away and he turned away briefly, but returned to steal glances at her skin and try to figure out the colour, because it glimmered in the electric light. He held her hand and they walked around the lit room, wordless.

He stretched his right hand forward and clasped his hands into a lock like he was wrapping his arms around her, but he held nothing. He opened his eyes. He was alone. She was not there with him. The door was ajar. 'Even in my dreams, she torments me,' he snivelled.

Prof walked to the door and looked out into the surroundings which were covered by the darkness of a moonlit night without electric power, hopeful that she might still be around, somewhere. Then, just for a moment, he thought he saw a shadow on the last step. He didn't have the courage to follow it, as he feared it was his imagination again. He closed the door after him as he walked into the house.

Although the power was off, he went to switch off the lights, and trembled, craving the small space between life and death. He whimpered, 'Desire.'

There was something he noticed about himself, which could have always been there, but which he only became aware of since she had stopped coming. He realised that his palms became wet quickly and he was now always wiping them against the sofa or against his trousers before standing up again to face his set challenge.

Standing before the switch, his hands shook. He looked at the knob of the switch extending out like a stub. Prof placed his hands at the back of his head and locked his fingers. His skin rose. He felt his strength return and he again placed a hand on the switch, letting his mind concentrate on the will to push the button. But each time the thought of the cane on his skin came to his mind, he trembled and even as he thought of how much he wanted the lights on, his mind continued to wander to his days in Maiduguri Prison.

'It's your heart beating not soldiers coming. Press down the switch,' a voice in his head said. As the moment of indecision followed, he felt as if Desire was standing close to him, as he repeated her words in his head; 'I don't like staying in this darkness,' and he remembered how the noticeable lack of lustre that accompanied those words highlighted a disappointment he never noted before then, in her voice. He looked towards the window blind which he had tied in a bunch, and then at the grey which made it difficult to stretch his vision beyond the dim light of the stars outside. At that moment, he foresaw the long nights he would spend alone. He walked outside and knocked on the door, trying out a deliberate bang, like he felt Desire would make in her desperation to get back into the room. With each bang, his hands grew weaker and he rested his head against the wall, sobbing loudly.

His shoulders landed in a droop and his knock-knee bent slightly to carry the bulge of his stomach.

He winced and closed his eyes tight, determined to light up the room. He placed his two hands on the switch, and with all the emotional strength he had, he pushed it down but the lights did not come on. Prof stared up at the switch and at the place where he supposed the bulb should be. His heart raced and he became so unsure of what could have happened that he sank slowly down, sliding with his back against the wall again to weep. Something was happening, he moved stealthily towards the door.

Kpa!

An amber brightness settled upon the room. Prof sprang up from his squatted posture as flushes of light penetrated his eyes and he blinked several times. He began to twitch uncontrollably as he adjusted his eyes to the light. He opened and closed his eyes to create a balance and make out a difference between light and dark. He became still, expecting something to happen to him. He waited.

Prof stared at the walls. After several minutes, of standing and waiting, a cry that had stood in his throat crawled to his lips and he wailed aloud. His hand returned to the switch and he flicked it on and off with his index finger, and then off, and on again. He stood with his back against the wall and slid down again, until he crouched on the floor with his eyes fixed on the bulb. He moved away from the wall and walked towards the light. He moved closer to the bulb and stared at it lengthily.

'Desire,' he whispered.

Her seat was empty and a depression on the sofa announced even more boldly her last visit. He wondered what Desire would do now that the lights were on. He could feel a slow pain rising in the lower region of his neck, he felt drained and when he looked around as the light cascaded into the once dark room, he felt like someone who suddenly realised his superpowers; perhaps now, he could stop remembering.

He also felt that now that the lights were on, she would be there, but after a long wait and not hearing her breathing, he walked to the switch and turned the lights off, and then on again and then, finally, off.

'Desire,' he whispered again and found himself sobbing.

He stared at the colour of the wall which he had once used as his defence, picked up his T-shirt, swung it over his shoulder and rushed out of the room, opening the door with such force that it banged against the wall.

As he stood on the stairhead looking around him, he realised that he didn't know where Desire's house was or anything more than the things they had discussed in his room. All he knew was that she was a neighbour from one of the buildings in the neighbourhood. He racked his brain to remember her last name, or something she might have said that could help him locate her. He turned towards the door and decided to go back into the house and wait till the next day.

A stream of sunlight fell on his face and the amber light from the bulb was buried in its brightness. He watched the electric bulb again and thought of what to tell Desire when he saw her.

The more he thought of what to say, the more he felt sweat all over, and this made it difficult to think, so that all he could murmur was the name, 'Desire.'

For the first time since he was released from prison, he longed to go out and rise with the sun, but he continued to lie down, thinking of the way she said goodbye. Finally, he stood up from the sofa and walked into the bathroom, murmuring, 'See you tomorrow.'

In the bathroom, he stood by the sink, ran the tap and splashed cold water on his face and then hurried out, because a sudden urge gripped him from within and he became desperate to get out of the house before it was too late. He ran into the bedroom to dress. He settled for a tie and a shirt that smelt of mildew, placing his hand flat on the cloth to smoothen it. The wrinkles remained, and the lines stuck out like disentangled, fine fibres attached to cloth, but he felt pleased with his attempt.

It was when he stepped out of the bedroom that he realised that he didn't even know where he should start looking for her. They never talked about her family, her house or who she really was. The only thing he knew was that she was a student of the Lagos State University. All the same, he walked absentmindedly towards the door, where he remained for a while with his eyes closed, savouring, since his return from prison, the true sense of being free. He walked down the stairs, humming a sound that made no sense. With each step, as the grey covering of early morn slipped away, he feared someone might recognise him as Professor Eniolorunda, the activist.

The main road had many potholes. It was the same road he had walked shrouded in cloth, but in the light of day, it was different. The puddle of brown water which sat in the hole stank like a bowl of rotten beans. He stood in the middle of the road and looked around the same row of the Lego-like blocks of flats, many of which wore faded paint.

Prof turned in shock to watch a man who walked hurriedly past him after they nearly bumped into each other. The man had a faded, black police beret on but was dressed in a long sleeved blue shirt, folded at the elbows. He didn't look back. He didn't really care what time it could be. He just felt safe, knowing that she was somewhere close and he would find her. He walked until the dawn slipped between the cracks of silver lining the skies.

He walked towards the bus stop carrying his legs like he was following orders in a military drill. He walked in slow steps and with his mind wandering in and out, he did not realise when he reached the bus stop where everyone seemed in a hurry. It was not the hurry of trying to make it to an appointment. It was a rush that seemed injected into the lives of the people. Prof looked around him at the women, men, teenagers, even children—some being dragged along, smiling, but in an irritable sort of way, and they turned aggressive each time he tried to be friendly or introduce himself to them. They all struggled against the sun, which seemed intent on draining them of their strength.

He looked around with the hope that Desire would shout from among the people on the street and call his name. Twice, he looked around abruptly when someone shouted, but it was just a woman shouting down an *okada* rider, who sped off on his motorcycle. There was also a girl calling on her sister to wait for her. Prof moved past the people rushing to and from the bus stop, unaware of how he slithered through them so that he could escape their strained necks, as their struggle to get onto the buses made him feel different.

The people on the road, running off to their different commitments, reminded him of his days as a university professor. He remembered how he left for campus at 5am or 5.30am to meet other comrades with whom he put up revolutionary posters on the campus before it was peopled. The security men never told on him.

'Prof! Our correct *padi-man*,' they singled him out and saluted him among other lecturers, with much verve and animated familiarity. Two of the security men visited him in prison in the early days. None of his "comrade" lecturers did.

From the letters he got, they explained that they were equally hunted and it was important that they stayed away. Since his release, still, none had visited.

'Most of your comrades ask after you. But, you know this darkness,' Kayo had said, during one of his early attempts to renew their friendship upon his return from prison. 'All of them are now minister of this or that. The president offered them a chance to rebuild the country with him.'

Prof smacked his lips as his thoughts turned to his youthful days. Those days spent chanting revolutionary songs in front of government houses. He could see all of his comrades again, standing behind him as he rendered his speech with a stuttering anger.

He shook his head and whistled, then tucked his hand into his trousers as he regained awareness that he was on the street, walking among people he wanted to be away from. His fear of being recognised returned, but though the number of people at the bus stop increased, they stood apart from him and he felt that they eyed him nonetheless. It felt like no one recognised him, or if they did, they were being rather polite about it.

Prof watched as new faces came to the bus stop and the way their spaces were then replaced made him think of himself. If, with those sufferings, he had died in prison, would society just have filled his space?

The dry harmattan air blew gently against his ears and he drew his shirt closer. Desire, again, crossed his mind; a small stirring tingled slightly between his loins. After a while, he decided that it was simply how Desire concerned herself with him and his well-being that kept him confounded. He couldn't be in love with her. Love was too expensive a gift of the heart. It was the love for their country that bonded them.

A car honked behind him, he moved away from the bus stop sign and crossed over to the other side of the road where traffic was building. The two police officers directing the traffic did not appear too pleased with it. They remained at their post chatting idly. Soon, vehicles were locked bumper to bumper, and many *okada* riders had to turn off the engines of their motorcycles. Even pedestrians struggled to walk in the jam, as they tried to negotiate the potholes in the road.

Somewhere in this gridlock, a man in a rickety Peugeot 504, with a moustache set like Charlie Chaplin's, shook his index finger in warning at an *okada* man trying to ride his motorcycle through a small space between his car and a brand new Toyota Avensis, whose driver looked straight ahead like he wore a neck brace.

'Fool! Don't you see there's no space there?' Chaplin spat at the *okada* man.

'Sharrap! Person with correct car no complain. Na you with old *tuke-tuke* car dey talk, talk!' The *okada* man attacked; intent on passing between the cars.

Chaplin yelled, 'Man! If you scratch my car, I will bless you with slaps this afternoon.'

'Sharrap you...' the *okada* man barely completed his sentence, before losing hold of his motorcycle, which hit the bumper of Chaplin's car. He hurriedly rose from the ground, balanced his motorcycle, and inspected Chaplin's car for any damage.

He sighed, and turned to Chaplin, 'No dent, only small scratch.' If Chaplin heard him, he said nothing. He simply climbed out of his car, walked to the bumper and ran his two hands over it. He noticed a negligible scratch, yet he felt the need to punish the *okada* man for his rudeness.

He removed his chequered shirt, laying it on the driver's seat of his car, leaving a sweat-drenched, once-white vest covering his chest, then he charged at the *okada* man, grabbed him by the collar and screamed at him, 'Do you want to die? Yes or no?'

Prof thought of going to the man to plead on the *okada* man's behalf, but seeing how he did not budge when other passers-by went to him, he remained at the bus stop and watched.

Chaplin held the *okada* man tighter. And before anyone could say, 'Free traffic,' he had landed a hard slap that left the imprint of his fingers on the *okada* man's left cheek. It took about ten seconds before the *okada* man regained slight composure, 'You slap me! For what? Ha! Is it because I have motorcycle and you have motorcar?'

He wiped the side of his face like he needed to check if Chaplin's slap had left a stain. He was five inches shorter than Chaplin, and in a fair fight, he would be the casualty, and as if in realisation of his disadvantage, he shouted, 'I go show you today!' He rushed to his motorcycle, opened a plastic box tied to the back, rummaged hurriedly through it, and in a flash, swung something at Chaplin. Chaplin ducked and stepped back to see what it was.

'Rat?!' Chaplin screamed in shock.

'Yes. Rat,' the *okada* man said, chasing after Chaplin with the poor animal squeaking and squirming in his hands, 'I will show you that as I can conquer rat, that same way I will conquer you.'

'Rat! Help-o! Rat! Help-o!' Chaplin shouted as he struggled to climb up to the roof of his car, trembling. The idea that anyone could go travel around with rats carried the message that it was something sinister. Chaplin, evidently, didn't want to see the outcome of this *juju*, or what it could do to him.

Everything became chaotic in a matter of minutes. The road was now a flight of tightly packed cars and pedestrians moving in and out of the jam as they walked to their destinations. The other side of the road, which appeared free earlier, was now as jammed. The run became more intense, he heard a driver who was not aware of what went on earlier yell, 'Ha! *Ole ni o*, ha! *Awon ole*. It must be armed robbers-o. They must be shooting like mad in front. That is what caused the traffic.'

From the position in which Prof stood, he watched as the driver's assumption passed as message by word of mouth and in very few minutes, the gridlock that had kept vehicles in a three-hour jam suddenly dissolved, leaving Chaplin on the roof of his car, in the middle of the road, screaming for help from the hysterical *okada* man who was swinging the rat he held by the tail at his face.

It was a sad walk home. He unlocked the door with more

anger in him than he ever thought he could still have. There was confusion as he realised he didn't know anything about Desire, other than that she visited him at 9pm every day. He took a seat, and slowly, all the pains of the past years, which didn't even come out in clear pictures, made his eyes damp and he began to cry.

His anger was not a violent anger. Instead, there was a little distortion which brought on a smile. It was submissive and patient. She once told him that the most popular saying in the country was, 'Times are hard,' that the sentence may soon become a greeting shared on the streets. It would become the chief compliment thrown around if things went on like this. He watched out for signs of this as he walked the streets—she had prepared him ahead of time.

She laughed whenever he said she should stand up for the rights of the people, because he was no longer relevant. He listened to the cackle of her voice breaking into a shimmer. It came with a rhythm and he watched her with the absorption of a nature lover appreciating the sunset. From her visits, Prof knew she was one of those people who couldn't laugh in small bits. She laughed in a rush; and when she laughed, she swayed and shook the seat she sat on. He recalled how her voice rose from chuckles to giggling, to open-mouthed smothered screams of delight. He loved her naivety. There was an openness to her questions. It was that of someone who had read of practical lessons in theory textbooks. It was soaked in a native intelligence of having acquired knowledge by listening, perseverance and consistency.

He imagined himself stroking Desire's face, and defining the contours, one of those times she visited, just to show that he felt her anger, and telling her everything would be fine. Then it struck him that he had never seen Desire's face, in the light, in its full form, unaided by his imagination. The darkness buried her complexion, the shape of her face, the form of her body. He opened his eyes and stared at the white ceiling cluttered with peeling plaster.

32

Desire rolled over as she lay on the sofa, dreaming of lights flushing her face. She blinked several times. It took several minutes to fully awaken. Her eyelids were weighed down and her head groggy. She had been in a room that was not his or hers. She sat on a chair looking around. The room was lit with a fluorescent lamp which flickered frequently. It was lightning after the thunder. Prof walked in from somewhere, Ireti was with him. Prof sat on a chair beside her, while Ireti, looking quiet, stood behind him. The lights went out. The armchairs they sat on became as cold as ice. She fumbled between her reality and her imagination, as the abnormal temperature of the chair increased by the second. She moved to the edge of the seat in fear and nearly fell off, because the chair rose slowly into the air. She jumped down from the floating chair and bumped into him. He remained silent; a smirk on his face. She wanted to know what was amiss.

'What's happening? Prof?'

He said nothing to her, only stroking her left cheek with deep breaths escaping his lips at intervals. There was a feeling like nothing she had ever felt.

Desire hurried towards the switch only to find Ireti's hands on it. He blocked her from flipping the knob and stared at her with such cold eyes she shuddered. She was shocked that he got there before she did and then...

* * *

Remilekun lay on the bed with her left hand supporting her head as a pillow. Desire watched her as she stirred, only to search drowsily for her pillow which had fallen from the bed.

When she did not find it, she placed both her hands under her head and carried on sleeping. After staring at her friend for as long as her attention could hold, Desire turned her own pillow from the side dribble had spewed on and changed her position until she lay on her side facing her friend's bed. She removed the pillow from under her head and placed it on her chest, and then tightened her arm around it. She observed how sunlight trooped into the room through the window and again she let herself be distracted with the way it swallowed the light of the electric bulb. She wondered why she had never visited Prof in the daytime and tried to fold up the curtains at those times he went to the toilet.

She wanted so much to forget him; the way a young tree forgets a leaf when it falls, but the leaf never forgets the tree, it rots so that it can become nutrient—and strengthens the tree. There really is no forgetting.

She remained on her bed for a while, struggling to silence the thoughts of Prof. The sun rolled down towards their window and shone into the room. She sat up on the bed, folded her legs into a triangle, feet on her thighs, and picked at her toes. The heaviness of her fears made her restless, so she stood up and picked up a broom from under the bed. She began dusting, sweeping and cleaning, recalling as many of the things she wanted to do but could not. Remilekun woke and turned towards her, mouthing, 'Haan ha! Pull down the curtains, the light is blinding!'

Desire rested her back against the wall, but sat up on the bed, glad that she had pushed off the temptation to go and see Prof. She could not tell how the day passed as thoughts of him taunted her along with the burden of carrying Ireti's fears. She got up again and found herself drifting through the housework and then leaning against the window, watching the streets. She assumed she was doing the same thing he was doing; each watching for the other's visit.

Remilekun stood up from the bed and tied the curtain into a bunch, and in the process she bumped a book off the window sill. She flipped through it and laughed, 'So you have started writing poetry?'

'Just some thoughts. Nothing serious,' Desire replied, stretching her hand so Remilekun could give her the book. She flipped the pages as she tried to follow the trail of Remilekun's talks of cars, bag and shoe labels, best travel places.

'I also wrote poetry when my guy almost left me. Poetry like: "If you leave me, I will die," and "Your pupils are my sunrise."'

Desire shook her head and eyed Remilekun, who soon changed the conversation to how she wanted to get some money from her mother and her boyfriend for a bag that she saw in a boutique.

'Isn't it too early for fashion gist? You know I don't give a damn?'

'You know I give a damn. Not having an opinion to give does not mean not getting an opinion from someone. My friend, bring your body down, *joor*!'

At that point, Remilekun's talk was like a cloud that wouldn't arrange into neat layers in her head. And though she was not really thinking of anything else, she discovered she had stopped listening.

'Desire!' She heard the shout and came to consciousness. '*Haba*! What are you thinking? I called you, like, three times.'

'I was deep in thought...'

'Thinking of that crazy Prof, *abi*? After all I am doing to take your mind away from it.'

Desire spent a moment before she said, 'Yes,' although she was not in that moment.

'I think I need to find one fine boy to handle you properly. See, when sex only happens in your imagination, most of the time, you can only misbehave. You want to serve that Prof. I can feel it. What happened to your Ireti boy?'

'Nothing. We just minding our own corners of the world now.'

'Just like that?'

'Yes! Just like that.'

'You and that boy had potentials to take things far-o, at least that is my thought.'

'Friendships evolve. Friendships dissolve.'

'Into what? Madam philosopher—how does someone just disappear from your life. I don't understand.'

'Remilekun, please. I don't want to talk about it.'

'Okay. No vex. At least you can answer this one: who is *yanshing* you now?'

'Re-mi. Pleaseee!'

'Why don't you ever want to talk about sex?' The room was silent again, the only sound was that of their laboured breathing against the stifling heat. They were there for some minutes and Desire even dozed off, until she heard Remilekun's voice sounding through as if it was from the end of a tunnel.

'You're sweating like a goat about to be slaughtered. Come and lie with me on the ground. I will fan you.'

Desire climbed down from her bed sleepily and pulled the T-shirt she was wearing over her buttocks. She lay with Remilekun on the mattress spread on the ground. She remained quiet. They were opening the curtains a few minutes ago, she'd been listening to the crescendo of daytime and Pastor hold his services in the middle of the night. Every noise that was made was made outside their room.

It was Remilekun springing to her feet from the mattress, while also marching around the room with her feet thudding against the ground that made her stir.

'Is that mosquito?' her voice sounded like someone else's.

'No,' Desire shook her head and jeered, 'That is a crab. A crab that gives malaria. Buzzzzz.'

'Is that meant to amuse me? Not funny! Are you okay?'

'I should be the one asking you that question. You have been behaving like... what I don't even know.'

'Babe, what is wrong with you? Has that Prof transferred his mental illness to you?'

'Daytime feels like night,' Desire turned onto her side and

placed her hand under her head.

'Night-not! Turn here and look at me. See, I can't live in the same room with a mad woman-o. What is wrong with you? I have a feeling you will wake up one day and bite my ears off.' Desire laughed, then became quiet, again. Remilekun stopped talking. She looked at Desire for a long time before folding her arms over her chest. In that moment, it was as if something unsaid wished to crack the state of intimacy and mutual respect that always existed between them.

'Sincerely, what did he do to you?' Remilekun spoke as if she feared someone else was listening. She placed her hand on Desire's arm and when she felt no response she lay down by her and patted her head gently.

'Sometimes, I feel I should open you up and throw out the dirt in your life.' The few times that Remilekun offered serious advice or a listening ear, it was usually steeped in a philosophy she learnt from a teacher back in secondary school. She always said life should be lived like a detergent— 'Pour in. Wash. Pour out. Laundering is a reminder that we can always come out clean.'

Desire's unease rose slowly as Remilekun's hand soothed her. A small cry was stuck in her throat and her head wished to say so many things, but she knew there was nothing to say. She cried softly, thinking to herself, *She wouldn't understand the lights.*

'Is it Prof?'

'I don't know what it is. I feel empty. I loved going there and then I just don't know what happened. I feel very empty.'

'*Pele*. Don't cry. Don't cry.'

'I am just crying.'

'For nothing?'

'Yes.'

Desire let Remilekun's hand circle a pattern against her neck and the sensation made her ease a little. She was not ready to be left alone.

'Have you ever tried to call your father "Daddy"?'

Remilekun's fingers were no longer forming a pattern on her skin, she simply stroked up and down, like she was giving her words direction.

'He was never really a father,' Remilekun said, sucking in her breath. Desire moved forward on the mattress like she needed to put some space between them. Her heartbeat increased as a story came to the tip of her tongue and she wondered if what she was about to reveal would make Remilekun behave differently towards her. Her lips were weighty. She was rethinking her actions and thinking of saying something about how much she wanted to go to see Prof when Remilekun said, 'Lean on me.' She chuckled, 'My dad used to say that a lot, now that he's got a second wife, who is doing well leaning on his arse, can you imagine she—'

Remilekun stopped talking when she realised that it was Desire who needed to talk, 'Sorry. I am listening.'

Desire placed the pillow under her head and moved back to her former position. She cleared her throat, closed her eyes and imagined she was in the room with Prof. She recalled the ambience: a sigh, a long-drawn breath, and then silence. She started her story.

'My mother killed my father,' she began and it sounded true to her ears. Desire felt Remilekun's body hardening. Her hand lay immobile against her neck. Desire didn't say another word for a few seconds. She wanted the import of what she revealed to fill the room—and it did. She said nothing more until Remilekun, sounding like a child who was being teased for her fear, spoke.

'How? How did it happen?' But Desire didn't say anything. She paused to indicate that she wished to explain further but needed a moment. The silence lengthened as they lay side by side on the mattress. Remilekun drew closer to her and then cuddled up to her and held her tightly around her waist. 'I want to release you,' she cried softly and began again to pat Desire on the head like a baby.

Desire stopped for a while. She played with the story in her head before she started it.

'You see, it is kind of complicated. I didn't see it happen. You know, I wasn't there, how can I explain this? I was there. I just knew. It was as if I made it happen,' Desire sighed.

Remilekun said, 'You scare me.'

Tension entered the room. Desire waited, unsure of what her roommate was up to. She feared disgust and anxiety, and as if Remilekun realised that she may have made herself an inappropriate listening ear, she tickled Desire on the waist and said, 'What's with the suspense now? Is this a gen-gen film?'

'What's a gen-gen film again?'

'Don't you know those old Chinese action movies, when they are changing scenes, you just hear the sound before the action— "gen gen..."'

Desire shook her head and said, 'You'll never change.' She turned and adjusted the pillow under her head.

'Okay. I'm listening. Tell me the story.'

Desire noticed a little hesitation in Remilekun's voice but started her story anyway. She couldn't help but wonder, as she spoke, if her memory had in any way reinvented the things that had really happened to her father.

She began by telling Remilekun how it all started one night. She was alone in a room with her mother, who fanned herself with a cardboard in silence to keep the heat away. Sometimes, her mother blew the fan towards Desire. The flapping of the paper against her mother's hand and the distant hum of generators from the other room provided foreboding of what was to happen. She and her mother both lay on a single mattress, ignorant of how the night would unfold. She placed her head on her mother's lap, enjoying the way she pulled her hair playfully, leaving her to waddle between sleep and wake.

It was one of those nights when Babangida came home late; she and her mother had spent the night waiting for him. Several times, she dozed off, only to be finally roused by a kick, which was her father trying to find a place for his feet as he staggered into the room. At first, the scene went according to script; her mother stayed a few metres from him, as he threw curses at her and he stumbled towards her to swing a punch or slap anywhere his hands landed. Then, there would be the stifled sobs, a sudden scream that faded into repressed cries, that would follow Desire into sleep. Desire's mother would express, years after, that Babangida's problem was a "soft brain" that could not deal with alcohol.

'He drinks just one bottle. His problem is his wild temper.' Yet, alcohol oozed even from the pores on his skin.

That night, electricity came on just as her mother complained about the little kerosene left in the hurricane lamp. The usual scream of 'Up NEPA!' in the neighbourhood, which followed electricity being restored came, as did the squeal of their fan as it laboured to start. The room was not lit. The bulb in the sitting room had burnt out the previous night and her mother hadn't replaced it, so the room relied on the light coming from the bedroom. The room-and-parlour flat had two entrances; a burglar-proof iron door that led into their flat and a flush door that remained permanently open, because it could be brought to the ground with one breath. A blue curtain with paisley patterns of pointed arches hung down from it and divided the sitting room from her parents' bedroom. A number of times, funny noises from the room reached her ears, without her trying hard to listen.

In a few minutes, after the electric power was restored, the noise of television sets from neighbours watching late night shows drowned the noise of their fan. It divided the silence between her and her mother. Neither of them thought of switching the television on. Her father's rule was that the television should be off at 8pm, unless of course, he was home. Desire could not remember any neighbour coming to their room to rescue her mother when the fights began. Her mother didn't share house gossip or her provisions and was seen as a proud and troublesome woman in the self-contained flat of a multiple-storey face-me-I-face-you building, with two rooms and a separate bath and kitchen.

Each night, since he started beating them, Desire daydreamed of how he would die in his sleep or of her mother overpowering him. That night, as her mother played with her hair again, she stirred as she heard the distant voice, 'Desire. Are you awake?' Desire was quiet. She didn't understand why she pretended to be asleep at that time, because usually, she would have answered her mother with a grunt, but at that moment, she remained still.

The darkness covered her pretence even more.

'Your father,' her mother said the word, "father" with much emphasis. Before adding, 'I have never slept with any man apart from him. Is it my fault that nature gave us a dark child, even though we are both fair?' Her mother's voice shook, and Desire shut her eyes even tighter. Her mother stroked her head. First, it came with tenderness but soon her hands kneaded her flesh, and the stroke of her hand appeared to be dictated by the rush of whatever she felt inside her.

'He was never like this. Babangida was such a loveable man. It is that friend of his,' Desire's mother said. 'I was a prostitute and Babangida said he would die if I didn't marry him. I was the one who was worried about what people would say.'

Her mother gripped her hand hard and she wanted to tell her to stop, but all she could do was stay still and pretend she was asleep. Her mother patted her head. She felt a strange sensation that ran down her spine. She listened as her mother continued to talk.

'He beats me so hard. I don't even know myself any more. Desire. I feel like I'm eighty-five and I'm just thirty-one. He thinks I slept with someone else. We used to love each other.' Her memory took her to the few times that she called Babangida Father, the days before he started to behave like a jealous stepfather, hankering for his wife's attention.

There was a time, once, after a bout of beating, when her mother's eyes had a purple glow beneath the eyelids for several days. She had said with usual childhood innocence, 'I think you should run away-o.'

'And who will take care of you?'

'What if he dies? At least someone will take care of me.'

Her mother pinched her nose slightly, 'What will kill him? He's your father, okay? Don't say such things again.'

'He's not my father. He says it. If I was the one he beats like this, one day, I would just kill him.'

'Shut up! What do you know?' Her mother then put her to sleep and walked into the kitchen saying, 'I need to prepare his food, before he comes back screaming like something bit off his penis.' Then she added, 'Sleep.'

Desire slept for a while, and stirred, but she did not know why. It must have been her father's thundering presence. She closed her eyes tight and prayed for sleep to take her back to that land where nothing happened. She pretended to be asleep as the usual shouting and cursing flew over her head. It tore her heart to shreds.

'Bastard woman. *Were.* Mad woman, *oloshi.* Carrier of misery. Until you confess, I will make life hell for you.'

Desire heard the thumping, and the muffled shrieks of her mother, like something was between her teeth. When she screamed, it sounded as if there was a hand placed over her mouth hindering her from sounding it out.

That night, like other nights, Papa in his drunkenness beat her mother. Desire knew she couldn't run into the room, to plead that her father should leave her mother alone, like she did in the past. She knew better now, that they would both come out bruised, from under the weight of her father's worn leather belt. The first and last time she tried to come between them as they fought, he pushed the two of them together— mother and daughter—and swiped the leather against their skin. Desire closed her eyes tight and prayed for sleep to return as she listened to the sound of the leather belt on her mother's hide. That was the last she heard, as she either fell asleep or fainted. By the time she woke up, it was to her mother's soft cries by her side.

'Desire? Are you awake?' her mother whispered and

nudged her slightly on the shoulder. The night became quiet in a guilty way. The power went off and the televisions died. The church sounds stopped. It was like everything connived in an act it shouldn't.

The watchmen forgot to beat the hourly gong that night, the gong whose metal rasping created echoes that reverberated into her ears and woke her. After the fight, her mother came to Desire's side of the bed. She held her in a close embrace and rocked her gently from one side to another; like she was a cloth swayed by the wind. She continued to rock her, but all through, Desire shut her eyes as if she was indeed drowsy. She was thankful that the room was dark and it shielded her, until she fell asleep.

Later into the night, after the sudden quiet, her mother's body-trembling sob forced her into a sitting position. Then she hugged her and clasped Desire's hand in her own. The sweat on their palms mixed and their pain came together. As her mother cried, Desire cried. They both cried into the early morn. They then nestled against each other, sniffling themselves to sleep, each knowing that the morning would be different.

The following morning, Desire's mother swung herself against the doorpost and screamed into the air; neighbours scuttled out from all around as she led them one by one to Babangida's body, stretched on the bed like he was pulled at both ends by two very strong men, shouting, 'Wake him... please, somebody wake him up!'

'It's almost over. It's almost over,' she heard again, her mother whispering into her ears. Desire remembered that she almost opened her eyes to ask her mother what was over, because she couldn't understand, but she remained still, even when the woman stood up from her side.

'Please, never you tell a soul this story.'

'It's safe with me,' Remilekun whispered.

She felt she needed to make her story even juicer, validate her reason for visiting Prof even more. This is how she wanted to remember it if she could not forget.

'You know, there's something I never told you, Prof gave us our house in Maroko and provided food for us. He even sent me to secondary school. You see why I can't leave him.' Desire felt the weight of the story she had just made up seep through her veins. Even her mother's depressive rants never contained her father the way hers did now. One thing she felt was good, however, was having her mother kill him, as this made her look like one who fought back for what was hers.

'Babe, no soul shall hear this story from you.'

Remilekun nodded and wrapped her arms around herself. Desire moved towards her, offering herself as warmth.

'I only wished your Prof wasn't that strange. I'm sure it was the prison.'

She moved closer to Remilekun and held her and a small sob passed through her throat before she said, 'I never want to be married. I have the fear that I will kill my husband or maybe my child.'

'What?' Remilekun jumped up from the sleeping posture she was in and pinched Desire's cheeks. She lay back on the bed.

'Don't say that, babe!'

Desire did not reply. Instead she sniffed. Remilekun raised her head and peered into her face.

'What are you looking for in my face?'

'Checking to see if you have the face of a killer.'

'What do you see?'

'The face of a woman who can be anything she wants to be,' she said, a snort accompanied her words.

'Thanks,' and then she added, 'You better tell me now-o. You know the blood of a killer is inside me.'

Remilekun tickled her again. She tickled back. They giggled and fell in a swoop off the mattress with their arms around each other. The air from Remilekun as she exhaled on Desire's shoulder made her body tense. She lay with her back to the ground, slowly, and as their bodies met, their perspiration mingled.

Desire covered herself with the bedspread and tightened it around herself.

33

Desire stood up from the bed and looked into the street. She listened to the news filtering in from the other room on a popular radio station.

'Remilekun, are you listening to the news?'

'Where?' she asked.

'On radio. Labour says there would be indefinite strike action to protest the fuel hike. ASUU strike plus Labour strike is equal to dead country. From what I'm seeing, people have started the strike. The street is dry. No hustle. No bustle.'

The blocks of flats which made up the estate stood around like observers to the units of activity going on: boys played football, and then, in an instant, they scattered in several directions. It didn't take long before the siren of a police patrol van filtered into her room. It stopped in front of her block. Except for the cans which served as goal posts, there was nothing to suggest that ten boys had just been there. Two policemen jumped down from the van and laughed like they were opening their mouths to the skies for rain. The one who seemed shorter of the two, placed his AK-47 properly behind him, stretched his hands into the air, and pushed out his paunch rather than his chest. She watched them and was about to close the window, when they flagged down a man dressed in fitted jeans and an oversized sleeveless shirt. He had a black laptop bag hanging from his shoulder. He walked past them with an almost unnoticeable stoop. As he walked past, the shorter of the policemen appeared to feel insulted. He dragged the man back by pulling at the back of his trousers. Some words were exchanged. Man-in-jeans nearly fell, yet he didn't struggle with them, he simply opened his bag and the taller of the policemen looked inside and waved him away.

The shorter policeman, who first pulled him, asked him to come back. He unzipped the now closed bag and dug his hands inside. He brought out a laptop and placed it on the ground. He said something to the man—Desire assumed that he was asking him for receipts.

At this point, Man-in-jeans shook his head vigorously and the short one pushed him. He fell to the ground. She didn't hear what they said to him, but from studying their movements, she understood what was going on. The policemen were accusing the man of having stolen the laptop because he did not carry a receipt, and he was arguing that the laptop was his. She could see it in the way the man threw his hands about, with so much vigour and desperation to state his innocence. His mouth moved very fast and his stoop was straightened. The shorter policeman pointed a finger in his face and he brushed it away. His tall friend held him and he threw his hands frantically in the air. The taller of the policemen, whom she thought was calmer, initially, brandished his gun before the Jeans-man, who continued to flay his arms about. His hand seemed to have met the face of the tall policeman. At this, three other policemen, who all the while were watching the incident, jumped down from the van and began to push him into their vehicle. He held on to the iron that was used as a step-in and fought not to enter.

Desire sighed. The second term of democracy, and each day, freedom still appeared to be a foreign tongue. The president was the type who always wanted to be right, so he could offer an I-told-you-so to his competition, while the masses suffered. If she were to visit Prof that night, she knew she would have told him about the incident. They would have discussed bad governance and then one thing would have led to another. She remembered the very few times, those instances of frivolous abandon, when she forgot everything—her past, the dark, the room, and just laughed and shared jokes with him as a friend. Sometimes, her hand would hit his playfully, and he would slip it off so she hit the chair rather than him.

But once she remembered that his room had no light, she became quiet and as if he had sensed her change of mood, they resumed the whispering and became cautious of running into each other's skin. She shrugged, as she reminded herself that he was now to be forgotten. Prof would be forgotten—and forgetting meant rewriting her narratives. Prof was now just a part of her imagination.

Desire rubbed her hands against her skin and watched the policemen, as they succeeded in pushing the man into their vehicle. His laptop was on the road. They drove a short distance away, reversed, and then the short policeman hurriedly picked up the computer from the ground and jumped back into the van. Desire sighed and drew the curtains. She eyed the towel which hung above the door, but she didn't stand up to enter the bathroom. She walked to her bed and sank into it, observing everything around her but finding nothing tangible to hold her focus.

Her eyes panned the piles of unwashed pots, dishes, dirty clothes, and the piles of books mounted in their different spaces, forming little hills. Finally, she rested her gaze on crumpled pieces of paper on the floor, around the waste basket. Desire wondered why she never noticed that the room needed some tidying. Remilekun was not one to lift a broom, even if the house became a garbage dump. She picked up a bucket and walked towards the door to fetch water which she could use to clean the room.

'I need to fetch water,' she said, even though she knew Remilekun was not listening.

Although people walked around, she still felt as if the place was empty. Even the air seemed languid. She felt like she could notice the thick balls of sweat hidden behind shirt collars and hung across the faces of people on the streets. It appeared as if everybody around walked with their heads bowed and their shoulders drooping. The sun came out fully. A hawker selling oranges screamed past, undaunted by the potency of the sun.

It was interesting how the burden of one's fears appeared on everything around one.

When Desire arrived at the public tap, she slapped *tintin* insects that bit her leg where she sat on the raised platform, glancing at the running water intermittently as it rolled into the bucket like a ball of yarn. Human memory connected the unlikely. It amused her that the water reminded her of Sarjee unfurling the smoke of weed into the air in Oshodi. She shook her head and saw how easy it was to wear the blame of what we cannot explain. She couldn't even tell what had been wrong with him.

She bit her fingernails, one after the other, and as she waited for the water to fill her plastic bucket, she decided, *This will be my last trip to him. I will apologise for telling him nonsense about his son. I'll just go inside and lie down.* Then she thought, *But what if really he's the father?*

She made two trips and then she waited for the bucket to fill a third time, while she watched a group of five teenage boys with plastic buckets and bowls coming towards the public tap, but instead, stopped to start a two-a-side football contest on the road.

When she lifted her head and stared at the rows of blocks with longing, it was with much courage that she stopped herself from putting down the bucket and walking towards his house, to see if he would open the door in the afternoon, and she would be able to catch a glimpse of him.

Later that night, when she would visit him, she would ask if he missed her. Then she wondered if Prof would indeed take her back in his room after they had both decided she was not to come back again. It had not crossed her mind all the while, but now, she felt he might be offended by her disappearance and would not open the door to her. The more she thought about this, the more she prayed that it should be to the contrary. She was so engrossed in her thoughts that she jerked when the hawker girl she noticed earlier stood in front of her and screamed her out of her dreams, 'Sweet orange here! Buy your sweet orange!' After several more cries and the same futile result, the girl directed her question to her in Yoruba, 'Aunty, sweet orange? Three for fifty naira.'

She shook her head and replied to her in the typical Yoruba farewell for persistent hawkers, 'Thanks. *Wa a ta.*' Not just a wish, she really hoped the girl would sell some.

The girl moved on, walked a few metres from Desire before she stopped to pick up something from the floor, with the tray of oranges balanced on her head. Desire kept looking at the girl, up to the time when a taxi nearly knocked her down, and she fell flat on the ground. Her oranges rolled in a hurry towards the open drain. The taxi driver jumped out of his car towards the girl, and he, with a few other people, helped her up as some others took her fallen oranges from the ground and placed them back on the tray. A small crowd surrounded her, straightening the girl's cloth and checking her body for any injury. That was where she first noticed him: a man dressed in an oversized, purple shirt and pink tie over green trousers, watching from a distance. His afro was a thick sponge of white hair, and a careful look at him showed that he limped when he walked. He stood behind the crowd helping the girl, watching them, but in no mood to offer help himself. There was something familiar about him and she could not even place the somewhere-ness that connected her with him. The man stood away from the crowd, yet appeared to be in deep observation of the things happening. Then, he turned. She looked away from him when it appeared that he caught her staring, focusing her attention to the gulley forming in the middle of the road because of unattended potholes.

From the side of her eyes, she tried to see if the man was still looking at her.

Finally, water spilled from the bucket and Desire rolled the piece of cloth she used as padding for her head. She folded it into a ring to protect against the friction of the bucket when she carried it on her head. With this headgear, she bent all her concentration on the bucket in a bid to avoid the man who, though she was not looking, continued to stare at her. She was so engrossed in forgetting him, that she did not notice the strange man moving towards her.

Desire bent over her bucket. She stretched her hands, jutted out her buttocks and spread her legs for balance in order to lift the bucket onto her head, but her eyes found audience with the strangely familiar man. She found herself bent over her bucket, her heart ramming and she did not move.

The man came closer. Her hands twitched. She forced her eyes to become icy, to hide her mounting fear as he walked towards her. There was something about him that reminded her of someone who meant something to her, someone she felt she knew. Like Prof? She repeated to herself that he could not be her Prof. She shook and looked around her but no one was watching. The street was minding its own business.

The man still walked towards her. She stood away from the bucket and held the tap tightly, like she could pull it out and hit him with it if he tried something malicious.

He stood in front of her.

She lifted her eyes and looked straight into his. He did not react as she expected, so she turned away. Yet, staring at him pulled at her heartstrings.

'What?' she said. It was a sudden defence and a plea for better revelation.

The man wiped his hand against his mouth, smiled at her and bent down to the tap. She moved away and watched him wash his face under the running water.

When he straightened up, she noticed the scars all over his face and on closer study, she realised he was bent to the side, like one leg was shorter than the other. She observed as the crease on his brow folded into haphazard rows as he stood watching her. She suddenly did not wish to know him. This was not Prof. As Desire watched him a little more, bending down and splashing water over his face again, she made up her mind that she would visit Prof that night, more convinced than ever. She was ashamed for him and of herself; that she could compare a vagabond to him, a world-renowned professor.

She bent over and lifted the bucket of water to her head in one swoop, before he finished washing himself at the tap.

A few metres away, she thought she heard her name, 'Desire.' She turned to the direction the voice came from. The strange man was closest to her, but he did not appear to have said anything. He stared at her with a resonance that shot at her mind. His heavy moustache fell over his mouth, so it was impossible to discern if his lips were curved in a smile or a frown. His eyes carried a distant look, and occasionally they twitched, like they were bothered with what they were seeing in her. She could not get it out of her mind that there was something so familiar about him, and it almost made her go to him and hold his hands. Yet, she remained where she was. She always knew how to read feelings through the eyes—she always believed she did. She looked into the man's eyes and they held a brief hold—his and hers, and she saw shame and confusion. She turned to go, these were not the ones she had wanted to see. She left him with the feelings she saw in his eyes, too. She understood that when you learn to read a man's eyes, you must also learn to forget some of the words you find in them. She took one long look at the man and moved away from him.

34

Prof stood at the door and watched the neighbourhood briefly, before he walked down the stairs, taking slow steps, with his eyes following the clouds like they were the thoughts floating in his head. He stumbled twice, then he held on to the banister so as not to fall and lifted his feet from one step to another. At the last step, a girl sat with a bag by her side. She turned all of a sudden, as his steps got her attention; then she ducked, as he drew closer to her. He felt shame at the fear he made her feel and so he stretched out his hands and helped her up.

The girl stammered as she stood with a bend, her weight resting on her right leg.

'Your mother sent me. She said this is for you,' she pointed to the bag on the ground.

'Tell her I miss her,' he said.

The girl looked at him with her eyes enlarged. She was still shaking when he collected the provisions from her grasp, her hands holding on tightly to the bag.

'You bring the food, right?'

'Yes, I drop it sometimes. I knock and run downstairs,' she said with her eyes on the ground.

He looked at her. She could not be more than 18 years old. Her skin was the colour of an over-ripe pawpaw, and each time she talked, it appeared she made a desperate effort not to show her teeth.

'Thank you,' he finally said. 'You can take it upstairs,' he extended his arms to return the bag to her.

The girl did not move. She watched him with a mouth wide open, 'Upstairs?'

'Yes, upstairs. Where I stay.'

After what seemed like a considerable amount of deliberation, she dropped the bag, rushed down the road and did not look back.

Prof picked up the bag of provisions as he watched the girl disappear. He muttered prayers for his mother, as he once again remembered a time he stayed on at the university instead of going home for the holidays. At the time, he made himself believe he was trying to earn himself some of the independence he believed she took away from him. He had no money on him, and though he could do with some money from her little earnings as a teacher and market trader, he told himself he would survive without her. One day, as the strike action intensified and his fellow comrades in the student union left for their different homes, things became more dire, as he didn't even have anyone to turn to for assistance with the transport fare. She came searching for him. He was outside on that day, calculating what he needed to do to raise money for his trip home, when he saw her walking towards the hostel with a big bag on her head.

'Maami! How—' his shame and totally dishevelled look kept him from looking at her as she reached him. His eyes could not hide his joy.

'My son, *Abiyamo kì í gbo ohùn omo re ko ma tatí wére.*'

A true mother she is, whose ear hearkens to her son's agony, he thought again, as he walked back into the house with the provisions the girl brought, before deciding on his next point of action. He rummaged through the bag and realised that his mother had also put a small purse with money inside. He shook with sobs, left the bag with the purse in the sitting room and hurried out of the door and down the stairs.

The rows of blocks and different activities perplexed him— hawkers, laughers, pedestrians—all of them assured him of how difficult it would be to know where Desire lived in the estate. Where does one start knocking in an estate with over 150 houses, each housing over 12 blocks of flats? It was a daunting task.

'I just need to tell her the room is lit. That's all,' Prof muttered to himself. He calculated the number of days he would spend going around, and how many flats he needed to visit.

He walked down to the block closest to his. The block was one of the few painted ones in the neighbourhood. It was painted in many colours; each flat was painted according to its resident's discretion. Prof walked to the flat by the right-hand side on the ground floor. He knocked on the door of the flat like someone who had come for a bad debt. A woman in a hijab peered through an opening, and before he could say anything, slammed the door in his face. On the third block, a few metres away from his, was a flat where the doorway was protected by a wooden door that looked like a single kick could blow it open. When a woman came to the door to open it, she remained still and mute for about five seconds. He watched as her eyes roamed over his body, from top to bottom, until he gulped the big blob of phlegm that had lodged in his throat. As he was deciding to state his reason for coming to her doorstep and break the silence between them, she screamed in a way that brought the rest of the family running to the door. Prof watched them gesturing wildly and speaking in an unfamiliar Nigerian language he couldn't place.

He stood by the door thinking of how he had assumed his knowledge of languages was vast, while also taking in the shock on their faces, before he said to her, 'Hello.'

He stopped when he said it. It amused him even when he didn't intend to, to see the sudden flicker in their eyes, and he caught a spark of surprise in there too. This was an emotion he couldn't understand, though. He ignored the disbelief in their eyes and continued, 'I'm looking for my friend, Desire. Her name is Desire Babangida?' he continued, and then he went on to explain. 'I can't describe her face. We always sat in the dark. But I know how she laughs, she laughs like a car spurting. Her voice is not thin, but it sounds thin because she speaks in a pitch.' He paused for the woman to talk, unsure if he was making sense to her. The neighbour simply shook her head and slowly shut the door in his face. He moved away from the door, backing away slowly, before he walked on, unsure of what to feel about the way he was treated. He continued his search.

Prof ignored the fingers that pointed at him as he walked the streets. It never occurred to him that he looked strange and considerably different from his earlier pictures. In this kind of neighbourhood, where the blocks were interlocked, their lives would be chained into a flow, also, of gossip. In a place like this, rumours would have flown around about him and Desire's frequent visits, and now, his sudden search for her. He noticed how surprise evolved into disgust in the way in which they looked at him when he arrived at each doorstep, bearing his mission. He was unwelcomed at one house after another—each dismissal more painful than the next. Prof put his hands together and put on as much of a pitiful look as he could. He pleaded with everyone he met, as he described her in detail, as far as his idea of her and intuition could take him, with as much embellishment as his imagination could conceive. It was when he got to the fourth house, and he was about to knock on the door that it suddenly hit him, that he knew more of her voice than anything else. In all his asking, he had made no description of her features. Each time he met a new neighbour, he felt he saw it in their eyes that they knew who he sought, yet they weren't ready to tell. It seemed like it was a communal decision to save her from him. Still, he persisted in his inclination to find Desire and tell her of the now lit room.

He stopped to watch a group of boys playing two-a-side football. Although he focused on the game, it was not out of a sudden interest in the sport, but as an interlude during which he could strategise his next move in his search for Desire. After a few moments of "ooh-ing", and "ah-ing" over the way the boys played, he walked over to them, who awaited their turn in the game, and spoke to the slim boy who stood against a power pole with his hand shading his eyes from the sun.

'Do you know Desire?'

'*Desire?*' the boy repeated and then shook his head, 'What kind of question is that? Do I know "desire"?'

Prof thought of a way to clarify it to the boy, whose eyes, though attentive to Prof's every move, were also on a mission of inspecting Prof's entire body. Prof, repeated, 'Desire,' and after a short pause, said, 'it is someone's name. Just tell me if you know a woman with that name. She's a student in LASU.'

The boy shrugged off the hand of the friend who tapped him on the shoulder, to talk to Prof.

'Ha, I don't know-o. Do you know her block, and the flat number?'

Prof shook his head in the negative.

'Ha! That one is hard-o. Where would you see her in this estate, without an address?' he said with a little chuckle in his throat. He eyed Prof from his head to his toe once again, and then said, 'You will search far-o.'

Another boy came to him, and pulled him by the shirt and ran off, screaming, 'Kolo! He no well-o.'

The others made signs to the boy, who listened, and he looked at Prof's eyes and said, 'Sorry. I can't help. You talk so well, I didn't realise...'

'Realise what?'

The boy was soon pulled away by his friends—whose impression of his assumed condition rested on the contempt which was openly displayed on their faces—and he ran to join them as they decided on the new set of players for the next game.

He resumed his search from one block to another. And at the last floor of Block Four, he stopped when he reached flat number 12. He slipped his hand into a space between the iron burglar-proof to reach the wooden door which had a sticker that said: "2005, MY YEAR OF TOO MUCH MONEY."

He knocked at the door, and then waited for almost two minutes before a squirrel-toothed woman opened the door, still chuckling from some inside joke. Her eyes opened wide,

wider and then wider still as she looked him down from his
bushy uncombed hair to his uncut toenails sticking out of his
rubber flip-flops. She stopped laughing as their eyes met. Prof
noticed that her cheeks assumed a puff, although she tried to
put her laughter in check. Her eyes retained a certain glimmer
though, and this brought to futility her struggle to appear stern
and impatient. She stepped outside the room, but made sure
a noticeable distance remained between her and Prof. All this
time, her left hand remained on the door handle.

'What happen?' she asked.

He was going to tell her about himself, when a voice called
from inside the house

'Maria, come see... come now! This show is just funny
mehnn!' A slight pause, and then the voice spoke again,
'Answer the person at the door quick nah?'

'I dey come,' she shouted, and then she turned to him,
her eyes scouting him so much that he felt her pick on every
part of his body, reminding him of how he did not bathe for
three days at a time. She didn't say anything to him except
through the eyes on his body, keeping her gaze from his face,
not in avoidance but in a settled conviction to avoid contact.
She then seemed to remember there was something she was
missing indoors.

'Can I help you... S-sir?'

Prof cleared his voice to state the reason he was at her
doorstep, but she did not let him express himself further
before she muttered, 'I think you should try the next flat, they
are the ones that trade old stuffs.'

Prof found himself staring at a shut door, mumbling to
himself. He stood, arms akimbo, for some minutes, before
he decided there and then that it was time to go back home
and re-strategise on his "Desire mission". He leaned against
the banister and shut his eyes. While he tried not to worry,
his mind remained heavy—as it consumed the honks from
vehicles, the screaming kids returning from school and
hawkers shouting their wares. The countless activities going

on around him clouded his head in that moment when he shut his eyes. It took the place of that which he wanted but could not have. It filled his mind gradually and he felt as if something inside him would soon explode. When he opened his eyes and looked down the stairs on which he would walk, back to his now lit room, he felt heavy. Prof descended the stairs with a bowed head and weighted feet. Drops of sweat dribbled after one another from the middle of his head down his sideburns. He wiped the sliding water off with the back of his left hand.

'Desire?' he thought to himself as he walked home. He lifted his face to view the block of flats and tried to work out again how he would tackle his search the next day. But the magnitude of what he was trying to do hit him just as he looked straight ahead at the houses which stretched down into a fading perspective in front of him. It chipped away at every bit of optimism he had built, and he shook his head.

He broached the thought of going to the LASU campus to find Desire, but it didn't take long for him to push that thought away. He didn't want people hovering about him, asking him questions about life after prison. He could almost determine the outcome of such a visit. *Me? I will never go back there,* he thought to himself. His former colleagues, students and God-knows-who would come before him, to see that renowned troublemaker. He pictured himself walking onto the campus, and students rushing down to catch a glimpse. Prof shook his head, *No. I can't do it. Not even for Desire.* Yet, he knew that his longing to find her ate up every other thought in his head. There was no conviction there.

Prof stroked his beard, lost in thought, when the loud wail chorused by passers-by, traders and men and women on the veranda of their houses stirred him from his reverie. His mind processed the unsettled ripples in the muddy water in the pothole, the passers-by uttering obscenities after the fading back of the *danfo,* to the animated looks of the few faces he caught trying to regain their composure. He touched his wet trousers and tried to remember what had happened to him. It seemed he had wandered onto the road or a car wandered into him. Prof didn't know what to think, especially with the sympathy the onlookers gave in his favour. He decided a car almost ran into him. He blew air from his mouth in exasperation and bent down to brush off the muddy water splattered on his striped cotton trousers. His concentration on this singular activity stole him from his absent-mindedness. He stood up straight, turned his head to the left, only for him to see that an orange seller was actually the one people were concerned about. He stood watching the audience given to the girl for a while and turned to move on. That was when he saw her—the woman by the public tap at the other side of the road, who looked like one capable of helping.

Mindless of the road which divided them in space, there was a momentary lightness in his head when he looked into her eyes. This was followed by stiffness in his chest which left him breathless for a moment. Just looking at her, for those brief seconds, left him fazed; he forgot about Desire. He felt something had indeed happened between them, or was it just his imagination? That "something" was heightened by the inappropriateness of his feelings. And with this thought in his head, he faced the disturbed waters in the potholes, and thought to himself, *It's the shouting that is having an after-effect.*

But he lifted his eyes to steal a glance at the woman by the public tap and again his eyes met hers, or so he thought; but that instantaneous feeling of some mutual knowing floored him and disrupted him for a while.

'That is Desire.'

He was sure. The woman by the tap carried a sense of familiarity that made his heart leap. He slowed down his steps, standing in one position, like he was observing something around the place. He stood and watched her. Slowly, he defined her classic guitar-shaped body structure, under the white T-shirt she wore with brown combat shorts. Her arms and legs, which exposed her skin, were for him iridescent against the sun sinking into the clouds. Prof savoured what the darkness in the room had hidden from him again and again. He studied the way her nipples poked against her T-shirt. They sprouted from her breasts, outlined under her T-shirt, which stood on her chest like twin hills. He stood without moving, and kept staring, until she stood up from the concrete built around the public tap, to lift the bucket onto her head. His eyes stayed on her as she bent forward and attempted to lift the bucket onto her head again. Her breasts shook and leaned forward with her in a cultured elegance, as she bent over. He stared at her, at her chest, without shame or guilt. He wanted to walk up to her and hold her in a tight embrace. The type long lost friends gave each other. He wanted those breasts of hers to breathe next to his chest.

As he changed his gaze from her chest, their eyes met again; this time they locked for much longer. As he looked into her eyes, he saw all those days she had spent with him in the room flash before his eyes—the sighs, her exhalations, her shuffles; and without being too conscious of it, he stretched out his hands to feel her. His hands floated in the air without touching anything until his consciousness again reminded him that he was on one of the many number-named streets in the estate he lived in. Though he was not close enough to elicit the kind of reaction that his body might intuitively have wished to express, despite the distance between them, he felt a bubbling inside him, and finally developed the courage to walk up to her. He walked towards her without thinking. His strides were wide as he moved towards her, and he analysed the things he would say to her. He debated with himself how the conversation he would have with her would go. *Do you know Desire? No, I'll rather say, 'You must be Desire'. That's more assuring.*

He stopped thinking. He had absentmindedly crossed over and was now standing in front of her. He felt her eyes on him. He exhaled and it sounded like a murmur, but no word escaped his lips. Instead, he remained in place, gesticulating with his hands, moving his lips and clearing his voice again and again until it became sore; finally he muttered, 'Desire,' before he moved away and watched from a distance, as she sized him up, from his bushy head to his dust-polished sandals, before she hurried away from him.

Prof remembered that he did not tumble the lock when he left earlier. He looked on in the direction of the departing girl thinking, only imagination can destroy its own creation. He took a deep breath and considered going home to lift the curtains of his house, so that the lame lights of the moon could walk in.

Acknowledgements

I started writing this novel because a friend offered me a place to relieve my burdens. A space to listen to silence and speak into the dark without fear. I'm grateful to you Albert Obi, wherever you may be, for trusting my ears to listen to you, and for inviting my silence into your house. Your invitation to "talk" opened my imagination to abandon my trauma and seek shadows that tell stories. I am indeed grateful.

For Aduke: the one I prayed for.

For Papa V and Mama V—my shoulders. Father and Mother.

For Show, Verie, Showski—brothers, friends, army and cheerleaders. Blood.

For Tayo, friend and sister. Fellow traveller.

Odia, friend, kindred spirit. Support.

For Bibi, whose words echo in my ears when I am almost lost in transit.

And to my editor, Layla, for accepting this story as ours, and leading it to a place it can breathe.

My journey couldn't have begun without the support I received from others. I am a body of gratitude to many people whose kindness has helped me find my way in difficult times. Hence, I am grateful to everyone who has shown me support, including you reading this book, for investing your time and money on me.

I speak into the world; I'm grateful.

We keep moving!

Support *A Small Silence*

We hope you enjoyed reading this book. It was brought to you by Cassava Republic Press, an award-winning independent publisher based in Abuja and London. If you think more people should read this book, here's how you can make sure this happens:

Recommend it. Don't keep the enjoyment of this book to yourself; tell everyone you know. Spread the word to your friends and family.

Review, review review. Your opinion is powerful and a positive review from you can generate new sales. Spare a minute to leave a short review on Amazon, GoodReads, Wordery, our website and other book buying sites.

Join the conversation. Hearing somebody you trust talk about a book with passion and excitement is one of the most powerful ways to get people to engage with it. If you like this book, talk about it, Facebook it, Tweet it, Blog it, Instagram it. Take pictures of the book and quote or highlight from your favourite passage. You could even add a link so others know where to purchase the book from.

Buy the book as gifts for others. Buying a gift is a regular activity for most of us – birthdays, anniversaries, holidays, special days or just a nice present for a loved one for no reason… If you love this book and you think it might resonate with others, then please buy extra copies!

Get your local bookshop or library to stock it. Sometimes bookshops and libraries only order books that they have heard about. If you loved this book, why not ask your librarian or bookshop to order it in. If enough people request a title, the bookshop or library will take note and will order a few copies for their shelves.

Recommend this book to your book club. Persuade your book club to read this book and discuss what you enjoy about the book in the company of others. This is a wonderful way to share what you like and help to boost the sales and popularity of this book. You can also join our online book club on Facebook at Afri-Lit Club to discuss books by other African writers.

Attend a book reading. There are lots of opportunities to hear writers talk about their work. Support them by attending their book events. Get your friends, colleagues and families to a reading and show an author your support.

Thank you!

Stay up to date with the latest books, special offers and exclusive content with our monthly newsletter.
Sign up on our website:
www.cassavarepublic.biz

Twitter: @cassavarepublic #SmallSilence #ReadCassava
#ReadingAfrica
Instagram: @cassavarepublicpress
Facebook: facebook.com/CassavaRepublic

Transforming a manuscript into the book you are now reading is a team effort. Cassava Republic Press would like to thank everyone who helped in the production of *A Small Silence*:

Editorial
Layla Mohamed
Bibi Bakare-Yusuf
Katlego Tapala
Temitayo Olofinlua

Design & Production
Michael Salu
Tobi Ajiboye

Sales & Marketing
Emma Shercliff
Kofo Okunola

Publicity
Halima Shode